EMMA ELLIS

The Poison Maker

First edition

Cover art by Miblart

This book was professionally typeset on Reedsy. Find out more at reedsy.com

1

Prologue

A bead of sweat dripped from his chin and hit the tabletop. The air con was broken again, and the heat made the cramped space a miasma of vinegary stench. Undeterred, he wiped the back of his unwashed hand across his face and carried on. The notes written on his wrist left ink smudges on his stubble and his sagging cheeks as he pored over a memorandum of proceedings and summaries. He had secrets to release. He needed a potion to flow deeply, brain-altering stuff with no antidote.

Computers stuttered in the humidity. A sliver of moonlight fought its way through the dusty blinds, casting shadows in the dim room. Just twenty minutes until the deadline. No distractions were allowed. He mixed and stirred, frowning with concentration, spinning the required fusion of reality and make believe. The hour was late, but his time was fixed. The venom at his fingertips would expire soon.

Sitting back to admire his work, he peered through bronze-rimmed spectacles, grinning as he evaluated his success.

His unruly teeth giving evidence of his poverty. He was unmotivated by money: only a bloody fool works for money. He did it for power, for liberty, for a kick.

At eleven-thirty, he was finished. He left the room and walked home, unfollowed, not sneaking around the back alleys or hiding in the shadows, for he was not like the rest of them. Vulnerability knew no place in his persona. He walked down the main road, lit by street lights, sterilised sidewalks clean and free from rubbish. The cleaners would be helpless against the dirt he was unleashing. He smiled as he walked home, sanitised, with a salubrious stride, his filth contained for now. He looked up at the street-cams and winked as he passed. Autocars seemed to keep their distance as they passed: no road spray would dirty his shoes.

He went by many names, was known by many guises. Most referred to him as the Poison Maker.

2

Chapter 1

I do not mean for this book to justify my actions. Far from it. It's more of a simple explanation, an education for future generations, so they can understand how things are in this cruel year of 2112. I suspect that, if you are reading this, history lessons are even more scant than they are now. Glossing over the tyranny and bloodshed. Dismissing the loneliness we all feel. Eliminating any sense of nostalgia and filling that void with a feeling of united responsibility. Our negative thoughts diffused into nothingness.

Perhaps I'm writing this to vindicate myself, so I can read it back and know that I had no choice. Did we ever? Choice is an illusion now. We are part of something bigger, greater, a collective ambition to keep us safe.

Safe. Another illusion.

There's a chance I'll make it into the history lessons, unlikely as that seems: a woman of my breeding can't afford the price tag those column inches command. But my scientific achievements are of note and my research enabled us to feed the country. Famine is one less thing we die of now. But the gluttony of the company's balance sheets will be my actual legacy. There are parts of my work I hope will be forgotten so my failures can die with me, be lost to the ashes. The world is burning anyway; let me join the cinders. At least then I'll be free.

I can barely remember what life was like before, although I try. Before. When I was punctual, well rested and naively ambitious. When my nonchalance came with confidence, my integrity with reverence. When I retained some belief in fairness, and felt the future was a place we should aspire to be. Before I knew that the future meant being so brusquely dismissive of the past. Before Grace seemed so sublimely happy.

I'd like to remember how I felt before I knew too much. When I stood at the bottom of the rocky cliff face of ignorance. I climbed, hurling my limbs over every sharp ledge, bloodying my hands, eager to get to the top. Then I stood on the narrow precipice for a brief moment before falling into the pit of knowledge. But it's impossible. The pit has a lid. There's no way out. You can't unknow something, like you can't remember what you believed before you knew the Earth orbits the Sun. You can't regain ignorance. I'm not even sure I want to, really. Perhaps I just want a day off; a day free to laugh and take joy in little things without the hollow feeling. I wish the hopelessness would go away. I wish there was more I could do. I wish I could tell her.

The day before I started to climb that cliff face, I went to work as usual. I had worked in the same lab for twenty years, so my mornings always conformed to the same schedule. I itched with discomfort as I walked to work. The buildings threw a shade that offered little relief and only restricted the sultry breeze a little. My shoes squelched in the dampness of disinfectant, the street spray misting and reaching as high as my knees. I kept my head down and plodded on, coughing with gravelly lungs, chafed skin grating with every step.

Something in the air caught my attention. A speck. Naturally, I assumed the worst, jumping to red alert. But it was fine. Not a crawler or a grain of filth, just the air pollution playing its usual tricks. The sterilised streets should have relaxed me, their barrenness a lure for comfort instead of distress, but it was hard to relax in such crushing heat.

The grey high-rises gave way to BioLabs, a huge glass building that had saved so many lives. As always, I went to the Selfie Station before going in. A futile task: the years had not been kind. My short hair sat like a lank mop, my skin blistered and scabbed. My vitality had been lost long before, blown away by the endless smog. The Raft's Perimeter was caked with the stuff, one of the many burdens those born in the Centre were spared.

The Selfie Station near the lab was one of the best in the area, well maintained and brandishing hair products and beauty aids. Everything you needed to look your best in the shortest space of time. The photograph frame had the lab and factory in the background, an impressive building of gleaming glass. This cropped view gave the impression of eternal, beautiful architecture, as if we lived in a world where design and aesthetics mattered. A morale-boosting image for anyone who would see the photo. I suppose it was a break from the ceaseless matt grey of every other stretch of The Raft.

My wan complexion was as enthusiastic about the day as my mind, but the Selfie Station's filters added enough fakery to make me bearable to look at. I uploaded the photo to my social media, heavily filtered and accompanied by the expected array of enthusiastic hashtags, then entered those huge glass doors to BioLabs.

'Microbes!' I cursed under my breath as I arrived, punctual as always, to find the interns already waiting. I stepped up to the monitor, held a finger out for the prick test, and let the robotic arm take my daily mouth swab.

'Thank you, Professor Selbourne! Your cortisone levels are normal and your blood test is average! Have a great day!' It had more manners than most of my colleagues.

I could see the interns' eager faces through the glass corridor, their youthful brains full of promise and idealism. Some stared back, others dared not look. I sighed and walked to my office. Soon we'll turn those lights off. I painted on a smile, which was considerably less animated than the array of smiles the interns presented. Then I slammed my office door behind me and yawned. That was about as much enthusiasm I could manage on a Monday morning.

I despaired at how special they thought they were, and how sheltered they actually were, how keen to take part in this charade. They were groomed to perfection and believed themselves the most capable, the most deserving. A class full of idealistic princes and princesses, promised the world by parents who had barely left their homes in a decade.

The parents had all attended the open day, some with their precious child, most in place of them.

'What duties would my daughter be expected to perform? She is top of her class.'

'My son is top of his class, so I assume he'll be given the respect he deserves?'

'My son is top of his class, so I expect him to have a position above his peers here.'

In the five years I had run the internship programme, I had yet to see an application without a parent's metaphorical hand-holding and every single applicant was, apparently, top of their class.

Waiting on my desk, underneath a cup of MimikTea, was a stack of files, topped with a note from the receptionist reading, '*For you to babysit this year.*' Piled underneath were the cover letters singing the twenty interns' praises, most likely written by their parents. I walked over to the glass and peeked through the blinds. They waited outside, rigid, still, silent, anticipating my instructions.

They can wait a bit longer.

I nursed my MimikTea until the clock said eight-forty and I summoned the energy to start work. I had interns to inspire. Maybe this would be the year of breakthroughs, the year of a worthwhile internship program. Maybe...

* * *

'And this is where the microscopes live—intern nine, please keep your goggles on, and taking selfies in the lab is prohibited. The e-pad next to the microscopes is what you need to look for, so it is easily identifiable. You will find the instructions next to the burners, and at each stage of the lab there is a fixed e-pad with the instructions on the screen, like so.' I demonstrated the software, and the interns stared intently. 'Intern seventeen, now is not the time to text, please put your device away.'

'I wasn't texting, Professor, I was making notes.'

'I believe the orientation of the lab is simple enough that notes are not needed. If this is too complicated, you might as well leave now.'

The intern hastily tucked her device away, red-faced and bottom lip quivering. Across the room, Penny, the wellbeing manager, glared at me. Her instructions had been to treat the interns sensitively, as studies showed they had a fragile nature at their age. The last thing the company needed was another suicide. I glared back, then thought better of it and softened my expression as much as I could.

'All instructions are on the app and website if you need a recap.' I took a deep breath. That was about as much empathy as I could manage.

'And here we have the product testing.' The interns followed me, shuffling along in unison, none wanting to be first or last. When they arrived at the desk of coloured pots of various sliced and minced this and that, a resounding 'Ahh' rippled through the room. I couldn't help but smile. This part I actually loved.

'Are these new, Professor?'

I nodded.

'Can we try some?' one asked, his chubby face reminding me that the years of famine were definitely over. Synthesising food for the nation had not happened without some victims of its success.

'Sure.' I fetched a petri dish and spoon for each of them.

'Mmm! Carrot!'

'This orange is so sweet and tangy.'

'This is the most wholesome-tasting potato I've ever had.'

'The latest in fibre synthesis and starch simulation is producing excellent results,' I said. 'Not only are the flavours very exciting to the palate, the digestive benefits are also excellent. Can anyone tell me the latest bowel cancer rates among the over fifties?' Twenty hands holding spoons shot in the air. 'Yes, intern two.'

'Forty percent, and a five percent increase each decade.'

'Excellent. And what about scurvy and other vitamin deficiencies? Intern one?'

'Forty percent of under twenties have had scurvy, and vitamin A deficiency accounts for poor eyesight for life in thirty percent of the Perimeter population.'

'And that,' another intern said, 'equates to an economic impact of eighty billion pounds a year.'

'Very good.' I forced a smile. Reciting facts gave the interns a feeling of self-worth, improving their confidence and ability to speak in front of others. That's what Penny told me, anyway. In one of her meetings, the belligerent and pompous woman had instructed me to be more approachable, to bolster the interns' delicate demeanours with praise. Applauding spoon-fed facts was akin to commending my computer for sending an email, I argued. We should give accolades for initiative and brilliance, not mimicry. But mental wellbeing was not my speciality, she sternly reminded me. So, I asked simple questions they knew the answers to and congratulated them for their cleverness in knowing such simple, mundane facts. They would go home to their parents, delighted they had taken part in a discussion at an eight-year-old's knowledge level.

'Now, cast your minds back to your history lessons from primary school.' I changed my tone, giving it an ominous quality to prepare them for a more challenging subject. 'What is carrot flavour?'

The interns looked at each other. None wanted to be the first to respond. After an extended silence, intern three raised a shaky hand.

'Carrot flavour is based on the vegetable carrot.'

'Yes, continue.'

'Carrots were grown...' She gulped. 'Underground... in dirt.'

'Exactly,' I said. 'As I'm sure you all know, the planet used to be covered in dirt. There was so much dirt that this very Raft that was once Britain was connected to the bottom of the ocean by it. Food was grown in dirt, and as such, people were covered in dirt. And with dirt came germs.'

The interns shuddered. I avoided looking at Penny, but could feel her icy gaze shooting daggers at me. *They're not ready to hear about such gruesome things! You've upset them!*

'This lab,' I said, 'and others like it can be credited with ridding the world of germs. Food is made and packaged in sterile conditions, so it arrives at your plate clean, measured, and free from germs.' I took a sip of water and watched the interns absorb the information. 'Now, can anyone tell me more benefits of lab-made food?' This time several hands shot in the air, the interns keen to talk freely. 'Intern ten, your turn.'

'Space, Professor. Lab-made food means more space for people to live. The land is not taken up with useless fields of dirt.'

'Excellent, number ten. In fact, the factory connected to this lab, about seven hundred square metres, can produce enough clean synthesised food to feed a million people around the clock. That frees up several million acres of otherwise useless land to house our ever-growing population. What other benefits to lab-made food are there? Intern number eleven.'

'A lab is not bound by weather, daylight, or growing patterns. It doesn't need to be left fallow and doesn't need fertiliser.'

'Excellent point, eleven. Can you believe that, in the eras of disease in the nineteenth and twentieth centuries, people ate fruit and vegetables grown in animal dung?'

Gasps of horror and shock exploded from the interns. 'No! Surely they didn't!'

Intern three gagged on his synthetic potato. I revelled in their disbelief.

'It's true,' I said. 'Filthy creatures producing filthy piles of excrement, which was then ploughed through fields of dirt to grow food to put in their mouths. And it surprised our ancestors when plague after plague struck them down.'

Several interns ran to a bin to retch, while others began sobbing, their tears dripping onto the polished steel tables. Penny, making a flamboyant spectacle of her attentiveness, supported one as he almost fainted. She propped him up against a wall, then faced me and scowled angrily. I shrugged in response.

'Try not to squirm from this news,' I continued, despite Penny shaking her head frantically at me and mouthing *enough!* 'Use the reality and lunacy of the past to propel your learning. History teaches us. Where our ancestors failed, we excel. You must understand how ignorant to the harshness of nature our ancestors were. When the climate bent and buckled, when the floods came and storms whipped the ground, they wanted to save the filth and the filthy creatures they fed on. Filthy creatures and plants were kept in pots of dirt in houses. They collected filthy creatures to show in museums and would pay to look at and touch them. They even thought if there were more filthy creatures, there would be fewer plagues.'

More gasps of horror sounded across the lab, some interns holding hands to their mouths in fear or wiping away tears. I gave them a moment to compose themselves, but just a brief one. I wasn't about to let those fidgeting backsides get too comfortable.

'Indeed, it wasn't until the bacterial infestations began in 2075 that humankind saw sense and eradicated other creatures. Before this, they believed that the more filthy creatures there were, the more dirt, the fewer germs they would get, as if these filthy creatures absorbed all the diseases like a sponge.' Giggles and laughs replaced the gasps and whimpers. I held up my hands. 'I know, I know, the hilarity of the past. It is the truth. Remember, until then, humankind was still feeding off dirt-fed animals, sucking on bones, ingesting their juices and even wearing their skins. Can you even imagine? Eating animal flesh, feeding on food grown in animal excrement, drinking animal juices, wearing animal skins and then being surprised when they became riddled with bacteria.'

The interns were quivering, some shaking their heads in disbelief. I couldn't help but smile. Their terror was my pride.

'Humankind of the past even used medicines to treat the filthy creatures prior to killing and consuming them, so much so that those medicines stopped working on people. They set our fate in motion. The bacteria became supercharged, resistant to treatment. Antibiotic medications could not keep up when the world was one giant petri dish of filth. Bacteria was taking over the planet as the strongest living thing on earth. There was barely a human alive who wasn't rife with infection. Coughing, pus, gingivitis, incontinence, impotence,' I continued, despite the cries of distress from my little audience, 'blindness, disability, sterility, seizures, paralysis.' Some interns started wailing. 'All from the pathogens that humankind harnessed and ingested. Once the traditional medicines stopped working, they realised that the germs they'd been harvesting through their filthy habits were becoming more powerful than humankind itself.'

I paused, allowing time for two interns to finish vomiting into a sink and a furious Penny to attend to the most upset. The rest wiped their brows, practised their breathing exercises and blinked away tears.

'Luckily for all of us, they changed their habits.' I walked over to a gap in the shelves of glassware where a blue square hung on the wall, along with the inscription '*With Sterility Comes Liberty.*' 'We progressed, and progress is paramount. Modern thinking caught up with science and education. The Blue Liberation party united the country, and the Great Sterilisation Project began.'

The mere mention of the Great Sterilisation Project was enough to put the interns at ease, and a ripple of relieved sighs spread through the lab. Colour returned to their cheeks, and the retching ceased. 'So sleep easy, interns. Everyone is safe now. The world you live in is clean thanks to labs like this and the great work of the Blue Liberation party, and the scientists and engineers thereafter.'

The interns clapped at the happy end to the terrifying story. 'With sterility comes liberty!' they all shouted.

School history lessons washed over the goriest parts of the story, and avoided upsetting the youngsters. But being told the truth on this, the first day of their internship, was a rite of passage into adulthood, I believed.

I stepped back and allowed the interns to explore the equipment for a few minutes—those that had recovered from their nausea, anyway. They stood up silently with their shoulders hunched and made their way to the computers and lab equipment. My assistant Marcus showed them how to work the burners and showed them where the beakers and flasks lived. A few interns found the courage to ask questions, speaking in whispers, keeping their eyes fixed on the floor.

I retreated to my office for a few moments alone in delightful peace. The glass-walled space was too big for the limited amount of furniture I had, but it conveyed the desired atmosphere: cold and unwelcoming. I had a desk, one chair and a backdrop of framed certificates and awards. My ego wall was the stuff of dreams to the interns outside, and a focal point for their parents on the open day: 'Here is the office of our top nutrition researcher. I'm sure you've all heard of Professor Selbourne, a long-term employee here at BioLabs. She is a shining example of what can be achieved here!' And the parents all stared wide-eyed with their 'Oohs' and 'Aahhs'. I once made the mistake of being in my office on an open day—one I have not repeated. Being the victim of doting parents' overbearing praise for their precious offspring, being the subject of their aspirations for their protégés, was as asphyxiating as walking through the Perimeter's smog.

I knew I couldn't hide for long. It was only day one of that year's programme, after all. Checking through a small gap in the blinds, I could see Marcus's panicked face as one intern started to cry again. I sighed and stepped back out into the lab.

'Alright, interns, I hope you've all enjoyed familiarising yourself with the equipment. Any questions? Yes, intern four?'

'Professor, if this food is all so cutting edge, why do so many people suffer from vitamin deficiencies?'

I exhaled slowly. Every year they ask this, and every year I have no response.

'Good question, intern four, good question.'

Chapter 2

The interns moved away, their bewildered eyes taking in the lab. The shelves and shelves of glassware, computer screens, burners, distillation setups. After a moment of looking dazed, they began touching and moving things, curiosity giving them some courage. Marcus stared rather dumbfounded at the clutter twenty new employees could create in such a short time. His organised oasis quickly turned to chaos.

All too soon I heard Penny's footsteps approaching, her distinctive scurry unmistakable, a discordant noise against the backdrop of clinking glass and muffled voices. I walked to a corner of the lab away from the interns. The last thing I needed was a public dressing-down from Penny. Again.

'Ahem.' She cleared her throat behind me. I picked up a conical flask and inspected it, then took another to compare the two.

'Ahem!' Penny coughed louder. I found a paper towel and started polishing the first flask.

'Professor, I will not be ignored!' she almost shrieked. I

sighed, defeated, and turned around. 'I was hoping not to have my office full of panicked interns on the very first day of their programme.' Her frizzy hair vibrated erratically as she shook her head.

'Is there something in the air?' I asked in my most innocent voice.

Her face contorted in anger, and her shrill voice rose to an excruciating pitch as she attempted to keep from shouting. 'You know exactly why they are all feeling so unwell. You simply cannot expect them to cope with hearing about filth and dirt and the way things used to be. They are too young.' The emphasis on her last two words was more than a little condescending.

'They're in their twenties. If they can't handle the truth—'

'They weren't there!' Her voice reached an octave she rarely achieved. Interns' heads snapped around to look at us. Penny smiled back at them, her lipstick-smeared teeth making it look more like a sneer. Then she leaned in closer to me, bombarding me with her perfume, and whispered, 'They have no concept of it. It's too much for them to cope with, on top of everything else they have to go through here. Certainly, day one is too early. They are not hardened to the world yet. Over half of them have never even left their apartments before, as you well know. First day away from home and you tell them scare stories. It's simply not on. We're going to have complaints from the parents already.'

I rolled my eyes. 'Honestly, Penny, it's hardly a scare story.' Every year she bored me with this rubbish. 'They should've been taught this already. Their parents should prepare them better. Doesn't it say that in the welcome emails they receive? That they must know Britain's history?'

Penny ignored me and continued her diatribe. 'I cannot cope with another year of panic attacks. Marcus doesn't want to clean up vomit every day. This is a sterile lab. Vomiting interns are counterproductive.' She had a point about that. The previous year had been a particularly bad one for vomit. On several occasions the sinks had been blocked, and the plumbing had to be repaired. Poor Marcus spent days fixing them. He never complained, though.

'Perhaps we should have more sick bags and buckets available?' I said.

Her eyes widened and bulged with rage, her lips puckering. I was sure steam started coming out of her ears. Her annoyance almost made the entire conversation worthwhile. 'I'll be speaking to Greg about this,' she said. I could see her cheeks ripple over grinding teeth. Then she scampered back to her hole like some awful insect.

When I started the internship programme, I thought it would be genuinely useful. I could mould young minds that would go on to make a difference, and they would provide fresh eyes to gift us with inspiration and ideas. I thought young people meant progress. They all floated in on a cloud of pride and praise from their parents, their shyness and inexperience drifting below them, lagging behind, the awe and wonder of their cloud elevating them above any insecurities. Behold their splendour, the new interns on their pedestals of good grades and bookishness, for never has a lab coat been so white! Never has a shirt been so precisely buttoned! Their shoes gleamed with the brilliance of youth and parental affection. They shone with innocence.

The fall to reality got harder every year. The emotional bruises swelled and left them deflated, as useful and articulate as a prune. I am unkind; I know. I have little patience. I could spend a day listing my faults and still not cover all of them. My job description mentions nothing of being sympathetic (although Penny attempted to convince me otherwise). Succeeding in this world requires a lack of empathy bordering on ruthlessness, so I make no apology for my minor cruelties. We are all someone's underling, and chances are that 'someone' has several subordinates, all willing to wipe their shoes on you on their way up. The concept of friendship went out of fashion years ago. I am a woman of my time, trying to survive. This lesson might actually be useful for the interns. For five years I had seen little but minds encumbered by exam grades and conformity, eroding any hope I had of finding brilliance or insight. Now all I wanted was some lackies to keep the lab clean and organise my notes.

I loitered in the lab all morning. The solitude of my office beckoned me, but I stayed put. I paraded around, showing the interns how the software worked, what projects we were working on, and explaining the roles they were required to play. I liked to watch their jitters, their nervousness, to feel their awe of me and my modest reputation. For someone who looked so unassuming, short and borderline unattractive, I enjoyed this bit of authority. Knowing they would wake in the night in a sweaty mess, heart racing with the worry of my displeasure... Well, that took some of the dullness of my days away.

'Most important is to input the data correctly. You see, the results go here.' I pointed to one screen and twenty pairs of unblinking eyes followed my hand. 'All that needs to go through these calculations here. Work out if it's statistically significant, and that data goes here.' I pointed to another monitor. Not one intern dared to even breathe. 'This is incredibly important, and where you can really make a difference.' They all nodded, still not taking their eyes off the screen. I smiled, unable to hide my smugness. If I could get them to do the data inputting, that would be a seriously tedious task off my back.

I heard the main doors swish open as Archie walked in. He gave me a sarcastic grin on his way to his office, knowing how much I hated day one of the intern programme.

'Ah, and here is one of the talented engineers himself.' I gestured to Archie, and he hesitated before stopping. I smirked. *You're not getting away that easily!* 'Interns, say hello to Mr Archibald Reynolds.'

They all said 'Hello' in unison.

'Good morning, interns.' He smiled at them before addressing me. 'Professor, how's your tomorrow?'

'Uncertain. And yours?'

'As always,' he said, using the traditional greeting in a rare display of professionalism. 'If you have a moment, Professor, can I have a word?'

'Please excuse me, interns. Explore the lab. Marcus is ready to answer your questions. Familiarise yourself with the processes, as tomorrow you'll be starting to make a real contribution to food synthesis.'

As soon as they were out of earshot, I spoke to Archie. 'Thanks. Trying to summon enthusiasm for another bunch of adolescents is frying my brain today.'

Archie nodded, and we walked to his office. It was stiflingly hot in there, with sixteen computer monitors on. There was a tiny window where, despite the smog, the sun elbowed its way through. The blind was broken and hanging off to the side, making it as useful as the pathetic air-con unit that did little more than buzz and dribble.

'Jesus, Archie. How do you cope in here?'

'Power rations are allocated to the labs at the moment. You get used to it. Greg doesn't give a shit if we cook, anyway,' he said, a bitter edge cutting into his usual cheerful tone. 'As long as the computers can cope, the staff can too.'

He was as pale and unshaven as any computer engineer, but a hell of a lot more charming. Most I'd worked with conversed in grunts and tuts, whereas Archie was thoughtful enough to make the MimikTea from time to time, welcomed conversation and was interested in people.

Archie laughed. 'Anyway, you moan about my office, but look how welcoming it is. At least I have seats.'

'My office has a seat,' I said as I collapsed into one of his.

He raised an eyebrow at me. 'Go ahead, make yourself at home.'

'This is hardly a seat, Archie. This is the corpse of a seat. Look at the state of it.' I inspected the threadbare upholstery and extracted some stuffing.

'You scientists. Always wanting perfection.'

I grinned and continued to delight in pointing out the holes and stains, as if he didn't know. 'My office is exactly as I want it. Unhomely is the aim. Imagine if the interns thought they could come in and sit down and talk to me! I'd never get rid of them. I'd have to stick a "Go Away" sign to the door.'

'You'd never write something that polite,' he said. 'What about your dearest friend, though?' He cleared his throat. 'Where is he meant to sit when he wishes to escape his sauna and chat to you in your office?'

'You can bring your own chair.' I tossed a biro at him and laughed. 'Wheel one through when you bring me a cup of tea, if you like.'

Archie was headhunted for BioLabs because his skill set did not stop with computer engineering. He also had a degree in geology, something the army sponsored him through during his years of service. The entire land surface may have been covered in concrete, but underneath that, rocks still ruled (I never told the interns that, obviously).

I fanned myself: a futile action. It seemed ironic that one of the best people in the country to prepare us for the weather had the worst climate control in his office. He always had a bowl of IcyCrema on his desk, melting down to mush. He took out a tub of red fruits flavour from his bag.

'What are our coordinates now?' I asked.

He put the spoon in his mouth and raised his eyebrows at me. 'Do you really want to know?'

'Go on, hit me.'

'Drifting at about N34.212737, W31.591748 and heading further south. At this rate, we'll hit the equator in a month.'

'Microbes, really? The equator in a month!' I sweated more just thinking about it.

Archie's geology degree came too late to be useful. But then, no geologist could have stopped what was happening. By the time we knew the extent of the problem, Britain was attached to the Earth's crust by only a thread. For that tiny sliver of land, there was no hope. Our decaying root's fate was sealed by the corrosion that had been left unchecked for too long. The rot had set in.

I fanned myself some more and pulled my shirt away from my moist skin. 'What would our temperature be if we were still fixed to the seabed, or at least if the anchor bridges were still in place?' I asked.

Archie shook his head. 'I've said it before: there's no point dwelling on what could be or might have been. We are floating aimlessly, forever.'

'They still say it's temporary, that we'll re-anchor one day.' He pulled a face of exaggerated doubt. 'They do say that!' I said, his theatrical shock too funny to take seriously.

'Yeah, of course they say that. But after twenty years we've glimpsed the mainland only once, and that didn't go too well. So I'd say it's quite unlikely.' He ate another spoonful of IcyCrema and winced at the cold shock it gave him. 'Anyway, they'd never go to the expense of building anchor bridges again. Why bother? The old anchors were blown up after a year. You remember what nationalists were like, the protests. "Borders not bridges!" "Liberation not co-operation!" "Liberation not infestation!"'

'If we ever find what's left of Cornwall or East Anglia, they'll probably blow those up, too.' It was a poor-taste joke. Those lands sank beneath the waves the instant we broke away. Sometimes we find hilarity in the lunacy: the last human civilisation, drifting out to sea on a Raft covered in concrete.

'You found that weather report yet?' I reminded him.

'Give me a minute. Satellites aren't always that quick, especially when The Raft is in spin mode.'

'Aren't you meant to be the best there is?' I said.

He rolled his eyes and checked his monitors. 'If we were still attached to the seabed, or at least still anchored in place, it would be...' He drum-rolled on his desk. '...ten degrees cooler.'

I sighed and watched the last bit of his IcyCrema collapse into liquid. 'That'd be nice.'

'Storms, though. Look.' He pointed to one monitor with fingerprint-style coloured swirls. 'Loads of rain. Enough even to flood The Raft a bit, I reckon. If we'd re-anchored when we drifted close to Portugal all those years ago, right now, hmm...' He uploaded some more images. 'About the same as here: bloody baking hot.'

'Sounds about right. The entire planet is bloody baking hot.'

'Anyway,' Archie continued, chirpier. 'The real reason I wanted to speak to you was to give you a heads-up.'

'I thought you were being a hero and dragging me away from the interns.'

'Ha! No. I love how much they annoy you.' He poked his tongue out at me. 'I actually have some good news. I had a video call with Greg this morning. Bit of exciting gossip: he has a new assignment for you. Promotion, I believe.'

'Really? What is it? Anything is better than wet-nursing these interns.'

'Not saying.' He mimed a zip across his mouth. 'Greg will be in tomorrow to speak to you, so keep those kids under control. I reckon it'll come with more money, though. It's not like he'd reward you with an even bigger office. You'd get lost.'

Greg thought a large office was as much a reward as going up a pay grade. Appearing important and wealthy was as important as actually being so. Climbing the ladder for those born in the Centre was a much easier task than for those of us reared in the Perimeter. For us, each slippery rung was beyond fingertips away, and we needed to leap just to graze it. I could hardly pay my rent with the void that was my office space. Greg couldn't see that, however. His indulgent upbringing gave him the reach he needed to heave himself up two rungs at a time.

'Don't get my hopes up, Archie.'

'I'm serious. It's going to be good news. He must have noticed your consistent hundred-percent score on the employee social media. Kiss-ass,' he said. 'Greg did seem particularly pleased with himself, though. You know, in that pompous, entitled way of his. I didn't think those teeth could get any whiter, but they're pretty much fluorescent now. Blinding his assistant, by the looks of it, her eyes were all teary.'

'Another one? Really?' I sighed.

'Yep, the shit. That last one, Ella... Ellie...'

'Ellen?'

'Yeah, that one. How long did she last? About a week?' He shook his head. 'That man is so depraved he should be tossed into the sea.'

I shuddered. Greg worked his way through assistants quicker than the wind blew through The Raft. They all ran away within weeks, terrified when his wandering eyes turned into wandering hands.

Archie shook his head. 'Centre pricks get away with whatever. Even if they get found out, it gets forgotten in minutes. There's always something more important to concern them. And us.'

'Them and us. Exactly.'

'Same country, different species, I swear. That's why I don't suck up to these pricks.' He raised his eyebrows at me.

'Not like I have a choice.'

'I know, babe,' he said. His sympathy was genuine. He knew all about my home life, my wife and our troubles. 'How long has it been?'

I paused to think. 'Must be eight years. No, nine.' Nine years we'd been on the fertility treatment list. Nine years of Grace's sadness. Nine years of my corporate ass-kissing to get us the references we needed.

'Shit. They've got you by the rope.' He smiled a supportive

smile, though his empathy came without experience. I was sure he still wanted to meet someone. He paid careful attention to his hair, changing the parting from one side to the other daily, insisting this would slow its retreat. I teased him, but banter on such topics had worn thinner than his comb-over.

He winked at me, always such a flirt. 'Professor Savannah Selbourne climbing the corporate ladder. Who'd have thought it?'

I winced at my name. I hated it. Savannah sounded pretty, which I was not. Or like I lived in a yurt, which I also did not. A fairly typical name handed out by parents from a generation still clinging to nature, yet who died from the havoc it caused.

'Well, maybe I can look forward to you calling me "Boss" and making all the tea,' I said as he handed me his empty cup with a grin. I rolled my eyes and left for the kitchen.

At least the kitchen was slightly cooler than Archie's office. I sat at the table and waited for the kettle to boil. I knew that in a few days, the interns wouldn't even let me have these few moments of peace. Their first-day timidness was a blessing.

Out the window, the sun was peeking above the high-rises from a different direction to the week before. The Raft must have spun 180 degrees. We didn't feel such movements, the dips and sways going undetected. The country veered and bobbed even before we broke away. No one paid any attention then, either. Our ship was sinking, and no one noticed.

'Tea delivery!' I said as I returned to the sauna. 'Archie, you alive?'

'Huh? Oh yeah, thanks.'

'Weather that exciting?'

'Well...'

'Seriously, Archie. No way is the weather exciting.'

'Usually I'd agree, but those storms I was telling you about—I think we could be in for a rogue wave.'

'Really? How big?' I asked.

'Hard to say, big enough to be of concern, though.'

'Our end of the coast or somewhere else?'

'The Raft is spinning so much it's hard to know. I've told the water companies to cover the drinking water, to section it off just in case. There's a chance it could wash up quite far and cause a contamination issue.'

'Well, keep it quiet. We don't want the interns hearing about it. They'll all drop out from fear in week one and I'll never get this product launch ready.'

Archie nodded. 'It'll probably be fine, anyway. I'll know more tomorrow. Maybe bottle up some water at home, just in case.'

I retreated to the coolness of my office, peering through the blinds to further inspect this year's crop. The interns were engrossed in microscopes and computer software. No one was crying yet, nothing broken. So far, so good. They all had the keen and fresh faces that came with the first day. Some had even spoken directly to each other or made eye contact. Perhaps this year's bunch would show some promise. A rogue wave shouldn't cause too much panic. Perhaps it wouldn't scare them. Perhaps.

4

Chapter 3

It was rare, almost unheard of, that I was happy or excited after a day at work. The lab that had once been my sanctuary now felt like a prison. The beakers and test tubes felt more like artillery than tools. Screens and screens of data, mind-numbing lists of numbers and more numbers, a purgatory of monotony, punishment for some childhood delinquency I had little recollection of.

That day, though, I hurried from the lab a little too quickly, forgetting the wall of heat that awaited me outside. The air was sucked out of my lungs as the thick soup of pollution and heat winded me. But not even the repressive temperature could detract from my elation. I almost skipped, lighter than air, walking with a joyous stride, eager to see what the next day would bring. A promotion could be exactly what I needed, what we needed, to improve our application to the fertility clinic. Grace would be so happy, I was sure. Her normally solemn face would light up and a smile would spark into life.

The walk was only twenty minutes, but an Autocar—a

frivolous expense I wouldn't normally bother with—cut that in half. It meant ten more minutes at home with Grace, meaning I could tell her my good news ten minutes sooner. I was excited. A long-awaited promotion and the delight of telling my wife. What could be better?

Before getting in an Autocar, I rushed over to the Selfie Station opposite the lab. The lighting at the station was flattering and adjustable, a choice of filters at the touch of a button that changed with the seasons and trends. I chose 'Evening Elegance' before a quick spruce up, attempting to get some volume in my limp hair. Middle age replaces glowing skin with a sallower covering. Time erodes radiance. I couldn't smile away the years: the lines would dig deeper. However good your nutrition is, gravity always wins. I did my best, though, taking my time at the station, aiming to not only impress work, but Grace too. Then I posted the required picture. '*Great day at work today. What a fantastic bunch of interns! #biolabs #greatday #lovemyjob.*' I got an instant thumbs up from the company's social media Autobot and maintained my hundred-percent employee credit score. I remembered Archie's comments. Never would he stoop so low as to visit a Selfie Station and hashtag work. Perhaps my years of devout selfies and corporate schmoozing were finally paying off.

The strip billboards that spanned the length of each building were reciting the news headlines on a loop, as always. Projected at no one in particular, yet piercing the mind of anyone in sight. I can't recall what they were that day. They can't have been too dramatic. The headlines of the days that followed dominate that part of my memory.

As the Autocar trundled closer to my street, the roads became bumpier and bumpier. The new quantum cables had been laid months before and the street still had not been repaired. Hardly anyone left their houses so they didn't notice, and didn't complain. The Autocar was programmed to avoid the worst of the potholes, but it was impossible to dodge every one. Salt is corrosive, and heat makes asphalt buckle. The combination had turned the road surface to dust. The Autocar threw me around as it swerved, and I hurt my elbow as I collided with the side of the vehicle. I should have just walked.

We pulled up at my apartment block and I got out, disinfectant road spray immediately soaking my ankles. It didn't sting like the old brands. Pity. There was something reassuring in the sting. The street was as quiet as always. A silent bliss where I could watch the dust particles catch the last rays of sun drifting up through the air above me. The particulate matter pollution was getting worse, I noted.

My parents had reminisced about busy streets and rush hours and queues like they were good things. They had missed the hustle and bustle, the fumes, the engine noise, the crowds and the din that came with them. My father would even groan at the lack of bird noise—the 'evening chorus', he called it. He would play an old recording on a loop in the evenings while we sat in our house, enshrouded by the silence outside. He said the birdsong brought him joy, but he choked back tears. I always thought it was strange to take comfort in something that evoked such sadness. 'Nature sickness', the doctors called it, or 'environmental dementia': when someone becomes so obsessed with the old world, it drives them crazy. The world progressed while my father's mind regressed. His thoughts could not escape the dirt. I was too young to comprehend. He slipped away before I was old enough to explain things to him, to help him understand.

Silence reminds me of my parents, their antitheses sparking their memories instead of their delights. But then, they took little delight in the world by the end. Better off, I'd tell myself.

I could hear Grace shouting in the Interactive Cupboard when I walked in the door. Our IC was top of the range. Archie had set it up, and it was impressive, even though it was over three years old. There was a switch on the stand with an orange button that, if pressed, would make Grace's voice boom, so the children jumped in shock. 'Riley, will you pay attention!' was her most common orange-switch statement these days, and that's what I heard as I walked through the door. History was this afternoon's lesson, by the sound of it.

I tiptoed around the apartment, getting changed and preparing dinner, not wanting to disturb Grace. I winced when I loudly clinked glasses and plates. Our apartment was compact and cluttered, inherited furniture making up a chaotic jumble of hand-me-downs. A mismatched array of shiny plastic and brushed metals, bookshelves housing photos and devices, a table too large for just us two, a stiff pleather armchair that was still dented with the imprint of my mother.

There was a real book hidden somewhere among the mess. I'd concealed it well, of course, as I had no licence to possess such a hazardous item. It was decades old, its paper made of archaic tree carcasses that curled at the edges and smelled like dust. I should just burn the thing, I knew that, but some things are too hard to let go.

I found a pack of Realios Protein Bits in the fridge and a box of Syntho Spaghetti in the cupboard. I opened a bottle of BordeuNo and got the glasses ready. Grace emerged from the IC looking tired and sat at the window. I went over to give her a kiss and was offered a cheek.

'Good day?'

Grace replied with a sigh, and I handed her a glass. She slouched low in her chair and resumed her usual state of staring out of the window. She always stared out of the window then, or down at the floor, rarely straight ahead. Like she didn't want to see what was right in front of her, trying hard not to acknowledge the present.

'I have exciting news.'

'Unlikely,' Grace said. 'The email came. We're still bottom of the list.'

'Still? But it's been nine years.'

Grace sighed again and drank her wine. She had a beautiful sigh, like a sad, mellifluent little cry. Her long, elegant neck slouched, wilted, unable to support the weight of her troubled mind. It used to blush pink when I kissed her there. Now it looked pallid and withered from abandonment. 'They're never going to consider us while we're in a one-bed. Where would we even put a baby?'

'There's that new tower block being built by the coast.'

'Even more Perimeter.' She shook her head. 'That won't be good. Fish junkies on every corner round there.'

'It might be nice. I'll walk over tomorrow and check it out. They're really trying to clean the area up.' I almost pleaded. 'And they're two-beds.'

'Oh, what does it matter anyway? They'll all be taken already, by people more important than us.' Her bitter tone cut.

'Well, that's where I have some good news,' I said, trying to reach out across the vacuum between us. 'I think I'm being offered a promotion tomorrow, so maybe that will look better on our application?'

'Maybe.' Grace shrugged an empty shrug. 'Still, with our contract almost up, they might need some reassurance.' She offered no congratulations.

Our ten-year marriage was almost up. It was the first time Grace had mentioned it, though I was well aware. We could renew or go our separate ways. The government put no pressure on couples either way. The ten-year marriage was supposed to ease divorce rates, make the country seem like it had one hundred percent happy and faithful marriages. And it had worked, according to statistics. In the last two decades, divorce rates had dropped from seventy percent to just ten. The Raft comprised only happily married couples, or happily single people (besides the ten percent who couldn't stand each other for more than a decade). The last great civilisation on earth was not only safe but happy. Apparently. According to those stats, even Grace and myself were a happily married couple.

'I'd like to renew. What about you?' My voice bordered on the pathetic.

'I suppose,' she said, flatly. 'It's not like we have a choice. The clinic will never consider me if I'm not married. Getting too old now, too.'

She didn't look it. Her complexion did not reflect how troubled her mind was. Staying indoors all the time had that one benefit.

'It could also be nice. It might make you happy. We could even have a ceremony, if you like?'

'Whatever you think.' Her expression didn't change. She continued to stare outside, her hands fidgeting restlessly.

I pulled my chair closer to her, my eyes willing her to look my way, to feel the love I was trying to send to her. 'Maybe they'll open up the schools again soon. There hasn't been a bird sighting in years now, not even a bug. The streets are clean enough. You could see the children again, not just in the IC. You might enjoy it, leaving the apartment again. Going outside.'

'You think that's some magic cure? Baking in the heat and breathing in the smog outside? They're never going to open the schools again anyway. They've built tower blocks where most of them used to be. You said so yourself. There's not even a playground now.' She let a tear fall down her cheek.

It had been gradual; her sinking into this cave where I could not reach her. Her loneliness was impenetrable, however much I tried. Melancholy hung off her like a shadow, her light obscured by her internment. She had turned to ice.

'We could see a doctor, Grace. You know, the clinic. They might not care if we explained why. Loads of people have therapy, loads take medication to help them cope.'

She shook her head quickly, making her golden curls bounce, conveying a joy her cries did not. 'No, no, no! We've been through this. I can't. We'd never get fertility treatment if they think I'm crazy.'

'You're not crazy. It's just, I can see it. You're not coping. Grace, please. You can't be this sad forever.'

'Forever?' she spat. 'You think we're never going to get the treatment?'

'No, no, that's not what I'm saying. But what if... what if your depression—' she recoiled at the word, '—affects you after the treatment too? Surely it's better to get on top of it now, before a baby comes along.'

'No.' Grace stood up, but her shoulders immediately fell in a defeated slump. 'We'd be struck off the waiting list if they diagnosed either of us with mental illness. Nutcases aren't allowed to breed,' she yelled through tears. 'Anyway, I'm not depressed. I'm a mother without a child. There's your cure. Fix that problem.'

She swallowed her wine in one mouthful and went for a shower.

I knew Grace blamed me, though she'd never say it directly. As sad as she was, she would never be so heartless as to say it out loud. 'Fix that problem' was enough of a hint. Whatever my achievements, I felt sure that the clinic saw me as little more than having the blood of Alternates. Legally, it wasn't supposed to work that way. I'm an individual, not my parent's clone, but my accolades were outstripped by my parents' reputation. I couldn't erase them. They had died years before, but had left a dirty mark against my name.

I took down an old e-pad from the shelf and brushed off the dust. I turned it on, the start-up screen taking ages to load, found the app I was looking for and pressed play. The music sounded tinny and the lyrics clichéd. Everything joyful sounded dated at this point. No new music had been made in decades. But it was a tune I knew Grace once loved. The volume button was unresponsive, but with a bit of persuasion, it complied and the melody rang out louder. I heard the shower turn off and Grace appeared in the doorway wrapped in a towel, wet hair down her sides.

'Why play that tune?'

'To remember.'

'I can't remember.'

'Yes, you can.'

'What's the point? Remembering happiness from before doesn't erase the sadness of now.' She hung her head low, staring at the water pooling beneath her. I walked over to her, taking her hands to dance. 'No, Sav. I don't want to. I can't.' She snatched her hands back. 'Playing some tune from a lifetime ago can't fix things.'

'You used to laugh at these lyrics. Your laugh was sort of wheezy, it sounded like a steam kettle,' I said and stroked her cheek. She pulled away.

I remembered that Grace. She found everything funny. Once her laughter kettle boiled, she would be left breathless, teary-eyed and flushed-cheeked. A decade later and that laugh was a distant memory. Her optimism had run its course, yearning turned to bitterness, cheeks once rosy turned sallow. I remembered the days when her eyes glowed with mischief rather than radiating misery.

'I've nothing to laugh about.' She wiped her eyes. 'We just need to be richer. If we were Centre, we'd have a baby by now.' She turned away and went back to the bathroom.

I sat on the sofa and sipped my wine. She had a point. Producing gametes from stem cells was easy. Affording the price tag was not. Never in a million years could we afford to pay for the treatment. Skirmishing fruitlessness with lab technology was so commonplace that people had become squeamish about the original method of procreation. Over ninety percent of children were made this way. The cleanliness of the clinic seemed a more reassuring way to produce a baby, rather than the traditional, unfashionable mess.

Grace's science-history syllabus skirted over the details; the reasons why were too obvious and deplorable to mention. Dirt was the answer. They all knew it. Centuries of eating animals that ate dirt and drank dirty water.

I went to bed that night refusing to be sucked into Grace's

despair. She slept as heavily as always as I tossed and turned. The next day's promotion felt like our last hope, and I allowed myself that: hope.

5

Chapter 4

The following morning, I dressed quietly so as not to wake Grace. She was a late riser, sleeping away her existence. As I left the bedroom, I glanced back at her, the pillow underneath her head visibly damp from tears. I had slept but felt barely rested, scenarios and possibilities swimming in my mind. What could it be? What sort of promotion? How vile was Greg going to be?

I left earlier than usual. I decided to take a look at the new housing development I'd mentioned to Grace, hoping that seeing it would help me feel, and act, inspired. The sun was barely up, but the temperature was already stifling. The roads glistened from their early morning spray of disinfectant, adding to the humidity. Where the sun hit the pavement, the sanitiser misted up and moistened my legs as high as my knees, sticking my trousers to my clammy skin. The hum of air conditioning was constant. Windows shut, inhabitants sealed inside, only filtered air allowed in. I checked the news on my phone. Nothing alarming. The calm before the storm? It had been a while since a disaster had hit the National Press, but from experience I knew that as soon as we dared to breathe, we'd be winded again.

Businesses had not yet opened for the day. The MindSpa was getting ready, and through its windows I could see the fluffy towels being neatly folded and the lighting altered until it was a relaxing shade. Their daily online meditation classes would be held in the private rooms for those using the services at home, a 24/7 service pitched as 'A Lifeline at any Time.'

The only other humans outside in this part of the neighbourhood apart from me were attending to the Selfie Stations. There were plenty of stations, and they were alarmingly well used, considering how few people went outside. Keeping up the pretence of perfection, helping with an employer's social media presence and shouting from the rooftops about how wonderful it was to work wherever, were often the only ways to get noticed in a company with thousands of Perimeter employees. Certainly, not partaking in this daily pursuit of pomposity was a way to label yourself as not a team player, not engaging, unreliable.

I, as always, engaged in the charade. I adjusted my hair and makeup, my cropped pixie-cut long overdue a trim. My makeup, applied in near darkness as I tried not to wake Grace, was brightened and touched up. I had scrubbed off the worst of my peeling skin that morning, but the abrasion left me blotchy. I smiled an effortless-looking smile (which actually took a lot of effort) and took my photo. '*Can't wait to achieve today!*' I wrote. '*#biolabs #foodforthought #Behealthy.*' I chose the Morning Glow filter, clicked to share, and looked at the image of the stranger in the picture. Her dark circles had been blurred out by the filter, a glint in her eye added by the lighting, a healthier hue applied to her skin. She looked excited, motivated, with a sincerity that welcomed conversation and felt the warm pride of achievement. The company employee app pinged to confirm I was doing a great job at work today. At least I would go meet Greg with one hundred percent maintained.

I meandered down the paved street, surrounded by grey, homogenised buildings complete with never-used Juliet balconies that lay in front of doors sealed with iron bars, a relic of the looting fears when food shortages were rife. No one had bothered to remove the bars afterwards. Why would they? The unvarying stack of tower blocks at least gave some shade, casting their grey shadows across the grey pavement.

The air was scorching, and the baking asphalt radiated up through my shoes if I stood still long enough. The polished streets became rougher and the road surface more worn as I headed towards the peripheral streets of the Perimeter. Loose gravel kicked up in the dust and I tightened the mask around my face, wheezing against the humidity. A warm wind whipped up some smog and carried with it a warning that I was walking closer to The Raft's edge. Even through my mask, I could taste the salt.

Despite the sea air, the walk to the edge felt safe. The heat and the salt I could tolerate; the thought of filth I could not bear. But I stayed alert, as always, my eyes darting from side to side with every step. Smog. Dust. Gravel. That was all. Every speck had a name. Inanimate, sterile debris. The buildings were reassuring in their bleakness, the old, frilly surfaces of the past smoothed off, scrubbed. Nowhere for vermin to hide.

The country's renovations had driven my father to the brink. All the trees being felled, the landscapes gradually changing from green to grey. The silencing of the countryside. It was hailed as progress. 'Progress is paramount,' they had said. It's modern, more convenient. Cleaner. If anyone complained, they were assumed to be uneducated, nostalgic, relics like my father who still delighted in seeing insects creep around. Weirdos, in other words. The sort we know as Alternates now, living unsanitary lives, not contributing, merely useless consumers. Sceptics, inciting fear and unfounded cynicism.

My father's sanity hung in the precipice between progress and nostalgia. I remembered those days so well. How things could have been so different for us, if only he'd learned to keep up. His stagnation stupefied him as the world changed. I dreamt often of the days before, of my parents, like they were reaching for me through time. A loneliness that transcended decades being tended by kindly hands, fumbling for acknowledgement. Reminding me of them, of an unrecognisable past, of our progress. Of what we had lost.

I am a small girl, walking down the street holding my father's hand. He bends down to pick up a tiny insect.

'Woodlouse, Savannah,' he whispers to me. 'A very important little thing for making compost.'

'What's compost?' I ask.

'It's earth that helps us grow plants.'

'What's a plant?'

He doesn't answer. He glances over his shoulder, then pockets the mini-beast. A scientist always, an entomologist, he hopes his work will help save species, not eradicate them. But the world is changing too quickly for him. He never looks up to see it, too busy searching in the dirt.

When we get back to our house, he makes a home for the creature with all the others. Shelves and shelves of insect houses. 'The hotel,' he calls it. Boxes of dirt and vegetation filled with crawlers and flyers and burrowers. He tells me their names and shows me their pictures in the book he published back in the days when people wanted to read words about filthy creatures, printed on paper made from filthy plants. The book I will cherish for years.

The day passes as he tells me about all of them, instilling a love of science but a distrust of his field as I watch the critters creep around their little cages. In a short time, their corpses litter the hotel's floor.

'This is the honeybee. It pollinates flowers, which makes fruit and gives us honey. This is an earthworm, which improves the soil. This is a fly, which helps decompose dead things.'

I screw my face up. 'What's "decompose"?'

'It's when microbes break down dead things, so they give their nutrients back.'

I blush at his candour. 'Microbes are bad,' I say with certainty.

'Not always, Savannah.' He buries a sigh.

A similar script dominates most of our evenings. My father is pleased by my intrigue, my young scientist's brain, eager to learn. But I have been taught so much else. Microbes are bad, that I know for sure. Poor old dad, confused as always. Give their nutrients back to what? He speaks in riddles with archaic words.

And then evening comes and there's a knock at the front door of our little townhouse. Father opens it and a man barges in. He is tall and smells strongly of soap. His shoes shine so much I can see the reflection of his chin wobbling.

I get sent to my room. From the doorway, I hear them argue.

'These are important species. They play a crucial role in the environment.'

'That environment doesn't exist now, Bill. These species have no place. You know they're illegal.'

'They have a right to survive.'

'As do we. The country is reaching its maximum biomass, it simply can't support everything. Human life is all that matters now.'

'But insects keep us healthy.'

'Not anymore. They spread disease, they're food for vermin birds. Their role in nature is no longer required. We have technology now. They are useless parasites using up precious resources.'

And then more men come in. They don't knock, just enter. They take the insect hotel. The first man says it'll be inciner-ated. They leave, and father cries.

Mother sits and says nothing except, 'I told you they'd come for them.'

Father is never the same again. He is quiet, barely speaking to anyone, even me. The whole country is hushed now. The land is still and quiet as the world loses the last of its colour. His research department closes, and he gets a new job as a caretaker at the school. Scrubbing the pavements and disinfecting the chairs. Ridding the building of the filth he tried to save. He looks more tired every day, spending evenings going through his old book, studying pictures of his insect friends, the only creatures he seems to care about. Long gone.

Time doesn't stop. It whizzes by, imperceptibly at first, but faster and faster until I realise how much has happened and how little I appreciated the velocity of it all. They take our house and put us in a small two-bed apartment. My father's tears are a constant soundtrack to my youth. Then the apartment blocks in our neighbourhood get hit by a bacterial infection for which no antibiotics work. My father is blamed. There are suspicions of illegal insects hoarded in the house. He wishes it were true, and he did have insects that cause people to die. The national news says he has caused disease. He doesn't care. He has no time for humans.

Our home is searched for more disease-carrying insects. I never find out if they succeed as I'm at the hospital, watching my father die as his whole body turns purple and black and his skin blisters off like old wallpaper. Eventually, he stops crying for good. He just coughs and slips away.

By the time I'm ten years old, it's just me and my mother. We walk to our old house and watch as they knock it down to make room for another apartment building. She doesn't cry; she has no tears left these days. My mother's literature collection is still in the house when they bulldoze it. As the dust settles, a few pages float in the turbulent air and land at our feet. She looks down at them, pages with words that serve no purpose anymore. She didn't speak again after that day. To her, without poems and literature, there is little point in words.

The sanitation laws get stricter, the medicines are better. For every new disease, the world gets smarter. That's what they tell us. Clinics pop up for monthly injections and they find more ways to make drinking water as the air gets hotter and hotter. Desalination plants dominate the coastline. Storms make landslides so they concrete over the land and that fixes that. The drainage is better, so there are fewer floods. The air pollution gets worse, so no one goes out anymore. Agriculture dies as the land doesn't work anymore. The food labs aren't in full swing yet.

The country's foundations rot. There are protests and riots until the anchor bridges are destroyed. My brother takes his family and they run across to France, just in time. He is much older, and I never knew him well, so I barely notice his absence. Despite the concrete and iron girders, the western and eastern corners of the country break off and sink away. Masses of people migrate inland and are packed into tighter and tighter spaces.

In the blink of an eye, my mother is gone too. I don't even notice her get sick. The food shortages wipe out her energy, but she was always so lethargic, anyway. So many never leave the house now. Her solitude seems normal. My mother withers away without me even realising.

But I have grown up enough. I am more young woman than child and can be independent. The country carries on and I am calloused against the calamity. And before I know it, I have finished my studies. Time has raced on before I can catch my breath. I start work and get published and get married and now I'm here, watching Grace's unhappiness as if through a lens, still with a faint golden tint in the apples of her cheeks. All I see is her. Despite the darkness that she feels, the gloom that enshrouds her, against the greyness and the opacity of the world—to me, she glows.

I continued to wander past the rundown street where that old school used to be. Absent of children for some time, it was inhabited by jobless artists who refused to do a degree of any use. I stopped to watch a young girl, probably about sixteen, stare into the school then walk in. Her clothes were tatty, her facemask decorated with doodles and symbols. As she walked up the steps, the crowd of Alternates actually hugged her like some oracular saviour, without a drop of disinfectant first. They won't last long with habits like that.

The salt was now leaving a residue on my skin as I dodged the discarded, rotting fish bones littering the street. I tightened my facemask against the smell, but the putrid stink elbowed its way in. The street sanitisers worked from the Centre out towards the Perimeter, so wouldn't get to this mess for an hour or so yet.

As I approached the fencing around the new development, I peered up at the concrete construction. Sure, the neighbourhood wasn't great, but the floor plan for each apartment was twice the size of our own. The stem-cell waiting list was sure to view that more favourably. However, the block was just two streets away from the old docks, with their derelict trawler frequented only by fish junkies after their next hit.

Drug-testing kit wrappers drifted in the breeze, the medicinal shower disclosing the truth about what was happening there.

A man, likely my age, his face creviced like paving slabs, approached me.

'Fresh catch today, high readings of benzodopamines and codeine.'

'No, thank you,' I replied as politely as I could.

'After a bit of FatAway, perhaps?' He pointed a dirty finger towards my midriff.

'No,' I said, trying to hide my disgust, but recoiling instinctively. His fingers were grubby and he stank of the sea.

Alternates. Eurgh. That is what happens if you don't get the appropriate education. I shuddered and scurried past him. Drawing pictures for a living, writing fiction, just absurd when there was so much other work that needed to be done. A whole country had to be catered for. Useless consumers, all of them.

I wondered if my interns had ever witnessed an Alternate eating a fish carcass, feasting on the drugs inside. I doubted it. It was a disgusting sight. Teeth tearing into flesh, ripping apart the corpse in barbaric fashion, releasing shiny scales to rain down onto their laps. Bite marks exposing blood vessels and bones rife with narcotics and filth. I gagged as I saw another Alternate wipe entrails from her mouth with her arm, high on dopamine or opiates, most likely. She flicked remnants onto the street in a shower of grime. An insult to all we had achieved.

I took some photos of the development for Grace, then made my way back inland, attempting to keep my mind focused on my day ahead: my daydreams had distracted me for long enough. I scanned the headlines on the strip billboards. Greg was bound to bring up something from the news. Current affairs gave him a chance to namedrop.

Bird Seen Ten Miles Offshore, Shot Immediately. New Developments Planned in the Perimeter: Progress is Paramount! Elections Looming, Blue Liberation Party Announce Candidates. With Sterility Comes Liberty! Street safety score: *4/5. Everyone is Safe Now.*

Nothing too alarming, really. One bird offshore was no reason for panic. The country was still safe, which meant the interns should be ready for that day's work. But then the billboards flashed to indicate a new headline.

Rogue Wave Warning! Stay Inside. Drink Bottled Water Only.

47

'Microbes!' I cursed. I had forgotten to bottle some tap water at home. I stopped by a vending machine to take a bottle with me and cursed again as I noted the price was already up fifty percent on yesterday.

I was still a few streets from work when I saw it. A fleeting glimpse at the edge of my vision, too quick for my mind to process. I continued walking for a moment before I froze. That wasn't soot! Something on the ground, crawling. A chill rippled up my spine. I backed away slowly. One step, then another, my shaking legs struggling at the third. I took a deep breath, attempting to summon some dormant courage, and turned slowly. My whole body itched. Sweat stung my eyes, and I wiped it away with my fingers. Blinked. There it was. A hideous, shiny, jet-black thing. With legs. Lots of legs. And other appendages that looked like legs. I remembered it from my father's book, now suddenly on display in front of me.

My breath came in shudders. I tried counting, forcing slow exhales, yet my heart hurried on. A cockroach! I felt my breakfast fight its way up and I swallowed hard. Filth! Vermin! The grotesque thing walked through a puddle of street-sprayer disinfectant like it was nothing. It didn't die. It paused, shook its legs off, and carried on.

We used to have drills for this. There were information sites. My mind went blank, hindered by panic and lack of practice. It had been too long, I couldn't remember. What was I meant to do? Call someone? Kill it somehow? Report it? Slowly, with no sudden movements, I fumbled for my phone with trembling fingers and found the government website.

Keep your distance. Do not try and capture or kill it yourself. Report it on the link below immediately. Quarantine yourself for two weeks.

Two weeks! I couldn't do that, I had my meeting with Greg, my promotion. Microbes!

A cold trickle of panic bubbled through me. Was this to be the start of it? A new plague? Food for birds, attracting more birds, meaning more vermin.

Think, Savannah. Think!

My father used to handle such things and look what happened to him. Surely, as long as I didn't actually touch the thing, I'd be fine. But I couldn't let it crawl away, to scurry off and find a mate and... eurgh. Even the thought of its hideous little legs wriggling made me heave.

I looked around for something, anything, to assist me. There were some broken bits of tarmac, one piece about the size of my palm. I could squash the cockroach. I didn't have to touch it to do that. Picking up the tarmac, I inched closer to the beast. It was standing still, parading its surplus limbs and feelers. It was disgusting.

There were no nooks or crannies for it to hide in. It was exposed, an easy target. Maybe it would bake in the heat before I had time to squash it? I crept closer still, feeling like the sneaky crawler I was hunting. Every inch of my skin was tingling, like a million filthy insects were clambering underneath, rummaging through my insides. No, I had to be sure; I had to kill it. I gagged. Reached out, then gagged again. My hand quivered as it hovered over the thing. Then, *crunch*. Its brittle body crumpled under the tarmac slab, the vibrations prickling my bones. I let out a little yelp, then released the tarmac and stood quickly, feeling lightheaded and backing away. I grabbed my sanitiser and coated myself with it.

Then I ran to work.

Chapter 5

The interns all stood to attention as I passed. (Why they did that, I had no idea, I never told them to.) Their admiring faces were so unaware of the dangers outside. I entered my office and shut the blinds, putting the lights on low and the air con on full blast, hoping the darkness and coolness would keep me calm. I raised my arms up to the breeze, willing my sweat to dry. Someone had left a cup of MimikTea on my desk, which I sipped gratefully. I held my breath, then released it slowly.

Calm down, Sav. You're okay.

The sounds of the lab seeped in: muffled conversations, boiling liquids, timers beeping. That familiar din I hated so much sounded comforting after my morning of panic. I closed my eyes for a few moments and felt my heart slow. I needed to focus. It was just one bug. One awful, repugnant little bug. We were still safe. I didn't touch it. I gulped more of my MimikTea and felt the last of my adrenaline dissipate. Time to concentrate. The day's headlines scrolled across the bottom of my screen. '*Bottled water only!*' On repeat, over and over.

Underneath, stuck to the monitor, was a note from Archie saying, '*Good luck!*'

Being comfortable to the point of boredom in my career had taken years of work. I was unstimulated and commanded respect only from my juniors. Prestige from higher up took a disproportionate amount of effort. The prospect of a new role left me feeling as if I was jumping into a void, and I didn't even know what was expected of me yet. Archie thought he was doing me a favour by telling me, but I fizzed with unwelcome anticipation. I briefly considered a quick visit to the MindSpa before noting the time. Instead, I finished my MimikTea and tried to find serenity in the relative stillness of my office.

I leafed through the interns' files once again, the dull information a welcome distraction, thinking that Greg might ask some questions about them. Unlikely, as his interest was reserved for balance sheets. Nevertheless, it was best to be prepared.

The pages and pages of information listed every one of the interns' flaws, both what they admitted and what the internet searches divulged. Their families, their medical records, their address history, familial fertility, any hint of a social life outside. All secrets bared like snarling teeth. The Private Investigative software we used to prejudge them was borderline illegal, so Archie made it impossible to trace. After the PI had done its job, the application form questions were selected accordingly. A level of honesty was expected, but be too honest, and the company's non-disclosure policy could be threatened. 'We need the right sort,' Greg would say. Holding on to a few secrets was quite normal.

I reached into my desk drawer and removed my ridiculously ostentatious Cartier watch, gifted to me by my brother. It had been an heirloom of his wife's, and I guess he didn't want it weighing her down if they ended up in the sea. I put on my impractically large engagement ring – remodelled from antique stones, too big for normal wear – and placed a loving photo of Grace and myself on my desk, posing in an exclusive holiday resort where we forked out for one night soon after our wedding, solely to get the picture. The photo showed the spacious courtyard lined with green outdoor carpet, a private swimming pool with bright blue water, umbrellas offering shade and drinks glasses containing brightly coloured cocktails. At least I, and my office, now looked prepared for Greg's arrival.

Greg claimed he could tell someone's postcode from their smell, although by the way he screwed up his eyes and scrutinised every last thread and hair, his other senses were clearly at play too. And he judged accordingly. 'A true patriot,' he called himself. And he himself oozed finery. Watches from a range the Prime Minister wore; scents not found on the mainland since years before the anchors fell; the finest suits, tailored to perfection, replaced or adjusted frequently to compensate for his ever-expanding waistline. His haters whispered that he was the only one in the country who gained weight during the famines. Food shortages did nothing except feed his appetite for more. A lifelong advocate for the destruction of the anchors and the drifting of The Raft, as well as donating to have the fence put up round the Centre, his 'patriotism' was tainted with flawed science and a love of money.

I walked around the lab and watched the interns wobble and quake. Had they seen the news yet? I wasn't sure. During the last round of internships, a rogue wave had washed a load of fish nearly half a mile inland and a bone had found its way into the freshwater supply. Sterilised water arrived in bottles and the streets were cleaned, but there were reports of stomach bugs. Three interns were hospitalised with dehydration as they refused to drink, too scared of where the bug had come from. The whole programme had to be delayed by two months and we missed a release deadline for a new synthesised milk drink. Calcium deficiency and osteoporosis still raged on, and I couldn't help but blame that delay.

None of the interns smiled or spoke. They moved like robots between equipment and stations, machines rather than people with not a gram of ingenuity between them. I flicked through more information from their files as I walked, putting faces to the numbers. Speaks four languages: useless. A born leader: troublemaker. A team player: lazy. Excelled at school: boring.

Twenty interns, all with straight As, all wanting to prove themselves as more brilliant than the rest. All sure they were worthy of the wonder and praise heaped on them by adoring parents, all on the verge of a panic attack at the sound of my footsteps. I saw the twitchy legs, the fiddling fingers, the breathing exercises. All completely indistinguishable from their peers.

Just as I was doing my rounds and giving instructions, Greg entered. With each heavy step, glass instruments jingled. The chime announcing his arrival. His voice was as big as his stature, yet had some catching up to do to match the grandiose scale of his ego. He paraded down the aisles, serving opinions and instructions as if distributing food to the starving. He was accompanied by two assistants, as usual. Always female. The one on his right – Elma, I think her name was – had been there for some time. She rarely ever raised her head, always engrossed in taking notes on her e-pad. The second I did not recognise, but Archie had warned me she was new. Another one. This assistant was young, eager, slightly panic-stricken and somewhat expendable.

Greg trudged down the walkway and squeezed past me. He had room to pass without contact, yet his oscillating gut still caressed me. Reaching his arm around me to hold the table, he heaved past as I tucked in. I felt his grunting breath on the back of my neck.

'Savannah, my office, ten minutes,' he snorted as he continued to flaunt himself around the lab.

Meeting Greg once in a lifetime was bad enough. The frequent interactions I had to endure were hideous affairs. My tolerance for him never improved. Even with the possibility of good news, I dreaded his company. Those ten minutes passed too quickly.

I walked to his office, the short stroll down the corridor not long enough to quell my dread. Elma was sitting outside. She didn't look up, her e-pad engaging her completely. I knocked softly and went in.

His office was an exhibition of opulence. The furniture was actual wood, fortified with ironwork. It must have been a hundred years old. It was so rare to see something like that away from the Centre. The grain, visible like a fingerprint, was still distinguishable through the many layers of solvent varnish. On the wall hung various framed printouts of the newspaper headline from when the anchors were destroyed: '*If Sea Levels Rise, We Rise With Them!*' Another showed a picture of people fleeing across one of the anchor bridges as it disappeared into the sea. '*Deserters Deserve to Drown,*' followed by, '*Britain Has Its Greatness Back.*'

The instant I met him, almost two decades earlier, I knew

Greg was from the Centre. His lips weren't chapped, his skin was smooth on fat cheeks. With each breath, his chest heaved, doubling its diameter, boasting lungs filled with air instead of soot. His legs walked in straight, proud strides, displaying the full benefits of vitamin D. He was spectacle-free. The most obvious sign of all was his teeth. Fortified with calcium, he spoke with them on deliberate display: no gaps, no decay. Even his hair shone like he had sourced some omegas from somewhere. 'They add omegas to the tap water in the Centre,' Archie would joke.

I stood for some time in his office doorway, unnoticed. Greg sat, his chins swaying slightly, as assistant number two, on all fours, cleaned his shoes. He was captivated by the view. A little drool wet the corners of his mouth. I coughed and cleared my throat.

'Savannah, what the hell are you doing walking into my office like this?' he shouted, jumping alert. He pushed his assistant to the floor and wiped the drool on his sleeve.

'You asked me to come in, sir.'

'Ah, yes. Right.' He shooed his assistant out and she scurried away, briefly looking at me as she passed, her damp eyes and furrowed brow screaming for help. Their silent plea was useless, though. I was as powerless as her.

Greg took a moment to compose himself, then said, 'Tell me, Savannah, the vitamin infusion. We have success?'

'Yes, sir. We're delighted with the preliminary results. We estimate the absorption factor is up forty per—'

'Yes, yes, yes,' he said. 'Now, there is an opening at the National Press, doing the biomedical press releases. I know what you're thinking: Kenzie, Hammond, Tris or even Cartwright would be better choices, and of course, that's what everyone thinks. However, we have a quota and the opening must go to someone from the Perimeter—the Government's idea of being more representative, since even you people get a vote. Which makes you the most sensible choice.'

I was taken aback. I did not know what to expect, but the National Press was way off my radar. 'Great, sir. Thank you, sir.'

'What pay grade are you on now? E? F?'

'G, sir.'

'G?' He almost laughed. 'Well, this comes with a D wage. Only for that specific work, though, which will be part-time around your lab duties. You may have to offload some of those hours onto someone else. Is there anyone capable?'

D wage! I fidgeted, wanting to leap for joy. 'I can certainly train someone up.'

'Good, good. That's settled, then. You'll need to pass the probation, of course, and you'll need to impress the Prime Minister since it's her neck on the line if the public gets the wrong idea through the media, you understand what I mean?' I nodded. 'There's a construction project tomorrow that the Ministers are interested in visiting for the photo opportunity. Some old derelict school, there can't be many left, I'm sure you'll know where it is. Why don't you come along and we can do introductions?'

Greg's offer resonated like music. 'Sounds perfect. Thank you.'

He hunched over his desk, his decadent gut restricting his access somewhat. A pile of paperwork was organised for him and he vacantly leafed through it. 'Are you still here, Savannah? I've got work to do.'

'Apologies. See you later, sir.' I turned to leave, but he spoke again.

'Savannah?'

'Yes, sir?'

'Get HR to put an advert out for a new assistant for me, I need one with bigger...' Both hands gestured in circles around his chest. '...abilities.'

'Bigger abilities, sir?'

'Yes, that's right. Bigger abilities,' he grunted. 'Now go.'

I left the room quickly, hoping he wouldn't decide to detail what 'bigger abilities' meant. The poor woman who had hurried from his office was the fourth assistant I could recall over the previous year, each one displaying an upgrade in their 'abilities' compared to the last. I mentally drafted the email I would have to send to HR, pondering how to make it sound like I was asking for something other than what he intended. Greg and the libel invincibility that came with being Centre-reared would never consider it a challenge. I would use quotation marks, I decided. His words, not mine.

Chapter 6

The rest of my day was joyful. I was ecstatic. Even interns asking me idiotic questions couldn't blacken my mood.

'Professor, what's a pipette?'

'Can my mother come with me tomorrow?'

'Professor, how hot does a Bunsen burner get?'

'Do the lab goggles come in different colours?'

Two interns spent most of the day complaining they were hungry. We weren't even synthesising flavours that day. The lab smelled of bleach, not food. One had their lab coat on back to front and insisted everyone else was wearing theirs wrong. Another got lost three times going to the toilet. The toilets were right next to the lab. It's a testament to how I felt that I made it through eight hours without screaming, throwing a beaker at someone or—my usual escape—shutting myself in my office and locking the door.

My walk home that evening was luminous. The streets seemed less drab, the hum of the air con sounded melodic. I skipped to it. The morning's trauma and news of the wave felt like a million years earlier. I bought some water on the way and didn't even grimace that the price had doubled again since the morning.

I imagined arriving home, Grace standing in the evening light of the balcony window, her golden curls silhouetted against the orange sky. Her smile would radiate, and she would hold me in a way that she hadn't for years. Because my news was good, really good. Those two-bed apartments were within our grasp. Pay grade D, even part-time, meant we would be considered. The foundations of each dwelling were several metres more than what we had, with ICs installed and a communal garden laid with soft asphalt.

I shut out the memory of the cockroach. It was just one. One bit of filth. It wasn't a plague. And it was dead, like the rest of the filthy creatures. Forget it.

Grace's excitement, however, was non-existent.

'It's a good promotion, Grace. More money. It'll move us up the treatment list, for sure.'

Silence was her only response. Her face was stubborn in its resolve, straining to keep any ray of hope out. Her eyes were glazed, seeing further into a bleak future instead of the hope I was offering.

'Here.' I handed her a glass of wine. 'Let's celebrate.'

My heart sank as with one hand she took the glass, and with the other smoothed her skirt over her empty lap. Her mind's eye looking for the child that should be there.

I went to fetch the e-pad. Grace had buried it under a pile of boxes the day before. 'Don't bother,' she said, without turning around.

'There must be one song you'd like to hear?'

'No.'

I sat, defeated. Silence crowded around us. 'How about this weekend? We could get up early, like we used to. Do some yoga in the morning.'

'Why?'

'Healthy body, healthy mind.'

She bit her lip. 'Better to sleep. Dreams take me away from this place.' She gulped her wine in one go and let the glass fall to her lap.

I edged closer and held her hand. She angled her head away from me, the last of the evening sun casting an orange stripe across her neck. How I longed to hear her sing rather than cry. I looked down at her hands and saw her bitten nails.

When we first met, I noticed her nails straight away. How short they were, all except the one on her right index finger, like my mother's. She played the guitar as well. I heard Grace play just a few times. She sang gently as she played, her voice small and sweet, singing songs about a future she wanted in a world that was better than this one. The first time she played for me, the first day we met, my nerves unwound in a flutter as she sat, bare-legged on an old stool, her skin radiant, her voice containing the slight hint of the sadness that would one day take over completely. At that moment, she sounded whole. Content. Like she was at home and safe.

Our engagement was brief, her joy even briefer. The guitar hangs in the apartment now, the strings untouched for some time, the nail that plucked them bitten to the skin.

* * *

61

The following morning, I spent ages at the Selfie Station trying to tease some extra volume into my flat hair. I piled on the face cream and rouge. My skin was barely visible over my clothing and coverings, but I was determined that whatever could be seen should look as radiant as possible. Just being another soot-covered, short Perimeter resident would not give the best impression. I tried to look as Centre as I could. I wore thick-soled shoes to give me extra height, and a brightly patterned neckerchief, as it was the least dreary thing I owned. It had belonged to my father's mother, made in the days when new fabrics were still available and clothing changed with the seasons. The fashion houses served only the Centre now.

Archie once sent me an app that clipped together every selfie from the last ten years and played them back to you in a video montage. I'm still not sure if it was meant to be funny or soul-destroying. Perhaps just purely educational. But playing back hundreds of corporate snaps, illustrating my fight for recognition that rewarded me more than just a larger office and a better job title, was exhausting. Watching a decade of corporate ass-kissing and the effects of the constant swimming upstream on my face was a disheartening revelation. It was like someone had painted my face ten years earlier, but it had taken too long to dry. Instead, the colours ran, the contours of my face drooped and bled as gravity sucked the paint downwards. Then, after a few years, the paint dried. It over-dried, in fact, leaving cracks like parched earth. It showed my face melting into a desert. Watching a decade pass in seconds made it seem like an eternity of stagnation. I think it was about then that my work motivation hit the wall it had yet to get over. Until now!

Shop windows were plastered with posters advertising their

bottled-water supply. Delivery Autotrucks were loaded with bottles among the packets of synthesised nutrition from BioLabs (complete with my signature of authenticity). The market leaders, we were usually in everyone's grocery shop. The packaging needed updating, I realised, as I looked at the sea of green and yellow designs. It looked garish these days, an eyesore against the monotone background. The water bottles appeared newly labelled in a sleek and glossy grey. Timeless, yet modern. Rogueless Water was the brand on sale, complete with the tagline '*Keeping Everyone Safe*'. A new trademark that sprung from the news as if sitting on file, ready to pounce at the first opportunity.

I bought a bottle for my bag and huffed as it was four times the usual price, then followed the din of police and security sirens down to the coast. The directions Greg had given me were sparse, but I knew the development he meant. Even if I didn't, I could just follow the street sprayers. They spluttered out of sync with one another, cleaning the streets ahead of their VIP arrivals. The stink of stronger-than-usual disinfectant erupted from their spouts. The Autosweepers had been out in force too, eliminating any trace of rubbish and soot from every inch of road the Centre vehicles would take. Following their course was easy: I just had to look for the cleanest roads.

The cars shone the way everything from the Centre does. They were huge vehicles, the kind of thing you never saw in the Perimeter, with silent engines, dark windows and smooth autonomous settings. Archie said that the cars knew when they had reached the Perimeter, and got louder and more juddery on purpose so they didn't look out of place. In the Centre they glided like oil on water. I didn't know that then as, up to that point, I'd never left the Perimeter.

The crowd was sparser than I'd imagined it would be. The news that morning would have left the whole neighbourhood rattled, the strip billboards flashing their alert, devices everywhere pinging with the announcement. A bird had landed on the shore. Luckily, it was a loud one that cawed to alert everyone to its presence. It was shot instantly, the area sanitised, and those within a mile of it taken for quarantine.

Memories of yesterday and the disgusting beast crawled back into my mind. A bug, and now a bird! There had been so few live-bird sightings on The Raft since they were culled, and barely a single reported bug. But how many were unreported, like my own minor act of treason? I itched. I felt that sub-epidermal wriggling feeling again.

Forget it, Sav. It's dead. It's done.

There were whispers in the crowd, murmurs of panic and denial. Disbelief and scepticism. Constant wary glances.

'Did you hear about the bird?'

'Vermin again, after all this time!'

'I knew the street sprayers weren't up to full concentration.'

'Filth! Can you believe it? Filth!'

'How can they tell us we're safe when there's a bird landing on the shore?'

'Not to mention the wave. Bet fish bones have washed up everywhere.'

'Not that you'd know. I mean, look at the place. Filth on filth.'

'The Prime Minister is still coming. They wouldn't come if we weren't safe.'

'It's just one bird. It can't be as bad as before.'

'The wave wasn't near here. It's all cleaned up, anyway.'

I messaged Marcus to check that the interns had made it

to the lab, and that we had sufficient stock of water. The last thing we needed was staff shortages due to one headline. They'd be too young to remember the horrors of the last bird flu and the gore of the cull. Of course, their parents would know. Our childhood memories had been contaminated with those images. We could never forget.

The people out that day had covered their faces more than usual, double-layering, and some wore full goggles. Hands in their pockets, their wary faces alert and watchful. A few had antiviral spray that they continuously squirted into the air ahead of them with each step. The strip billboards updated to report that life and medical insurance premiums had sky-rocketed with the bird invasion. ('Invasion', they called it. For one bird?) '*Buy Now Before Prices Rise Higher!*' the press encouraged, and the stock market was down fifteen percent. The fallout from the filth continued.

A message requesting calm had been released from the Centre. There was no need to panic. Testing was available for anyone who wanted it, and the antiviral drugs were vastly improved and stockpiled just in case. All street cleaners were called in, day off or not, holidays cancelled, and they trawled up and down, disinfecting every bit of pavement. The billboards flashed warnings to keep skin covered, alongside adverts for sprays and soaps, private doctors and counselling services.

It was just one bird, I reminded myself. One bird and one bug. No need to panic. The hysteria must be coming from the Alternates and computer engineers, who spent too much time reading crap on the internet instead of studies from labs. I kept my face covered and, despite the stifling heat, wore full-length clothes and gloves. I refused to get as rattled and scared as so many others did. So many years of disasters had hardened me against such tribulations. The exterminators and sterilisers did their jobs well. Yet still I shivered. Filth. Filth on our clean shores.

Drivers in full hazmat suits exited a line of vehicles, their polished white paintwork showing the characteristic dust and salt marks of the Perimeter. Nothing shines for long this far from the Centre. Armed with sprays of surface cleaners, they wiped down every inch of the paintwork, windows, even the tyres, before changing gloves and opening the doors. Out stepped the Prime Minister and her various staff members, all tall and strongly built with mouths full of teeth, constantly misting the air in front of them with antiviral spray rather than cover up. Their skin appeared rosy, unflaked, and smooth. Archie said that the street cleaners in the Centre didn't chafe like in the Perimeter, because of some pH technology and moisturising properties. Archie said a lot of things, but looking at this entourage, I could certainly believe it. They exuded health.

I held back, searching the faces for someone I recognised, my stomach cramping from nerves. I listened for Greg's booming voice, but couldn't hear it from the edge of the crowd. Even the amplitude of his ego wasn't enough to penetrate the throng.

Construction fencing had gone up around the old school. The artists I had seen the day before had been ejected, that sixteen-year-old girl and her newfound friends scattered to the wind. Demolition had been on the cards for years, a poster with the details outside the school for as long as I could remember. I supposed the Alternates couldn't read, or perhaps they chose to ignore it. Even my mother had the sense to leave our house in good time before the demolition crew came in.

There was a new poster up now, so large it was impossible

to read from the narrow street. Inside the school gates, where the crowd was gathered, offered the best view. It showed the Prime Minister with her stern face and folded arms, and the text '*Digging up the time capsule from class of 2010! Rejoicing in our history!*' The news spreading through the crowd was that children in 2010 had buried some work and artefacts, and before the building work could start, they must knock down the old brick plinth and remove the time capsule. There was some excitement. A load of junk buried by kids a hundred years earlier was the sort of historical find people loved. So much had changed, it illustrated our progress. It would be like digging up a dinosaur, the world it represented being equally extinct. The likelihood was that some of it would be from ancestors of people still living here. No one had moved very far in a long time.

I moved closer to the vehicles and into the crowd, where I found Greg among a group of Centre folk. His stature was the giveaway, although he appeared less imposing when next to his neighbours. As I approached, his thundering voice resonated clearly over the street sprayers and general chatter. He was lacking his usual two assistants; no doubt such obvious displays of chauvinism were not well received among his fellow Centres. As I advanced, I witnessed him complimenting the Prime Minister's advisor, with an enthusiastic, 'Absolutely ma'am, wonderful idea ma'am, I couldn't agree more ma'am.' His voice was loud but sounded restrained and humble, not the booming display of authority he exhibited in the lab. *Everyone is kissing someone's ass*, I thought.

A few deep breaths and, holding my head high, I walked towards their circle. They stood at least a foot taller than me, with more girth adding to their domineering presence. Their circle was impassable as it was patrolled by armed security. I had to call for Greg from the outskirts.

'Hi, Greg. Sir.' He didn't hear me. I tried again, louder, several times, to the annoyance of the security.

'Oh, wonderful.' With delight, he eventually acknowledged me. His usual inadvertent grope or rub was replaced with the Centre greeting of a hand air-shake, which I reciprocated. In the most cheerful voice I had ever heard him use, he cleared me with security. 'This is Professor Savannah Selbourne, my recommendation for the National Press.'

The circle opened, just slightly, so they could turn their heads to look at me. The advisors all stared, examining me for an uncomfortable amount of time, making small grunts and quizzical mumbles. I just gazed back, hoping it was obvious I was smiling through my face covering.

'Nice to meet you, Professor,' one advisor said, finally breaking the hypercritical stillness. I recognised her as the Minister of Impartiality from her characteristic red dress. That angular face was in the corner of every news article, adding her approval. Her voice sounded haughty and unfriendly: 'rather indifferent to meet you' is what she should have said. After looking me up and down, she refused to tilt her head to look at me when she spoke, instead peering down her nose. Her superiority was therefore displayed to me in the form of her nostrils. The entire circle looked down at me in the same way. Any hint of a smile came from one corner of their mouths only before they resumed their open-mouthed expressions to display their teeth. The two closest to me topped up their antiviral body spray. Fragranced with Chanel, I noted.

'No, that's not how they say hello here,' an advisor chastised the minister. Then he turned to me and cleared his throat.

'How's your tomorrow?'

'Uncertain,' I replied, my voice meek. I felt like a tourist attraction.

'Oh, how delightful! I've always wanted to say that.' He giggled and clapped his hands together with delight. 'Such a wonderful greeting for the Perimeter, and so apt, don't you think?'

They all nodded patronizing nods at me before turning away and continuing their conversation.

'This all seems a little sentimental to me.'

'God knows what ancient amoebas have clung to life inside that thing.'

'A load of Perimeter kids' garbage from a century ago. What a waste of time.'

'Bet there's a dead bird in there.' Most laughed.

'That's poor taste,' one said.

'Oh, lighten up,' another scolded. 'Look at this place. It's so miserable you just have to laugh.'

'The Prime Minister is very keen to seem in touch with the Perimeter, and besides the cost of the extra security and cleaners, it's basically free PR.'

'I suppose even these people get a vote.' They all sighed at that.

I stood quietly. Unfazed and listening. They spoke over my head, not bothering to involve me at all. I was a speck of dust wafting around them, disregarded, a miniscule irritant.

'This is certainly the furthest out I've been. Did you notice there's even a stem-cell centre here? They're actually still breeding.'

'Shocking.' They all nodded.

With that, the Prime Minister arrived at our group. The

advisors parted in rehearsed unison, their eyes squinted under the force of a smile. Up close, I noted their faces were covered in a thin protective biofilm, the likes of which I had never seen before. Their entire bodies appeared to be vacuum-packed and hermetically sealed, showing off their expensively cared-for skin with more safety than we in the Perimeter got from our paper and cloth coverings. With body-wraps like that, all the people too scared to leave the house would feel safer. I longed to have a close look at it, to take a sample away.

'Morning, Prime Minister,' the gathering said.

'Shame about that bird nonsense, today of all days.' The Prime Minister sounded agitated.

They all murmured in support. 'Still, our presence here must be reassuring to these people.'

'Yes, yes, quite,' she said. 'This part of the Perimeter is quite near The Raft's edge, I presume?'

'Yes, quite close, ma'am. That explains the smell, anyway.'

'Hmm. It's good to engage with such people, on the very fringe of civilisation.'

'Absolutely, Prime Minister,' said an advisor.

'I assume they have quantum cables by now?'

'Well, laying them throughout is quite expensive, ma'am. But some certainly have access.'

'They need quantum access for their jobs, do they not?' She frowned, her eyebrows coming together at the bridge of her nose.

'The mind of a Perimeter employee is a little slower than in the Centre. Such high speeds would be a waste.'

'I see.' She pondered this for a moment. 'And their weekly medicals? Are they showing any issues?'

'They're monthly here, ma'am. The Perimeter people are

hardy and go outside much less often. Monthly check-ups are deemed adequate. You'd be amazed, Prime Minister, some even fail to attend monthly. Even the home kits for those indoors full-time aren't all used.'

'Gosh.' The Prime Minister separated her eyebrows again. 'Well, it is certainly eye-opening to travel to such places. It is imperative we engage with these people. They do get a vote, after all.'

'On that note, Prime Minister, may I introduce Professor Savannah Selbourne,' said Greg, putting the emphasis on *Professor*. 'My recommendation for the medical press release job.' He nudged me forwards with his elbow.

'Pleasure to meet you, Prime Minister,' I said, and bowed.

'Yes, quite,' she said. She was shorter than the rest by an inch or so and lifted her chin to compensate. All the posters I'd seen of her showed her as broad shouldered, with a strong physique. Masculine poses and an imposing jawline. In the flesh, her posture appeared less intimidating than the others, soft bellied with a rounded back. The biofilm covering smoothed out her skin and I could see the same dazzling Centre teeth. The hair looked real, slicked back and hanging almost to her shoulders. Not a strand unaccounted for. She wore a collarless shirt buttoned up to her neck, well-fitted trousers, and a loose blazer that disguised her bosom. Her shoes, I noted, were platformed and heeled, giving her an extra inch.

'Speaking of press releases, where's Clark? He should be here to cover this. This is definitely his department.' The Prime Minister sounded petulant. *Some reputations are correct*, I noted.

'The bird, ma'am,' one advisor said. 'His child is a little fragile, and he was worried about exposure to the filth here.'

He looked my way and scrunched up his nose.

'Understandable,' she said, though clearly dissatisfied.

'May I make a suggestion, Prime Minister?' Greg asked. 'Savannah is here. She could cover this press release. We have photographers already.'

'Who?'

'Savannah, ma'am, my medical press release recommendation. Professor Selbourne.'

'Oh, her. I'd forgotten all about her. Where the hell is she?'

'Here, Prime Minister,' I said.

She looked down at me. 'Ah, there you are.'

'She's used to the Perimeter air, so that shouldn't be a problem.' I had never heard Greg sound so enthusiastic—when he wasn't inspecting new assistant applications, anyway. I could see the money signs light up in his eyes. His top scientist writing general news for the National Press—he'd be salivating at the thought. 'And it could be a good way to appeal to the Perimeter, if your press release comes from a Perimeter resident. Isn't that right, Savannah?'

'Absolutely. I'm keen to start, Prime Minister.' I attempted to make my voice loud and authoritative, but it came out as a squeak. Hardly a good advert for the Perimeter air. I winced at the sound of it. With my stunted height and bad skin, I felt every bit the ruddy Perimeter resident.

'Of course you are,' the Prime Minister said. I couldn't tell if she was smiling or grimacing. 'Well, if you're sure there's no other option, I suppose it can't hurt.'

I felt a knot in my stomach; I wasn't sure if it was excitement or nerves. Both, most likely. Imposter syndrome, Penny called it when counselling the interns. Right then, I was in their shoes. Out of my depth, the world looming high over my head as if I had a mountain to climb. I should be more sympathetic to them and their first-day worries, I thought. The overconfidence I usually felt at work was swallowed up by an all-consuming self-doubt and apprehension. But this was the sort of opportunity that was so incredibly rare for a Perimeter resident. I needed Greg's impolite nudge to bury my anxieties. I had to try. My name would be in print, writing authentic articles that everyone read, not just ones in science journals. The notoriety that came with that was sure to get me the references the clinic needed. My knees quivered with a mixture of excitement and nerves. This was my chance. For Grace. For us.

8

Chapter 7

I said at the start how little I knew back then. Recounting these events makes me cringe at my ignorance. How many red flags had to hit me in the face before I realised that all was not as it seemed? Remember when, as a kid, you found out Father Christmas wasn't real? Of course he's not real, you realised. How could you have been so stupid? It's so obvious. Then you tell yourself you never really believed, anyway. But I did. I really did.

The scant crowd fell silent as the Prime Minister made her way to the plinth, where some labourers were removing bricks. She stood behind them, waving to the crowd. She put on a long rubber glove and reached in, pulling out a chest that looked like it was made of wood. The crowd gasped. Many of them had never seen actual wood. The Prime Minister put the box on the table and stood back while two cleaners arrived promptly to spray the chest with disinfectant. 'With sterility comes liberty!' they said when they were finished and saluted.

'It is important to remember our past, as it tells us how far we have come. Progress is paramount!' the Prime Minister said. The crowd clapped at this. 'From a country afflicted with disease and suffering, where no one knew where they belonged or where to call home. A country invaded by foreigners, both human and germ—to this glorious nation of independence and cleanliness. Our last tether to the mainland took with it our parasitic reliance on muck. Like the magnificent structures we build, like a skyscraper reaching for the stars, we have risen above the dirt. A truly civilised society. With sterility comes liberty!' An enthusiastic cheer erupted from the crowd. 'Now let us delve into our savage past so we can feel evermore triumphant.'

The crowd clapped again as the photographers clicked away. The Prime Minister, behind a plastic shield, opened the chest with her gloved hand, her head arching back as far as her neck would allow, as if she feared a bomb. I held my breath, half-expecting to see vermin crawl out.

The heat was getting unbearable, and I could see the perspiration trickle through her hairline. It followed the combed lines of her hair, gliding down like little oil droplets. Under the biofilm covering, her face reddened. There was no shade on that platform, and I wondered if she'd ever known such heat without air con. She carried on regardless, a show of solidarity and strength for the Perimeter.

She pulled out a child's drawing, signed Emily, aged ten. It was of some quadruped creature, it was unclear what. The crowd gasped. Several similar drawings came out, all of various quadrupeds, some even of insects. One had the words '*Save the bees!*' signed by Maisie, aged ten. 'Poor little girl,' came the murmurings from the crowd. She likely died of a bee

75

sting, like so many. Deadly, pointless creatures. How foolish children were back then. Another poster said something about a hodgeheg, or hedgehog, I don't really remember what it was called. Children dream up all sorts of peculiar monsters. This one was spiked like an underwater mine, with eyes. 'Ooh' and 'ahh' emerged from the crowd, though most winced and huffed, especially when a winged, feathered creature was shown. How brazenly children portrayed such images. Drawn with love and sentiment, with no idea of the horrors that awaited them. How naïve they were about the dangers.

The Prime Minister shook her head in pity for the past. 'We can tell these youngsters lived in an age before such hideous beasts ripped the world apart with their diseases. Before birds turned truly evil and preyed on babies. If only they'd known the dangers.' Her audience clutched their chests and nodded.

There were lurid pictures of wiry, broad plants, most likely types of trees. Some pictures even showed the muck they grew in. '*Save the forests!*' one picture said in badly lopsided handwriting.

'Well. If...' the Prime Minister squinted to read the name on the page, '...if Elliot is still alive today, he must be delighted at how our technology has bested these "trees"! SolaArbs and ArbAirs lining every region and squeezed into every space possible. Giving us energy and cleaning our air. Why have the filth of nature when we can gleam with clean technology?'

'With sterility comes liberty!' we all said in unison.

Eventually the parade of pictures ended, to the relief of the onlookers, who all seemed to be struggling in the heat. The Prime Minister gave a last address. 'Today's headlines and the contents of this box certainly show us how much more educated, prepared, and clean we are. It's good to remind ourselves of the filth of the past to illustrate the progress we have made. The Great Sterilisation Project has saved us all. The filth is in the past. Everyone is safe now.'

'With sterility comes liberty!' we all said again.

The crowd soon dispersed. The gruesome display was too much for their delicate nature. They fanned themselves. Some had partners with them for support; there were no children, of course. No sense in telling children about the monsters that used to roam the world.

I saw one elderly woman in the crowd. Her worn face wasn't even covered. It hung and gaped like old curtains. She had a wide-brimmed hat and dark glasses, her minimal practicalities appearing more like a disguise. Her loose linen dress was too long for her, likely purchased in her younger years before her spine bowed and crumbled. She walked well, though, determination overpowering her frailty, her balance sturdy and assured. She departed the school grounds with the confident stride of someone younger.

I spotted the photographer with his National Press badge dangling from his pocket and grabbed his attention. 'I'm writing the article,' I said, and pointed to the old woman. 'Can you get snaps of her, please?'

I wanted to speak to her. Why would such an elderly person be outside on such a hot, dangerous day? She must have come here for a reason. I moved to stop her as she shuffled off, but Greg's looming mass blocked my way.

'So, Savannah, you made notes, I hope? The editor, Peter, needs this article by eight p.m.'

'Yes, sir, I was just going to—'

'No "just", no "going to". I will hear none of that passive, unmotivated nonsense you Perimeter people try to pull. This is important. Your name in the papers puts BioLabs' name out there too, you understand?'

'Yes, sir, but—'

'No "buts" either. I'm aware this is not your forte. It'll be easier for you in your limited experience to do the press write-ups for the nutritional news—even pharmaceuticals, at a stretch. This story is more cultural, and I know experience of culture for the Perimeter is somewhat limited, what with the lack of education and uncontrolled breeding. See this as a challenge…'

I stopped listening. His condescending, entitled Centre crap was a lot to take. The heat made me impatient, and his obtrusive frame was a formidable obstacle. I peered past his face and its punctured hole of a mouth lined with foaming spittle to see the woman disappearing behind a corner. The photographer was talking to someone he seemed to know in the crowd. He had ignored my request.

My note-taking had been meagre. What was there to say? I supposed they wanted me to capture the mood of an engaged crowd, say how the political presence lifted them on such a perilous day. Portray the Prime Minister as some knight in shining armour, saving us from our gloom. That's certainly how the Centre saw us Perimeter population: unclean, unqualified burdens. I had learned more from listening to their conversations than from watching the Prime Minister. Their pity and ignorance were outstanding, albeit not all that surprising. I had worked with Greg for years, after all.

I felt torn between my loyalties to the Perimeter and the task expected of me. I was to be the first Perimeter resident to write for the National Press. Our voices were normally limited to whispers on the dark web and the ramblings of the unregulated news. Uncredible and poorly researched, the Perimeter opinions were lost under the weight of the Centre clout. Mere mumblings silenced by our lack of authority. But I had the opportunity to give our point of view, to speak up for the Perimeter, not just spoon feed them the same old hogwash, unjust and biased towards the affluent.

Greg was right, though; this was well out of my comfort zone. I could write for hours on the benefits of vitamins, their chemical compositions and malnutrition diseases. Writing a press article about politicians and some kids' drawings was not something I was interested in, nor had any expertise in. I was merely a substitute for their usual journalist, who was too clean to sully his hands with the Perimeter right now.

By the time I reached the lab, I had decided to write the piece I knew Greg wanted from me, a piece that would satisfy the attitude of his superiors. After all, I was no renegade, and an article about some old school junk was hardly going to change Centre opinions of the Perimeter, however carefully I worded it. Plus, I only had until eight that evening to write it up, so there was no time for a moral dilemma.

* * *

'Hey, Sav, you hear about the bird?' Archie asked me as soon as I walked into the lab.

'Yeah, pretty terrifying.' I didn't stop, just kept walking to my office.

'Professor.' An intern grabbed my attention, stepping up very close to me and smiling brashly. 'I'm learning the se-

79

quencing for the vitamin infusion and I have a few questions—
'

'Ask Marcus.' I waved her away. Her face fell, and she retreated to her desk. I continued to my office, ignoring Penny's shrieks of disapproval behind me.

Door closed, shutters down, computer on. Just one afternoon to write my first piece. I needed to concentrate. There was a knock at the door.

'Go away!'

Archie poked his head in. 'Alright, Sav?'

'Sorry, yes, I'm fine. I have to write up this press release. New job.'

'Say no more! Cup of tea on the way, and I'll make sure you're left alone all afternoon.'

Breathing a sigh of relief when the MimikTea arrived and Archie disappeared, I began. I also emailed the interns, dishing out more responsibilities to some who were proving themselves capable—meaning the ones who could wear their safety equipment properly, hadn't cried yet or didn't need a parental escort. I asked Marcus to oversee the extra workload. And with that, I had freed up hours each week for my new role.

At a quarter to eight, I finished the article and clicked send. I felt pleased, particularly with the way I'd described the crowd's apprehension over the bird, and the Prime Minister taking precautions with her biofilm. Trying hard not to sound too much like a scientist and more like a spectator, I described the representations of the previous generations' creatures, the 'Save the bees' and 'Save the trees' musings by the children, and how the Prime Minister reminded us that technology had bested nature. I tried to include nostalgia and sentiment, mentioning the elderly woman in the crowd, although with no input from her directly, there was little I could say. It was an accurate and engaging piece. And then I went home.

I muted any expectations. I assumed I'd find Grace tired, distant, perhaps even in bed already. But, to my surprise, she was ecstatic. Awake, alert and on her feet to greet me as I walked through the door. She leapt over with her arms open, congratulating me with a spirited voice. She seemed thrilled, smiling broadly and radiant with excitement.

'I've been thinking about it a lot,' she said, barely able to stay still, 'and I think you're right. Your name in the press. This could mean good things for us. I mean, that carries a certain accolade, don't you think?'

'Yes, I do.'

'Not that your science work doesn't, not at all, just this does even more so. Much more, if you think about it. They can't expect a top journalist to live in such a tiny apartment forever. You have a voice, people will read your words. That's important.'

She sounded like poetry to me, musical and vibrant. Dancing as she spoke, the evening light bouncing off her, her shadow disappearing under her cavorting euphoria. She'd cooked dinner, opened wine, even prepared dessert.

'Just think, Sav, it could be soon,' she said as we sat down to eat. 'I really feel hopeful now.' I beamed in response, wanting to hear nothing but the song of her voice. 'I even went out.'

'Really?' I almost dropped my fork. This was monumental news. 'No way, really? Grace, that's amazing. You've not been out for years.'

'I know. But I did. I went for a walk, all the way to that new development, the one you mentioned by the coast, with the two-beds.'

'It's not the best area, but there are big plans to improve it.'

'It's fine, really. I could see the floor plans, the apartments. Loads more space than here. I could see it, imagine it. A little baby crawling around all that space. I could see where the IC would go. It's not perfect but, with a baby, it could be.'

I stared at her in awe. 'Well done, Grace. Going outside, that's just wonderful. Today of all days, too. That's such a big step. It's done you the world of good. I can see it.'

And I could. Her cheeks were rosy. She had seen the possibilities that existed outside our shoebox apartment. She was energised and alive with a vivacity that had been absent for so long. Genuinely hopeful and optimistic, she pranced around the apartment as if caught in a breeze. She had braved the outside world. I had new career prospects, and with all the good news she bubbled with elation. I laughed with her, at her, the hilarity of her buoyancy subduing any lingering gloom.

'And you'll never guess what,' she said, as she finished the last of her meal.

'What? Tell me.'

'That naughty boy, Riley, I didn't have to shout at him all day. He'd even done his homework.' She held her hands to her cheeks in mock surprise.

'Well, clearly you can work miracles. You're a wonder with those children. The patience of a saint. When our baby comes, it'll be the luckiest kid alive.'

She leant over the table and kissed me. 'I don't want to get my hopes up, but maybe soon.' She smoothed her dress over her flat stomach and then did the same to me. 'You wouldn't mind if it had to be you?'

I shook my head. 'Whatever it takes.'

I meant it, although I hoped otherwise. The literature said

that when there is a choice of carrier, if one of the aspiring parents conceived naturally, then often that was the most suitable candidate. I was unusual in that—according to my parents, at least—I was conceived the old-fashioned way. Grace, however, was not. I cringed at the thought of carrying a baby. I imagined it would feel like an invasion and an assault rather than a joy. But what seemed parasitic to me was an innate heartstring pull to her. For Grace, I would do whatever was best.

Her smile looked natural, her soft cheeks rising effortlessly, like she had hidden there all along. 'I suppose with your new job and the lab stuff, you'll be really busy for a while?'

'Busier, probably. With the infusion in its final testing and the launch afterwards, too.' The realisation of my workload suddenly dawned on me. I could offload more to the interns, most likely, if they had a bit of common sense to spare.

'Don't you worry.' Grace stood and cleared away the dishes. 'I can do all the cooking and cleaning. You just concentrate on work. I'm so proud of you. Leave all the household stuff to me.'

I could have cried with joy. There was so much love in her voice, and so much affection in her arms. Affection that had been absent for years. We made love, something we hadn't done in a long time. Contentment had been lacking in our lives but, right then, I felt complete.

9

Chapter 8

The Poison Maker pored over the recipes, the instructions he worked from, interpreted and devoured. The cramped room, buzzing with whirring machines, was suffocating. Undeterred, he continued. Relentless in his quest to find the perfect poison. 'Hit the brain hard, disable the nervous system, shut down thought processes,' he muttered to himself as he stirred. Any poison, no matter how painful and obscene, would do to turn the population's minds to mush. Followers, powerless, robotic and efficient. Take their pain away and with it their mental liberty. This would be his next trial. The next test in the sea of many. His database was bulging with results, good and bad, fuelling his desire to continue.

When he was done, he smirked. He released his poison, a mild dose, subtle, and left the building. Covering his face, disguised and shielded. He coughed as he walked as if to say: I am one of you, I am one of you.

* * *

My sleep was restless that night. Grace's joy lit up my evening, but it could not penetrate the night's darkness. I spent what felt like hours staring at the ceiling, watching the shadows creep across it, scurrying into the spaces where the light had been. The whole world seemed to crawl around like vermin. Every time I closed my eyes, that was all I saw. When I did sleep, nightmares barged into my thoughts.

I am a child watching the armoured, hazmat-suited soldiers with nets and shotguns, firing at anything that moves and scooping up the bodies that have succumbed to the poisoned pellets in heaps on every street corner. Flu rages like wildfire. Dead birds fall from the sky and their swollen corpses litter the streets, spreading their poison.

I woke in a sweat and shook the images from my mind. I needed to remember the action and the clean-up. The sterile streets should be in my dreams, instead of the filth haunting my nightmares. The carcasses and their mess were bagged up and undiluted bleach was poured over the pavement. The birds, the source of so much suffering, extinguished.

Everybody is safe now.

The sanitiser may have cleansed the street, but it couldn't clean away grief. Grief leaves a stain.

Eventually, the sun rose to chase away the shadows. I shuffled free from Grace's embrace, leaving her sleeping peacefully. My alarm had not yet sounded, but I reached for my phone, desperate to see my press release in the news. I scrolled and found it a few stories down. There it was, complete with my name in the credits: '*By Professor Savannah Selbourne,*

Perimeter resident, head nutritional researcher at BioLabs.' They had used my picture from the company website. I looked younger than I was. The picture must have been a decade old. My smile seemed authentic, and my eyes lacked the dark circles that had become so hard to disguise.

I had been published in science journals plenty of times, but who reads those things? Everyone reads the news. The Minister of Impartiality's photograph adorned the top corner, complete with her customary red dress, taut across her robust torso like she was bursting with objectivity. Her picture was smaller than mine, but she outshone me with her bracelets, brooches and charms festooning every inch of her. Despite my drab picture, I shone with self-pride and my vanity made me blush.

My heart fluttered as I read it through, dreading some spelling error that the editors had missed, but found none. The editor had reworked the story slightly, which was to be expected for a first submission. Nothing serious; rather than the crowd feeling apprehensive about the bird, it was delighted with the successful clean-up. A more positive spin. I kicked myself for not thinking of that. The nostalgia was replaced by the public finding the pictures silly and old-fashioned, and there was more emphasis on the Prime Minister's statement about technology besting nature. Again, the edited version was much more sensible. And probably more accurate: no one really felt nostalgia towards filthy creatures and it was silly to imply it. The reference to the Prime Minister's biofilm was taken out also. I supposed they didn't want to tell the Perimeter about safety equipment we didn't have access to yet. So, a few wise alterations, but the essence of my story was there, and my name was still attached. There were no spelling mistakes I could see. It flowed well and captured the spirit of the day. All in all, I summarised that I had a lot to learn but was delighted that my name was in print. For my first piece, I was thrilled. I left the page open on Grace's computer so she could see it when she started work.

On my walk to the lab, I dodged a small protest near the old school where I'd been the day before. Alternates, by the looks of it. They were bunched together, many of them with their skin on display, their body heat causing the morning temperature to escalate. I could feel it radiate like an inferno. Fools! They were talking, standing very close, and some were even making contact with each other. To me, they looked like a bacterial soup, an outbreak waiting to happen. I shook my head and walked past quickly, leaving their muffled chat behind me.

Archie greeted me at the office with a high five and a 'Well done.' The interns lined up and gave me a round of applause as I walked in. My cheeks flushed as I told them to get on with their work. Greg had been right: I represented the company, the whole lab, so it was good for all of us.

I opened my computer to find an email from Greg:

Well done. Less editing next time would be better. More projects coming, you are the new Clark for now.

It seemed Clark still did not want to venture to the Perimeter, which meant more work for me. Oh, I could hug that horrible bird! Who knew such filth could bring opportunities? I read the email again and scratched my head as I pondered what Greg had to do with editing the piece. Peter, from the National Press, was speaking to him instead of me, like I needed that arrogant showpiece as a middleman. *Don't knock it, Sav!* I told myself. This was good news, even if it came from Greg.

I spent the morning getting updates from Marcus about the interns, and he seemed pleased enough to take some of my workload. The interns were happy liaising with him instead of me, something about him being more approachable or listening more. The vitamin infusion was on track, and results would be completed within days. I was brimming with elation. I glided into Archie's office on cloud nine and sat with him for an hour discussing The Raft's current movement, although we mostly gossiped about what the Prime Minister looked like up close.

'Short? Really?'

'Yep,' I said. 'Not Perimeter-short, but not as tall as the rest.'

'She always looks huge in photos.'

'She's not some dainty thing. She's broad, clearly eats well. I wouldn't like to arm wrestle her. Definitely shorter than the rest, though.'

'They must make her stand on a box for official photos.'

'I thought exactly the same!' I said. 'She has quite a presence, though. They all do. They're so tall and have their chins so high, I could see right up their nostrils.'

Archie made a disgusted face. 'What a sight. I'll bet their nostrils can tell you a lot of stories.' We laughed again. 'Wonder what makes the big boss shorter? Stunted growth from some vitamin deficiency in childhood? What's your professional opinion?'

'Just luck of the draw, most likely. Surprising she got the job, really. They always prefer the tallest and biggest in power.'

'Do they, though? Maybe the top bosses have always been shorter. We never knew this one was until now.'

'I guess we only know what they show us.'

'And that is what's so wrong with the world. We only know what we're told.' He shook his head.

'Ha! That's hilarious coming from you, super-hacker extraordinaire. If anyone can sift the fact from fiction, it's you.'

Clandestine computer engineers were commonplace; ones as good as Archie, less so. His toolkit of software, satellites and limited-range drones was like a box of children's toys to him. A plastic train set and a five-piece jigsaw puzzle. Unstimulating and elementary to an adult with such expertise. The tedium deadened his neurones, one axon at a time.

'Who're you calling "hacker"? I'm just a weatherman.'

I laughed at the picture of mock innocence his face made.

'Not that they take any notice of me, anyway. Five times the price for a bottle of water now. If only they'd listened.'

I sighed. 'Even I didn't listen to you, Archie. I totally forgot to bottle up some water.'

He slapped his forehead. 'I should be used to being ignored. What's the point of being an expert these days? I'm not the only one, either. Others have been silenced, brushed under the carpet with the dust of doubters.'

'Well, they listened eventually. "Everybody is safe now." Even if they're a bit out of pocket.'

'No more waves on the horizon, at least,' Archie said. 'But you've seen the news? The bird?'

'Yes, of course. It's fine, the clean-up was thorough,' I said. 'I guess there are still birds out there. There were so many, some were bound to escape.'

'Bet no bird would ever land in the Centre. And their water is fine, the wave wouldn't have got into their supply,' he said. 'We're just a buffer here, cannon fodder for them.'

I nodded. 'They have literally no clue about what life is like for us here.'

Archie tutted and rolled his eyes. He had stood shoulder-to-shoulder with other Perimeter soldiers as we drifted terrifyingly close to the mainland all those years ago, waiting for the shells to hit. No one from the Centre was in the army. They gave the orders, safe behind the fence, detached and protected, the bravery of the Perimeter their main defence. After hearing the measly battle cry of computer engineers, seeing their uncertain handling of rifles, their hesitation and awkwardly orchestrated tactics, the mainland forces realised that 'keyboard warrior' rarely means actual warrior. No contact was made after all, and The Raft continued its anomalous drift that Archie was now charged with predicting.

'You seen the company email from Greg this morning?' Archie asked with a smirk.

'Of course not. I never bother with group emails from Greg. What's the point? I'll hear everyone else moaning about it, eventually.'

'Ahem.' Archie cleared his throat in a theatrical fashion, pulled his face in to mimic Greg's surplus chins and splayed his lips in the typical Centre sneer. I struggled to swallow my MimikTea as a laugh exploded in my throat. 'You will be pleased to know that BioLabs' factory will be bottling up the best, most popular, safest drinking water brand. Rogueless Water is clean, on-trend and safe from rogue-wave contaminants. For our lucky staff working for such a prosperous company, bottles of Rogueless Water will be available in the vending machine for ten percent off live price. BioLabs doing their bit to keep everyone safe.'

'How very generous of him.'

'Keeping everyone safe and the shareholders' wallets fat,' Archie said.

'The Centre bubble look after themselves.'

We both shook our heads and sipped our MimikTea.

'You see the protests this morning?' I asked. 'What's that about?'

'No idea,' he said. 'They'll be hot, standing outside all day, and buy more water. Either that or they'll die of heatstroke. Win-win as far as the Centre is concerned.'

'That's a bit harsh.'

'They're Alternates. The Centre doesn't like them. I'll bet the powerful would like a way to wipe them out, or make them contribute more. Taking away their healthcare didn't work, so they want rid of them.'

'Well they can hardly just round them up and shoot them. Anyway, they're useless consumers. Everyone thinks they should contribute more.'

'Just think about it,' Archie said. 'The bird. It's crazy that one has landed, and right in the Perimeter too, where Alternates live. Any disease that bird was carrying is only going to infect the sort of people the Centre wants rid of. I'll bet the Centre are always plotting ways to wipe out those that don't toe the line.'

I narrowed my eyes at him. 'I think you've been reading too much online hysteria.'

He shook his head. 'Look, just be careful when you're outside. And listen to those lanky Centre twats. I bet they know a lot more than we do.'

'Will do.'

I left Archie's office to gather my things and leave work for the day. The interns, to their credit, were a mostly self-motivated group, able to work on their own initiative and understand the instructions Marcus had given them. The one who'd asked me about the infusion sequencing the day before seemed to have figured out what to do. Besides a mild tantrum about a beaker spill, they appeared to be coping. A couple were tasting samples they'd made and, based on their facial expressions, the results were mixed. The ones inputting data were awake, which was exceptionally promising. In previous years, we'd had several fall asleep at their desks.

I had spent months with Archie and Marcus sorting out the software in the lab to make it user-friendly, the instructions accessible and the ergonomics idiot-proof. It looked like it was working. I glanced through the uploads and the note-taking was concise and thorough. The data was filling up quicker than I'd expected, and no one had left in tears yet. They seemed unaffected by the bird news, since they had turned up for work. Perhaps the youth were developing into a less hysterical generation, I thought. Any sceptics of the Great Sterilisation Project were being lost to logic. An excellent result of progression.

As I was about to leave, Marcus knocked at my door. 'Microbes!' I cursed under my breath, before calling, 'Come in,' a little too fake-cheerfully. Six years as my lab assistant, and Marcus still knocked so feebly it was as though he was as terrified as the interns had been on day one. He would painstakingly try to solve any problem before bothering anyone else, and for the most part, he succeeded. So a knock at my door was unlikely to be a good thing.

He entered with intern number four, a plain young woman with a bowed posture as if her head was too heavy for her thin neck. I made a mental note to check her medical records.

None of the interns had declared calcium deficiencies or spinal problems. Lying about their health was not a good starting point for an intern.

'Marcus, what can I do for you?' My false cheer quickly dissolved.

'Sorry to disturb you, Professor. This is Mabel. She's been working on the results for the vitamin infusion. I've been overseeing her work, and she has some ideas she'd like to share with you.' Marcus's short stature and dry, pale skin implied poverty. The wages he got from BioLab would have brought him more money than he'd known when growing up. These days, he could almost pass as someone from a well-tarmacked and fish-free neighbourhood.

I looked at Mabel. Her head sagged lower, like she was deflating. 'Go on, Mabel. I'm listening,' I said.

'Well, Professor,' she said, gulping hard. 'The results... erm, the results, you see... what I'm trying to say—'

'Spit it out, Mabel. I haven't got all day.'

Her trembling intensified, but she found her words. 'I don't think they're going to be as favourable as were hoped for.'

'They rarely are.'

'So, well, I've been looking at historical records from old food before the Great Sterilisation Project.' She stopped there, her pale cheeks flushed, and squeezed her shaking hands together. She was as inexperienced as the rest of the interns at face-to-face speaking. Addressing a superior was way out of her comfort zone.

'Listen, Mabel, science is about discovery. It's about asking questions, even difficult ones. If we don't ask questions, we get no answers. Inquisitive minds are a good thing. Please, continue,' I said, in a manner that even Penny would be pleased with.

'Yes, Professor. Thank you.' Mabel straightened slightly. 'Vitamin absorption seemed better than it is now. Food grown in f-filth seemed to be higher in vitamins, or at least vitamins were absorbed better.'

I suppressed a sigh. 'As commendable as it is that you've done further research,' I tried to conceal my impatience, 'this is not news. We are well aware of the limitations facing us when trying to replicate nature in a clean and safe environment. The very issue you've described is the problem we're trying to fix.'

'What I'm thinking, Professor, is that maybe there was some... well, some good function in the filth that we've since eradicated. Some b-b-bacteria that was important in vitamin absorption.'

I cupped my forehead in my hands. A groan caught in my throat. 'Well done for saying so. And, yes, of course you're right. It's something we've always known, but it's rare that such a young mind can cope with this news. The problem we have is that it's very difficult to reintroduce bacteria without creating a free-for-all. If we allow some bacteria back, we get loads. And before you know it, we're investigated for creating biological weapons.'

Mabel looked close to tears at my reply. I took a breath and continued. 'Listen, Mabel. It's brave of you to bring this up, and what an excellent mind you have. It's probable that we'll never match the absorption properties of the old, dirty world, but we must do what we can to get as close as possible.'

'Yes, Professor. Thank you.'

'Such a courageous mind deserves the clearance to investigate and research as thoroughly as it wants. Don't you agree,

Marcus?' He nodded. 'Keep up your research. Fresh eyes bring fresh ideas, which is exactly what this intern programme is about. Feel free to ask Marcus or Archie for extra supervised access, and if you have any ideas on how we can improve our results while keeping to the basic principles of the modern age, you have my permission to research it. Keep it quiet from the other interns for now, we don't want them getting jealous.'

'Of course, Professor, thank you so much.' Her posture straightened a little.

'Excellent. Good work, Mabel.'

After that intrusion, I left work only a few minutes late. On my first steps out of the building, I took a moment to allow the stresses of the day to leave me, and tried to take some deep breaths. It was so hot it felt like my in-breaths would burn my lungs. The strip billboard along the width of the building opposite displayed health warnings between the major headlines:

Stay Inside, Drink Water, Dangerous Heat. Everyone Is Safe Now! Let's Keep It That Way. Prime Minister Reveals Some More Filthy History.

My headline up on the billboards! Even the stifling heat could not stop me from smiling.

The streets were in shade as the sun set, but even the shadows were scorching. I walked a few steps from the lab, then turned to look back at the building and its thin chimney. The long edifice towered above all the high-rises, pumping out its blue smoke. The exact hue of a clear sky. I kept watching, unblinking, to detect the moment the smoke turned from blue to orange, just as the sun began to set. Changing the smoke colour to match what the sky should look like had been studied in focus groups. It reassured people it was causing less pollution. Of course, inspections and legislation meant there was less pollution anyway, from our factory at least. But public perception was the most important thing. 'Feel healthy,' was the pharmacist's motto brandished everywhere. 'Feel', I noted. Not 'be'.

I waited for the cooling effect of the sunset. But it didn't come. The heat was tenacious even as the sky dimmed. Resolved, I began my walk home slowly, watching my heart rate, splashing my face with water every hundred metres. My watch beeped at me, and through the sting of sweat in my eyes, I read the warning: '42℃.' No kidding!

The recently sprayed streets misted with evaporating bleach, the glistening buildings looking like they were sweating. Somehow, despite the temperature, the protest at the old school was still going. The people looked tired and drained. Alternates nearly always looked like that. At least most were wearing hats. They passed water bottles around like sacred chalices, monitoring every drop. The crowd seemed to have grown and still more were arriving. I supposed that night-time was preferable, avoiding the worst of the weather.

Once again, I gave them a wide berth, Archie's voice in my head making me cautious. Online nonsense or not, getting close to such a steaming horde of people was never a good idea. I tried not to gawk as I scurried past, but they looked so unclean and exposed with their uncovered flesh. Public-safety education was simply wasted on some.

When I arrived home, Grace was dozing on the sofa, one leg dangling over the side with her slipper half on her dainty foot. The fading sun cast a patchwork of orange light across her pink dress. Her arm lay across her waist with a green Christmas tea towel. There were many of her childish accessories around the apartment. Stuffed toys, glove puppets, dolls, toy trucks. Boxes of baby clothes were piled up in the corner of the bedroom, collected from second-hand sales and passed down from friends. 'Dress for the job you want,' she'd say. The clutter didn't worry me. She had a chaotic mind, passionate and unruly. A stifled creative shackled by modern-age practicalities.

Tonight, her face looked soft and relaxed, her worry lines giving way to comfort. Leaning against the wall was her guitar, a music book open on the floor. I just stood and gazed at her, the air con making some of her golden ringlets sway. Then the oven beeped, and she startled awake.

'Oh, you're home already! I meant to have this all ready and laid out.'

I smiled and laughed as she seemed flustered. 'I was thinking you're slacking a bit.'

She hit me playfully with the tea towel. 'I've made dinner. Got some nice stuff delivered.'

'It smells amazing.' And it really did, the aroma of savoury delights filled the room. So much of the food we ate was made in the lab but the smell of it cooking in a home setting was enticing.

Grace beamed. 'I just want to show how proud I am of you.'

The dinner was divine, the best SynthoMeat from the protein deli, the vegetable chunks rich in flavour. She was always such a wonderful cook before she lost all motivation and her sadness took over. That meal was like old Grace was back. I could taste joy in every bite.

However good the food was, I couldn't take my eyes off her.

She blushed and poked her tongue out playfully. The wine was from the boutique winery before it shut down. I missed their wines. Their fruit genomes had been sold to a big lab, and as such, they lost the finery in the boutique version somehow. Still, no one could afford much besides the mass-produced stuff. We had been saving that bottle for a special occasion. But my work success was not what I was celebrating with each sip. It was my wife. My love. She had her glow back.

'How were the interns today?' she asked.

'Annoying as ever.'

She raised an eyebrow. 'Were you mean?'

'Me? Of course not.' She rolled her eyes in response. 'And how were the kids?' I asked.

'Annoying as ever.'

'Were you mean?'

She copied my fake offence. 'Me? Of course not.' We laughed, her foot rubbing against mine under the table. Her flirty small talk was so reminiscent of years earlier.

Stuffed and enjoying myself so much, I went to the freezer to look for dessert.

'Don't go in the freezer!' Grace cried out.

'I was going to look for—'

'It's filthy. You'll catch something,' she said. 'I'll clean it and get some dessert in tomorrow.'

I smiled and went back to her. 'Aren't you just the perfect wife?'

At that moment, it felt like I had given her hope. A better job, more money and accolades would put us up the treatment list for sure. To have made my wife happy, to have restored her cheer—that made all the years of ass-kissing worthwhile.

Chapter 9

While I was at home enjoying Grace's newly regained happiness, Archie worked late at the lab, as usual. He could work from home if he chose, and was encouraged to, but rarely did. He had seen the effect of such a secluded lifestyle on computer engineers. Plus, the sporadic spurts of air con in his office were still better than what he had in his crappy basement apartment.

Once, in a quest for adventure, spurred on by boredom and inactivity, he'd taken an Autocar to the Centre. It shocked me when he told me. I would have tried to discourage him, and he knew it. Not that he would have listened. Our mutual stubbornness moulded our friendship.

He'd been spotted as a Perimeter instantly: it's hard to disguise yourself when you're a foot shorter and wearing more holes than clothes. Not having the relevant permits, the security at the fence sent him away, an outsider through and through. He'd only wanted a peek at the golden skyscrapers, the glass and the finery. Just one lungful of fresh air. The second time he armed himself with the required paperwork, doctored forms to say he was assessing their telecoms signal. Totally illegal: they'd have chucked him in the sea if they'd caught him, and he knew it. He'd also known that his permit would pass any scanner, and he had the charm to back it up.

He spent the whole day pretending to use a monitor and gawping at the tall people with mouths full of white teeth, even daring to buy a smoothie from a cafe, watching their street cleaners scrub the sidewalks until they literally shone. Perfect for those who wish to check their reflection at every opportunity. He told me that their Selfie Stations weren't the ramshackle mirrored stands with dim lighting and volumizers and radiance spritz that we had. In the Centre they were staffed, with stage-quality lighting and an entire array of cosmetics. Almost everyone on the street stopped and used them constantly. It seemed they had both the time and the cash.

As well as climate and trajectory modelling, Archie's job included vetting employees and searching the dark web for misinformation terrorists spreading damaging lies about the company and the industry. There wasn't a system he couldn't hack, or a firewall he couldn't break down. If he wanted to, he could find out your whole online dating history, your blood-vitamin count and when you last took a shit.

The year before, I had let an intern go for breaching secrecy rules. When their lawyer threatened court action, Archie provided evidence of them discussing innovations with some guy they'd fucked (in the flesh) a month earlier. That guy was a nobody, some coastal hipster trying to make ends meet doing graphic design for a budget cosmetics brand. It was a serious breach of confidentiality, and they sacked the intern without hope of severance. That was as career-ending as it got. Apparently, they were now working for the same budget cosmetic brand, doing skin tests on fragrances, and living in a squat.

Archie's brief spurt of air con spluttered to a stop, serving as his customary cue to go home. Even Marcus had left for the evening. Not wanting the entire workforce to note the rough location of his apartment, Archie preferred his walk home in solitude. People are so quick to judge.

After a decade of working with him, I knew his habits well. He always used the Selfie Station body spray on his way into work to disguise the smell of salty air. I knew that when he mimed zipping his mouth shut, there was no convincing him to tell. I also knew that, in time, I'd hear all the details.

Later, he would tell me the details of that evening. Relating it here serves to illustrate my own obliviousness. His version of events included references to his charm and suave demeanour. But as I said, I knew him too well.

That night, as he went to make himself a last cup of Noffee from the canteen, he spotted an intern still working away. Intern seven. It was easy to remember her: she was far prettier than the rest. She had pale skin, still smooth and as yet uncracked from the harsh Raft air. Such a clear complexion carried an impression of innocence, and her big green eyes reinforced an aura of naivety. She had messy blond hair clumsily scraped into a bun, with strands flying free and getting in her way constantly. She started when Archie walked through.

'Sorry, sir, I was just getting some extra hours in. Want to make a good impression.'

'No problem, you carry on.' He smiled in that charming way he does.

'Actually, sir, I could use some help.'

He nodded and walked over. 'Sure.'

'This computer keeps telling me I haven't uploaded the latest images, but I have.'

Archie moved in to have a look. As he did, she rolled up her sleeves, exposing a tattoo on her forearm. Such an act of rebellion in someone so young surprised him. The design was of swirling gold leaves, with the number '50' in the middle. It was a symbol he had seen before, but couldn't place it.

She caught his gaze. 'Oh, sorry,' she blushed, and pulled her sleeves back down.

'Interesting design.'

'Thanks. It's not mine, it's from the Fifty Golden Years group.' Archie looked at her blankly. 'It's not banned or anything,' she said. 'Well, not yet, so please don't tell the Professor. It's just a remembrance group, that's all.'

'It's your business,' he shrugged, 'nothing to do with me.'

'Thanks.' She leaned in closer. 'I'm Amalyn, by the way.'

'Archie.'

'I know,' she giggled. 'Maybe I could thank you for your discretion over a drink? Seems a shame to work this late and not enjoy a drink afterwards.'

Archie looked at the intern, her pretty purity, her face unscarred by truth. The confidence in her voice told a different story. She was half his age, maybe younger. He didn't know how to respond. 'A drink? In an actual bar?'

'There are still some around, you know.' She smiled. 'Let me show you.'

Was she flirting? Her innocent appearance now seemed anything but. She leaned in close, too close. Flesh flirting was so hard to read, it's much easier online. Archie felt his cheeks flush.

'Sure, why not?' He forced his shoulders to relax as he spoke.

'Now? Might as well, it's Friday night.'

Archie pondered his plans for the next day: sitting alone in his basement apartment, playing video games, maybe ordering some takeaway. A late night would not interfere with that too much.

'I'll get my coat.'

The bar was a short walk away, down a side street with graffiti over the sign, changing the name from West Street to SWeAt Street. Archie was required to sign in with his social media profile: 'Safety checks,' it said. He obeyed and entered his details onto the touchscreen, eyeing the auto-hacker software. Too out of date for any legit establishment, too modified to be looking for terrorists. They were looking for inspectors, he presumed. Inside, his suspicions were confirmed. The place had a level of sterility only acceptable to those with no memory of the last pandemic. People were squashed together, glasses were reused, and the toilets were not sprayed down with bleach between uses. The sanitation inspectors could earn their annual bonus on this place alone, Archie thought. He liked it.

He and Amalyn approached the stainless-steel bar, polka-dotted with water rings and spillages, above which hung a lit-up cocktail menu. It was extensive, boasting a range of tinctures for any ailment and inhibition. A cauldron of distillations and nuanced narcotics. The questionable combinations of pharmaceuticals, alcohol and vitamins made him at the mercy of the mixologist. At least he was with a biochemist.

'Try the Clean Machine,' Amalyn said.

Archie read the ingredients. Two shots of fifty percent spirit alcohol, mixed with green citrus juice and rehydration concentrate, and shaken with two drops of liquid amphetamine.

'Sounds delicious,' he lied. Amalyn ordered the 'Trippy Clean Machine: Warning: not for first-timers': two shots of fifty percent spirit alcohol with a hint of redberry flavouring, poured over ice and psilocybin extract.

The drinks arrived in tall stem glasses accompanied by a shot-sized glass of water each that doubled the bill. They found a seat in a booth and sat opposite each other on firm chairs designed to make them lean over the table. The red material was shiny and wipeable, yet the lack of hygiene enforced by the staff was evident in the splatters that decorated the surface. Archie sat with his hands in his pockets.

'Relax!' Amalyn laughed. 'Just don't lick the furniture and you'll be fine.'

She was right; he knew. Looking around, he saw the place was frequented by professionals. Everyone was smartly dressed, having just finished work, and appeared cleaner than the bar's interior. No Alternates in sight. They couldn't afford the drink prices, anyway. Amalyn's mocking put Archie at ease. *It's just a bar, for god's sake*, he chastised himself. As much as he had tried to avoid the reclusive habits adopted by so many, it was clear they had crept up on him.

He looked around the bar at the smiling faces, the laid-back postures, the ease with which conversation flowed. Life's unrests had ground social lives to a halt, but here they were, well-oiled, in frictionless frivolity. People stood close, and some made contact, others even more intimate than that. Archie found himself staring.

'Everyone has their monthly injections. There's no need to worry,' said Amalyn.

'I'm not worried,' he said, trying to hide his unease. 'Just surprised. I didn't know places like this still existed.'

'You don't get out much, do you?'

Around the carefree crowd, he saw exposed skin, arms and legs on display, necklines cut tantalisingly low, midriffs drawing in wandering eyes. Skin sparkled under the coloured lights, showing dampness from body heat and the struggling air con. Archie noticed the same tattoo that Amalyn had, the gold leaf with '50' in the middle. Fans blew noisily from the ceiling and walls. Amalyn's hair was loose now, blowing across her face.

'So, I hear you used to be in the army,' she said, her smile appearing to be genuine admiration.

'Yep, team leader for weather forecasting. Drone software, too.'

'Don't be so humble. I'll bet you were on the coast when we drifted near to Portugal?'

'Right on the water's edge.'

'It was so annoying when they implemented curfew. I wanted to see it. I was only a kid, I found it really exciting. I don't remember the mainland at all.'

'There were quite a lot of explosives chucked our way. It really wasn't safe.' He spared her the details. Archie had also been part of the squad that dissolved the anchors—whether or not he agreed with the act was a different story. He had watched people running for their families, falling into the sea from the bridges, having left it a moment too late before the anchors blew. Years later, when the shells came from the mainland to push The Raft away, the screams erupted again, but duller this time as most stayed inside. The shrill cry of a soldier being buried under a pile of rubble was a noise that still haunted his dreams. He had hoped the screams would stay in the past. He had tried to build a wall around those memories, to barricade them into a bygone oblivion.

Amalyn gasped and grabbed his hand. 'How brave you were.'

'Er... yeah, I guess.' Archie, more than a little unused to this level of forwardness, sipped his cocktail and fiddled with his sleeves. His body tingled, and the softness of her hand felt all the more inviting.

They ordered another round, then another. Unease just melted away. The beat of the music, the subtle colourful lighting, the cooling fans made Archie feel alive, and his worries washed away with every sip. Amalyn looked beautiful. Her skin was rosy from drink, her pupils wide, her hair falling in soft wisps over her face. She'd unbuttoned her blouse a little and he could see the tops of her pert breasts. The age gap didn't matter, even the educational difference wasn't important. He'd dated no one but computer engineers before, but that usual preference melted away. He stroked her cheek. They leaned in close, her hand grazed his thigh.

'They have rooms here, you know,' she said.

Archie gulped, his mouth suddenly dry...

There should have been a voice in his head telling him, '*No, she's a colleague. Worse: an intern!*' There should have been an element of doubt, a recognition of the age gap. She had been a kid when he was in the army. He should have been thinking about his hygiene, protection, the sanitation of the rooms in such a lax place. All these doubts should have been screaming at him, and, if it weren't for the cocktails, definitely would have. Instead, he felt comfortable, confident, lustful and reckless. He hadn't had flesh intercourse in a long time. Cyber, of course. Loads. But flesh? He struggled to remember how long it had been.

Amalyn didn't wait for Archie's reply. His voice lodged in his throat, parched with fervour. His wide eyes and smile said it all. She took him by his sweaty hand and led the way.

Chapter 10

It was the weekend, but that didn't mean a thing to Greg, who emailed me early Saturday, simply saying: 'Cover the protest.'

Great, not much of a clue. His weekly meetings with the press were Friday mornings; he could have given me a bit more notice. Still, I leapt into action, keen to get another story under my belt. A quick scan on satellite view and I saw the only crowd in the Perimeter. The protest I had walked past the day before was still there.

I didn't shower. There wasn't much point when I was going to be mingling in more bacteria than you'd find in a germ-research lab. The temperature outside was reported as thirty-three degrees: significantly cooler than the day before, still too hot for the head-to-toe attire I would have to wear. Grace was still asleep. I kissed her forehead and wrote her a note.

The walk from my apartment block was accompanied by the roar of air con and street sprayers. I loathed the street sprayers. They'd been installed throughout almost the entire Perimeter several years earlier after reports of an insect sighting. The piping was never buried into the asphalt, so what we lost in filth we gained in trip hazards. And after seeing that filthy crawler a few days earlier, I now seriously doubted their effectiveness. Sodden feet for minimal gain seemed a pointless inconvenience. I squelched my way along the road towards the coast. 'Microbes!' I cursed. I should have thought to wear rubber boots.

As I walked closer to The Raft's edge, I kept my gaze to the ground, willing my eyes to see nothing. The sea air whipped across the crumbling asphalt, the dust blowing up and adding to the smog, little specks flying about in my vision. But it was just particulate matter, nothing more. Neglected ditches lined every street towards the edge: the holes had been dug but the cables were still absent. In some places they'd buried the street sprayers when the quantum cables were laid, but in many others even those were still exposed. What remained were ditches with spray-painted outlines to highlight them. The little land we had left was drilled for no reason at all. The ditches seemed too deep to my untrained eyes. Still, if the extreme edges of The Raft broke away, who would care? Would anyone notice? No one had before.

It was just microscopic fissures at first, imperceptible. Natural flaws that no one spotted. Then they grew into larger imperfections, explained away with poorly researched excuses and belittled culpability. The fractures corroded into gaping crevices that became harder to patch over and conceal. Every time the ground seemed to loosen, they fortified it with concrete, coating over the top without ever checking what was happening underneath. Still, no one noticed.

Why is it we never notice things until it's too late? Humankind buried their heads in the dirt back then. Even when we all eventually noticed, no one worried. Our land was dissolving under our feet, but any hint of a problem was dismissed as ludicrous. We assumed what we had always assumed: the country was rock-solid.

I trod carefully around the holes, stumbling over the loose gravel. Despite keeping my gaze down, the headlines on the strip billboards grabbed my attention:

Heat Warning, Stay Indoors! Everyone Is Safe Now! New Drone Technology, Company Tops Rich List! Progress is Paramount! Prime Minister Condemns Mass Gathering in Wake of Bird Sighting! Street safety score 3/5 With Sterility Comes Liberty!

Having spotted no vermin, I felt a sense of relief, despite approaching the grimiest bit of The Raft. The protest had moved away from the school, the destruction of which I had imagined they were focusing on, to the old dock that clung on for dear life by the shore. A water desalination plant was installed around it, but since nothing had been done with the coast since, the dock had been left to ruin.

Dinghies attached by thick rope were bobbing excitedly on the murky water. Just offshore, nets were skimming the surface, scooping up the suffocating fish as they came up for a final gasp of air. The testing stands were lined along the shoreline and several streets inwards. Test wrappers littered the skies with every gust of wind. Each fish was individually assessed for pollutants and toxins, and graded according to which drug was most concentrated in its flesh. When The Raft drifted into shallower waters, as it occasionally did, explorations went deeper for mussels, which can have very pure sources of chemicals. Hair-dye fixers are especially prevalent, as well as the usual pharmaceuticals.

The protestors sounded angry, their hateful voices rever-berating as sweat dripped from their faces. They limped and shuffled up and down the street that ran alongside the old dock. The stench was overwhelming. It wasn't just a fish smell but general decay and rot, mingled with the unwashed vinegary stink from the armpits of the Alternates. Now and then, a wave would wash up over the concreted bank and rain its putrid waters onto the shore. My heart skipped a beat every time, but they were just normal waves. The usual thrashing The Raft's edge was accustomed to. The salty air left a residue on everything, and I could feel my hair getting sticky.

Bits of old plastic collected on the edges of the pavement, ancient dirty relics from who knows where, the sort of muck that lasts forever. The sweepers attended daily, but it wasn't enough to keep on top of the constant bombardment of ocean filth. The street sprayers were never installed this close to the edge, a dumb act of frugality by the authorities. The thriftiness of those in power left the unfunded streets to fester. Germs spread, and where the sprayer's mist began two streets inwards, it was turned up to full volume, creating a fountain of disinfectant bordering the squalor. I pulled my face shield closer, more to protect myself from the stench than anything. *If anywhere needs street sprayers, it's here*, I thought.

The protestors looked like they'd been out all night, clothes visibly unwashed and their faces hanging like old curtains. Their jawlines drooped down, their bottom lids following. They swayed on the spot, or hobbled in circles, leaving trails of old sweat behind them. A few sat or lay on the ground, which made my skin crawl. They barely flinched when they were bashed with gushes of sea water. They seemed to enjoy the cooling effect more than they abhorred the grime. I kept my distance, making mental notes, not daring to get out my e-pad in case I was mugged.

New posters had been put up since I had last walked around here. They showed pictures of how the new, cleaned-up docks would look, citing safety concerns and improved aesthetics. The new design would create more desalination plants and purification centres, as well as some high-rises and a hydropower station, blocking access to the water. A sensible progression for the population that contributed in a meaningful way. For the Alternates, though, it was a nightmare. The protestors who had the energy to chant rattled and spat in hoarse voices.

'Save our docks! Save our docks! Save our docks!'

Many looked too drained to do much more than mouth the words. There wasn't enough shade from the sun, and few of the protestors had water with them. They congregated in huddled groups, limbs strewn across others, mouths close to faces, faces close to hands. The entire scene was a festival of filth. Along with the chanting, I could hear other complaints coming from the crowd.

'How are we going to fish?' one woman was howling.

'They don't want us to fish. They want us to buy medicine we can't afford.'

'It's such a waste if we can't get our medicines from the sea!'

'I've heard that commercial ships are going to harvest the sea so we have to buy from them, and it'll be on our record.'

Ramshackle signs made of garbage read: '*Perimeter docks! Perimeter rules!*' I winced when I read them. So much treason in this gathering. If it was any further inland, the police would shut it down in minutes. But The Raft's edge was ignored, its voices small and actions weak, it just wasn't worth the risk to the police to come this close. We were expendable.

The impassioned protestors continued their chanting, scowling at those not joining in. I felt like an imposter, a spy, so I hid in what shadows there were behind billboards and banners, hoping to be eclipsed by them. The crowd was clearly made up of artists and thespians. The archaically idealistic sort that the modern world had left behind, their minds lost in the dirt. I wondered if my parents would have been here, pleading for the right to access foul waters and supporting the fish junkies. Probably not, I assured myself. For all their nostalgia, they understood disease and believed in hygiene.

I sighed at the sight of the waste, the arrogance of it. All these people were likely out of work, refusing to contribute to society in a meaningful way. They could have all the medicine they needed if they studied appropriately and put their computer engineering or biomedical science degrees to good use. I remembered my mother telling me how my grandmother had studied art at university. Art! Imagine. The privilege of uselessness was obsolete now. Choosing to put some creative interest above making a meaningful contribution was unthinkable. Like the interns who could speak multiple languages. All that time they spent on extinct words when they could have been studying science or coding. And now some romanticised ideals lived on in the likes of the fish junkies, who thought they should be able to study what they wanted and still reap the same benefits as everyone else. I clenched my fists as I watched the protest. A cockroach farm, that's what this was. My father's insect hotel in human form. Inept, filthy crawlers. I spotted a lump of tarmac close by and suppressed the urge to throw it at the crowd.

In among the unwashed Alternates, I saw a couple, their

young child hanging from the leg of the woman who was obviously her birth mother. To bring a child to such a place seemed reckless, yet the parents looked professional, clean, and healthy. One of the women bent down and plucked the girl from her leg, putting her on her back. The other put her arm around her wife and the little girl played with the hair in front of her, laughing as she yanked out the ponytail and made it messy. I felt a lump in my throat. It was Grace that yearned for motherhood, not me. But that little family showed me how wonderful having a child could be. The closeness those three shared looked so innate and pure. Why were they at the protest? No way would an artist couple have made the top of the fertility list. I took a risk and walked over to them, dodging rubbish and exhausted Alternates on the way.

'She's adorable,' I said.

'Quite the handful,' said one of the couple as she retied her hair.

'My wife and I, we've been on the list for such a long time,' I explained, unable to hide my sadness.

'We know that feeling.' They looked at me with whole-hearted empathy. 'I'm Cass and this is Sal, and this little troublemaker is Jocelyn.'

I introduced myself and gave little Jocelyn an air high five. 'I'm going to be four next week,' she said, holding up four fingers and demonstrating her counting skills.

'Wow, quite the young lady,' I said. Jocelyn looked proud. 'I don't mean to pry. Sorry to be so forward, but what's your secret?' I asked. 'The fertility waiting list is endless. How did you manage it? Do you work for the government or something?'

'Oh, god, no!' Cass laughed. 'I'm a teacher and Sal works

in a spa.' They saw the look of confusion on my face. 'No grandparents for the potential baby, I assume?'

'No,' I said. 'All our parents died before the Sterilisation Project was in full swing.'

'We're the same. But you know, the clinics really favour couples who have a grandparent. A babysitter, a bigger house to inherit. A grandparent really bumps you up the list.'

'Oh,' I sighed. 'I see.'

'Our parents are dead, too. But a recommendation from an elderly person, one with a bigger apartment, goes a long way.' I raised my eyebrows in disbelief. 'Really, it works. It helped us, anyway. You need someone aged over a hundred, and there's plenty of those. And it should be someone with no descendants of their own. There's a fair few who lost their whole families. They can sort of adopt you. And with their backing, the promise of a babysitter and a bigger apartment one day, you shoot up the list.'

'Really? I've never heard of such a thing.'

'It's hardly advertised on billboards. Check the dark web, but be careful, as it's often people who are quite outspoken about the government, which is why they want someone similar to leave their wealth to. Better to give it to a nice family than the leeches at the top.'

I nodded a little. Their candid way of talking was making me tense. Sal carried on with their tale.

'We met the most wonderful woman. She was a hundred and two and fit as a fiddle. She died a few months back, and we'd been raising Jocelyn in our studio until then. We've moved into her old apartment now, a two-bed place in a great part of town. All that space is just amazing. Jocelyn really has room to grow. And there are so many of Granny's memories around the house, photos and trinkets, reminding us of her stories about when she was a kid. Such a different world she grew up in. She used to babysit for us daytimes when we were at work and was a wonderful grandmother to little Joce. She was a big believer in access to healthcare, as that's how it was when she was young. That's why we're here protesting—for Granny.'

'For Granny!' Jocelyn said, clapping her hands.

'I get my medicines on healthcare, but Sal has to pay,' said Cass. 'We get our monthly vaccines, of course, but Sal gets nothing else. No degree, so no help. Her parents were writers and encouraged her creativity. Now she's demonised for it.'

I tried to look sympathetic. 'You could always retrain?'

'I had an infection as a teenager,' Sal said. 'It affected my memory. I'm okay, but I couldn't pass a degree.'

'And anyway, why should she?' said Cass. 'Her contribution is important. So many use the MindSpas, so it's not like Sal is useless. But still: no access.'

'I think when you have a child, your outlook changes so much,' Sal said. 'You want them to grow up in a world where they are valued, whatever their gifts, where their potential is not limited by their postcode. My parents were creatives. It's a shame we can't be like that now. We just want this little lady to be as happy and content as possible.' Sal tickled Jocelyn, who giggled and squirmed.

My politeness hid my reservations as I nodded. I thought I recognised Sal from the MindSpa I use. I had never considered the staff there might not have adequate degrees.

Their views were alien to me. They spoke about 'gifts', like individual merits were more important than The Raft. They weren't Alternates, not really, although it sounded like their Granny may have been. What kind of crazy old woman would we have to befriend? Someone with whimsical memories about the times when people lived in filth and visited other countries full of filth, spreading diseases and starving to death. Old people always viewed their past with rose-tinted glasses, remembering the joy of youth over the inconveniences that come with age. The world carries on spinning but, at some point, people do not. We stagnate in a pool of the past while time continues flowing. The stubborn rocks sit at the bottom of the river, eroded and immobile.

'That's great information. Thank you so much,' I said. 'My wife will be excited to hear it. We'll get searching for a grandparent straight away.'

'No problem. Here, take our email address.' Cass handed me her phone to copy her details. I hesitated before taking it, but Cass didn't notice. I had hand gel in my bag, I reminded myself. 'Any questions, feel free to get in touch. We know how hard the wait is.'

I thanked them again and retreated from the crowd, the stink becoming too much to bear. It seemed a sensible step. And it made sense. An inherited property, a babysitter: those things would help new parents immensely.

Having everything I needed for the article, I left for home.

12

Chapter 11

By the time I'd got home, stripped off my overclothes and coverings, and antiviral-sprayed myself down, Grace was just getting out of the shower. I smelled her cleanliness and knew I'd need more than just a spray to feel clean again. The stench of the crowd had soaked through to my bones. I scrubbed my hands until they looked red raw and threw my clothes straight in the laundry on a hot wash. Grace, flushed from her shower, looked fresh and content.

'Glad you're home,' she said. 'Did you pick up some water?'

'No, sorry, I forgot. I'll get some after I've showered. Can you believe it's eight times the price now?'

She shrugged. 'Sounds about right. Are Saturdays going to be a regular work thing?'

'Not sure, I think it's just ad hoc.'

'I'm not complaining.' She kissed me, she tasted like toothpaste. 'I'm proud of you.' She smiled and rubbed her hair with a towel. 'So, what's the hot story today?'

'The protests at the old docks.'

'Protests?'

'They're developing the area so there won't be access to the sea anymore. The place is filthy. It's going to make it a lot cleaner. There's dirty sea debris and fish muck everywhere. It stinks.'

'So there's going to be no access to the water at all?' Grace stopped drying her hair and stared at me.

'Not by the looks of it.'

'People won't be able to fish?'

'Nope. Rumours of big corporations doing it instead.'

'No more fish markets down there?'

'Nope.'

'How will people get medicines and drugs?' Her voice quivered.

'From the doctor or pharmacy like everyone else, I guess,' I said.

She stood motionless. 'When are they shutting them down?'

'Monday, I believe.'

Grace broke down. She held her chest like she'd been winded and struggled for breath. 'No, no, no. That can't happen.'

'Darling, why are you so worried?' I jumped up to hug her. Tears were streaming down her face. 'You don't have to worry, we have healthcare.'

She was trembling and barely able to speak. I tried to hold her tight, but she pushed me away. Her knees gave way, and she sunk to the floor. 'No, they can't do that.'

'They have to. There's going to be new apartments and a desalination plant. Its progress. Progress is paramount.'

I tried to hug her again, but she broke away, her weak arms rejecting me. Then she walked over to the freezer and pointed at the bottom drawer. She opened the door and pulled out a

119

tray. Inside, wrapped in several layers of plastic packaging, was a putrid revolting mess.

Fish.

'Grace, what the hell?' It was disgusting, a whole carcass, complete with glazed eyes and rancid teeth. Chunks of flesh were missing, the dirty knife still lying beside it. I gawped in disbelief. Then the penny dropped. There was a fish. Flesh was missing. My wife, my sweet wife, had dismembered and eaten flesh.

'I needed something,' she said through her tears. 'If I'd gone to the doctor, we'd be off the treatment list. And work kept saying that I need to be happier, how I'm unengaged.' Her speech was broken by sobs and cries, her shaking body trembled with every breath. 'Bad work reviews are reported to the clinic, too. I mean, they say they don't, but that's bullshit. Everyone knows the fertility clinic can get all the dirt on you they want. You have to believe me. I had no choice. I couldn't cope anymore. Even you said so. And the fish markets were so friendly and easy. I bought some with high ratings of mirtazapine, and it helped, it really helped.' She started sobbing again.

I gaped at her, trying to draw in air through my dry and coarse throat. Grace, my wife, was a fish junkie. She wasn't some artist or thespian, not some waste of space trying to rip people off by selling them poetry. She taught history and science to ten-year-olds. Hers was a proper job and proper purpose. She couldn't be a fish junkie. Not my Grace.

'What am I going to do, Sav? What am I going to do?'

I had no answer. The room spun as I felt dizzy. I looked away as nausea began rise from my gut. Our ancestors had consumed so much hormone-pumped flesh that they had bred us into barrenness. And now my wife was consoling herself by eating more flesh. What could I say? How could I respond to such a vile act?

'Don't turn away from me, Sav. Don't hate me. You know me, you know I had no choice.'

I remembered how happy she was, how she'd cooked with those hands that had touched that... that filth. She'd kissed me with those lips that had eaten it. I held a hand to my mouth. That carcass. Flesh. She had eaten flesh like some savage. I ran to the bathroom to vomit. Nothing came up, and I dry heaved. I rinsed my mouth at the tap, but the nausea wouldn't pass. It felt like a film of grime was covering me.

'Sav, please, you have to understand.'

Grace pleaded at the bathroom door, but I could not answer. I stripped naked and turned the shower up to full heat, burning my skin to scald away the grime. Sitting in the steamy room with the fan off, I hoped to cleanse my lungs with the mist. I breathed deeply as Grace's cries faded. My Grace, my wife. How could she?

I remembered how she had been. There was no doubt the medication, the fish, had helped. That carcass had consoled her in ways I could not. Her desperation in seeking such muck was not her doing, it just illustrated my failures as a wife, as a provider. My Alternate parents were likely a reason for the denial of treatment, and that denial had thrown my wife into the arms of the Alternates. Life had gone full circle. My heart heaved, my eyes wept. I was so mad, and Grace's sadness consumed me. Our lives, our wholesome lives that had begun together with such promise, had been ruined by a freezer of filth.

I wrapped myself in a towel and left the bathroom. Grace was sobbing silently on the sofa, her arms heavy at her sides. She seemed tainted now. I dared not breathe for fear of smelling fish.

'You hate me. You can't stand me. I can tell! You're disgusted!'

'No, I don't hate you.' I sat on the other end of the sofa. I couldn't bring myself to touch her. 'It's just... I don't know, Grace. It's just so disgusting! You ate that thing.'

Grace shook her head sadly. 'It made me throw up at first. Just the thought of it, the smell. I put it in the blender with some juice, but it was still awful. But I've felt so much better since. You have to understand. I just couldn't go on like that.'

Her despair overwhelmed me, her need, her vulnerability. 'We'll figure something out. It'll be okay,' I said.

How could this have happened? We weren't that sort of couple. We were good, hard working people. Our marriage contract was almost up, and part of me thought, *this is a deal breaker*. How can I renew vows with someone who ingests such filth? I shuddered. Still, I couldn't help but reminisce. She had been so vacant and sad. And how, lately, she'd seemed happier.

'I thought you were happy for me and my new job. I thought you were trusting me to work hard and get us up the list.'

'I am happy for you, you've been so amazing. My depression was just overpowering everything. Please understand, the medicine doesn't make the happiness false, it just makes the sadness easier to bear.'

I sneered at the mention of the word 'medicine'. It was fish. Dirty, stinking, polluted fish. And the toxic carcasses were now in our freezer. I gagged again.

I went to fetch myself a glass of water from the bathroom.

I couldn't face going back into the kitchen. She had been so happy. My old Grace had returned. How could I despise the thing that had gifted her with happiness? How could I recoil from those arms that needed me? It was not disgust at what she had done, not entirely. It was that my own failings had caused it, and I alone was powerless to fix it. The stinking carcass had succeeded where I could not. I had lost control. Grace had ventured outside, alone, her desperation conquering her fear of leaving the apartment. Those docks had given her a lease of life that I had been unable to provide. I had driven Grace to this as I had stunted my career for too long. My selfishness and wallowing, my boredom, were reflected in her despondency at home. My background meant I had to try harder, and I had failed to achieve what I should have. I had failed to provide. I had left her to wallow with delay, her life on hold.

The population had grown ever denser as she became diluted into the masses. A natural rebalance, said some. But the scales had pushed my wife to a place lower than I ever imagined. And still we would wait in line, as waiting is what was expected of us in the Perimeter. Resources were limited and stretched thinner and thinner as demand grew with every new soul created. For the greater good or for the good of the Greater?

Grace deserved more than this, more than me. I subdued my instinct to flinch as I put my arm around her. My voice soft, I told her about the couple at the protest, Sal and Cass, and little Jocelyn, about Jocelyn's giggles and the tenderness they all shared. Grace stared at me in awe. She had never heard me speak with desire for a child and a family before. We had always known she was the one who wanted a baby, while I just wanted to make her happy. She knew that deepest desire was hers alone. And then there I was, describing a family with a sense of longing, realising that, perhaps, I shared her want. A baby would fix Grace's depression better than a rotten old fish. If we could get up that list, there was hope.

I explained how Sal and Cass had made the list for treatment, how maybe we could find a grandparent to adopt. I gave Grace the couple's email address and told her to get in touch with them, and to search the dark web for listings while I went to write up my article.

My thoughts were spiralling, and my head hurt. I shut myself away at my desk, closing off the world outside, and sipped a cup of MimikTea. The computer stared blankly at me as I willed words to form, hoping they would find their way out of my brain onto the monitor by some sort of osmosis. Nothing came. I craved the MindSpa but told myself that if I got my article written, I could go to the spa after. Still, I was stuck. Language seemed inhibited and closed off in my mind. How to approach this? If I'd written the article a day earlier, I would have said how the protestors were idiots and foul, that they should train in useful careers and access medication in the same way as respectable people. But now. Now...

Grace wasn't an Alternate. She wasn't getting kicks from carcasses. She was ill, heartbroken, and struggling. The system was against her and she was just trying to get by. Cass and Sal weren't junkies. Sal worked in a spa: a useful job, really, if a little simple. Why shouldn't she have access to healthcare? And why should employers and fertility clinics have access to medical records?

It seemed to me, with the system as it was, that these people, the eclectic bunch that were protesting, might have a point. Who was I to judge those who bought fish when my wife had the need? And a genuine need. Grace now had the tools to cope with her despair, and the docks' redevelopment threatened that.

I wrote my article. It was an unbiased piece, giving both sides, all angles, explaining the need for confidentiality, for medicines for all, and the role that the docks played in that. I wrote of the tragedies that could lead people to such desperation.

I wrote as a scientist, how filthy this mode of drug extraction was, how variable in concentrations, yet how wasteful if all that is out at sea. I wrote of the need for more research and, if viable, how it should be seen as sustainable in a country where resources were limited and demand often outstripped supply. When I was finished, I felt exhausted. I read through it and shed a tear.

Poor Grace. Poor Grace and her desperation. How awful it must have been to eat that, to chew that flesh, the stodgy pulp sliding down her throat. I pushed it from my mind for fear of gagging again. But it would not be hidden so easily. I had seen the corpse and its entrails, its crooked face and tiny eyes, glazed with death and eternally encapsulated in its putrefied state.

I had never seen a whole fish before, not that I remembered. Their bones that littered the pavement at The Raft's edge gave no real impression of how a corpse would look. It was pitifully repulsive. Even the freezer's ice couldn't control its stench. I showered again and afterwards found Grace asleep, exhausted from her honesty. She still held the piece of paper with Cass's email address. I covered her in a blanket and left for the MindSpa.

My favourite MindSpa was a short walk from our block, not too near the coast. I visited most weekends. Although its effects were short-lived, the escapism it offered was worth it. It was a clean, white-tiled room with soft lighting and a smell reminiscent of floral additives. Sweet, but not overly sickly. The softly spoken young person at the reception checked me in and took me to one of the sunken chairs, wiped it down, then held my hand to help me climb in. The cushioning was soft and rose up around me in an embrace.

They gave me a pair of headphones and a fresh velvety face mask, weighted around the eyes and soothingly warm. As I fidgeted into comfort, a cooling breeze blew over me and my head was filled with the sound of rustling, like lots of paper caught in a gust. The sounds were advertised as 'clean and natural', targeting those parts of the brain that were still in tune with nature, where evolution hadn't caught up. We still craved certain sounds to feel at peace. The rustling was eventually joined by some musical cheeps and chirps, such strange sounds but so relaxing. I felt my stresses and worries melt away in the cooling breeze and floral scent.

After a couple of hours, the lights began to get a little brighter, an orange hue filtering through the mask and alerting my mind to awaken. I felt rested and prepared and wished I had the time to begin every day like that. All my neurones and thoughts aligned themselves in an efficient and motivated way, like every part of me had clicked together and was in synch. I felt ready to return home.

I walked down the grey pavement, the overly proficient street sprayers coating me in sanitiser. The smog was bad that day and the heat had risen angrily since the morning. We must be getting close to the equator, I realised. The low wind meant the smog wouldn't budge, and it hung like lace off the buildings and lampposts, dripping down the Autocars and SolaArbs. Even the ArbAirs were draped in thick smog. Overwhelmed, the Perimeter's older designs of artificial trees couldn't cope with this much pollution. Even through the bleach, the air smelled burnt.

The cheeps and chirps from the MindSpa quickly became an old memory. The hum of the air con was all I could hear.

13

Chapter 12

That same day, Archie awoke with a satisfaction he had not felt in some time. The poor man had gone so long without any action. I couldn't stop laughing when he told me. Refreshed, contented and gratified, he lay for a moment, the room silent, the morning light highlighting the crumbling decor. I chastised him when he told this part of the story: his out-of-character carelessness, wooed by some young beauty. Men are predictable, I justified. I squirmed as he reported the general uncleanliness of the place, the dust he could see on the mirror, and how a long-lost feeling of dread crept in.

I slapped my forehead when he told me. How could he have been so reckless? They hadn't even used protection.

Silently panicking so as not to disturb Amalyn, Archie's trembling hands lifted the covers, and he inspected himself. Any sores? Any itching or discharge? He felt his head for a fever.

'Relax,' Amalyn said. 'No one gets pregnant that way anymore, and there hasn't been a single recorded STI in years.'

Archie felt his cheeks redden. She must be right. If there were STI outbreaks, the news would have reported it. Anything to put people off such non-conformist behaviour. He lay back, allowing himself to unwind again. He wondered with bewilderment how it could be that casual sex was so rare in a world where it was so safe?

He turned to look at Amalyn, his head fuzzy with a mixture of perplexity and appreciation. Such a young beauty. How had he gotten so lucky? He tried to piece things together, from finishing work to going to the bar. He could not understand how he had managed to spend the night with Amalyn. She looked stunning, so much more beautiful than any woman he had been with before, even when he was a young man. Her sleepy face was so smooth and clear, she could be mistaken for a Centre. Ordinarily, he wouldn't trust anyone with such a silky complexion. With lines come wisdom and stories, each one representing a truth. Amalyn was as smooth as glass.

She rubbed her eyes and nuzzled in closer to him. Her floral shampoo scent was now masked by the smell of their evening together. He pulled her in closer.

'Tell me about when you were in the army again, at the coast with all those nasty weapons,' she said as she wrapped a leg over him.

'Well, it was really dangerous.'

'Oh yeah?'

'Yeah, for sure, only the strongest and bravest were there.' If the tough guy routine was what she wanted, he'd play along.

'Tell me more,' she said.

And so he did.

* * *

She smiled as they parted, and Archie couldn't have frowned if he'd tried. They agreed to keep work separate from whatever this was. He didn't know, having little recollection of the normal progression of such things, especially with someone her age. He admired the way Amalyn glided with ease over their parting. It was impossible for her to be awkward. She was not overconfident, but simply found interaction effortless, with a calm voice and casual expressions. She moved in a way that was inviting yet aloof, teasing yet willing, everything seemingly so natural.

Archie walked the hour to his apartment as if floating on the breeze. He didn't even notice the heat and smog. His absent-mindedness would last for days, forgetting to button his shirt correctly, neglecting his ironing. History was dominated by men, but the power women yielded was something quite different.

When he arrived home, he sat for a while, smelling his skin as the last of her scent lingered on him, then showered and logged on to play video games. But his mind was not the content and peaceful place it should have been. There was something he had to investigate, something he'd thought of, before he'd drunk too many cocktails, before they took away his inhibitions.

He had lost three games of *Foreign Invasion* and had a nap before he remembered the tattoo. The gold-leaf design, the numerals '50', on Amalyn and several others in that bar. To see a leaf drawn anywhere, even old graffiti, always provoked memories of archaic filth, of dirt, land collapsing and bacterial infestations. Leaves weren't symbols drawn light-heartedly; even speaking the word induced nausea in some.

A trawl on the dark web did not take long to throw up answers. It was the symbol of some cesspit organisation promoting physical touching and excesses in liberty. They slammed the government, the rules and restrictions, and made a taboo of taboos. It was aimed at youths and those burdened with nostalgia who longed for travel and germs. The members either had short memories or weren't alive in the previous pandemic. The politics he could understand: the authoritarian government that had been in power for decades hardly inspired future generations. There were elections, of course. Frequently. But all candidates were Blue Liberation and had been for some time. And everyone in power was from the Centre. It was natural that anyone from the Perimeter would be sceptical. However, condemning the rules seemed absurd. There weren't many, really. People weren't often banned from doing anything. They just chose not to, or couldn't access the facilities. You could swim in the ocean if you liked, but who would want to? You could walk the streets, go to bars, have an orgy if you really felt like it. This organisation wasn't doing anything illegal. Dissing the government wasn't illegal, it was just frowned upon socially, and could cost you a job. People prioritised their safety, that was all. And everyone was safe now. The Golden Fifty, as they called themselves, seemed to give caution a discourtesy.

Archie pondered the organisation and realised their thoughts and curiosities weren't dissimilar to his own. He hated the government and their spyware, and the power of the Centre, and was constantly exasperated with how the machine worked, the Perimeter pedalling constantly to provide for the needs of the Centre. He had seen the Centre, had witnessed its lavishness. Where the Perimeter was granted only what was necessary, the Centre had luxury. It infuriated him that healthcare was restricted, that careers were limited, that safety warnings were blasted into everyone's brains every minute. But a group of people expressing these views seemed extreme.

To see it in words made them seem baseless. He understood. The wanderlust, sure, and maybe years earlier it was justified. However, most of the land had been washed away or burnt to a crisp. There wasn't much to see off The Raft except fire and famine. They breathed the ashes of lost nations daily; their soot clogged every pore. What civilisations did still exist were inhabited by people still reliant on filth farming like dirty savages, living on the brink of survival. There had been recent reports of anarchists throwing bucket loads of crushed peanuts at people in Paris. Twenty allergy sufferers had died that day; it was a miracle that number wasn't higher. Of course, Archie knew this because he had access to confidential information that he had the illicit abilities to find. The likes of Amalyn and the Golden Fifty could only speculate. Envious minds, curious in their ignorance. If they could see the images he'd seen, they'd appreciate a bit more of what they had.

Reports of the organisation's promiscuity were plentiful. They promoted physical contact, showing skin, even kissing. And this all happened between people who were barely acquainted. Actual sex was common. Not online stuff: flesh sex. Archie's shock was hypocritical, he knew. He had indulged himself and enjoyed it immensely. But his satisfaction morphed into anxiety, and he inspected his nether regions again and showered for a second time. There were no reports of

STIs, as Amalyn had said. Still, he felt uneasy. He scrubbed himself for hours, took some prophylactic immune boosters, and doused himself in antiseptic cream.

He would tell me later that he never worried, but the look on his face when I told him to be careful was not of surprise, but one that said he had investigated and been reassured. His naivety had been removed by a search engine. He also put a reminder in his diary to visit the walk-in clinic for his monthly check-up and vaccine in the morning. A week early. Better to be safe.

* * *

I barely had time to speak to Grace for the rest of the weekend. Preparation for the week ahead took up every moment, and Monday morning rolled around all too quickly. I woke early and dressed in my smartest trouser suit, pairing it with the only heels I owned. My mother's old clothes were finally getting an airing. Five-inch heels would not be enough to get me noticed, but I hoped I would look slightly more authoritative, or at the very least less invisible.

I hadn't worn heels since my first day at BioLabs, and the shiny black material was thick with dust when I dug them out of the cupboard. The soles looked brand new, barely a scuff on them. My feet cramped almost instantly, I felt a pinch in my little toes and my calf muscles tightened in their new position. *Put up with it!* I chastised myself, admiring my new height.

My limp hair was as stubborn as ever. I did all I could to make it sit higher, setting it in rollers and spraying liberally, as even an extra centimetre or two of volume would help. My skin looked awful, pallid and flaking. The Perimeter air was harsh and the creams I applied did little to hide it. I had to accept myself the way I was. 'Perimeter and proud,' I told myself.

I felt a pang of nerves and excitement, my stomach twisting in knots at what was becoming a familiar feeling. I craved the MindSpa but had no time for such luxuries.

The early morning light made the shadows a brighter shade of grey, harmonising with the lingering fog of pollution. My story was due out in the morning news. I had an early meeting with ProLabs to discuss incorporating BioLabs' new vitamin infusion into their products. Then, in the afternoon, off to the Centre.

The Centre!

I checked my reflection for the hundredth time. With my slightly wavier hair and polished shoes, I felt foolish. I sprayed scents to mask the smell of soot and salt, but still felt like an obvious imposter. 'Everyone feels like that sometimes,' I told myself.

At least I could expense the Autocars to my work account. There was no way I could walk that far in my footwear, and the journey times would be significant. I opted for the door-to-door option, which was expensive but saved me the walk to the Autocar stop. And, most importantly, my feet would stay dry. There were plenty of Autocars available and one arrived at my block as I exited the door. I climbed in, and it was still slightly damp inside from its self-cleaning cycle. As we set off, I checked my emails, rereading the one from Greg I had received the night before:

Minister of Impartiality wants to see you in her office tomorrow afternoon. Don't fuck this up (permit attached).

Nice pep talk, there. I had tried to call Greg for confirmation of what it was about, but to no avail. Having never been to the Centre before, I had no idea what the procedure was. Greg, in his eternal ignorance and arrogance, hadn't considered the possibility that I might not be clued up. He never responded to my calls or emails, cherishing the weekend I was denied. Luckily, Archie was more forthcoming. He sent me some links and permit explanations he'd dug up from his own brief excursion.

'The information isn't available under normal search engines. Perish the thought of any old Perimeter resident learning the secret handshake,' he'd said. 'And don't wear a face mask. No one there does.'

Maybe this was a test, and figuring out how to get into the Centre showed either my intelligence or my ambivalence to security protocols. I kept my permit safe and hoped for the best.

Photographs of the Centre were emblazoned on every billboard around the Perimeter. The grandiose government buildings and luxury residences were supposed to inspire us to achieve, somehow. It was so rare for a Perimeter resident to get a pass to cross that fence. Besides Archie sneaking in, I'd never met any Perimeter resident who had been there, let alone been invited, and an invite from a Minister was unheard of. I concluded she must have liked my articles. Surely she wouldn't call me all the way in just to chastise me?

The short notice meant I had to have my swab tests done before my meeting with ProLabs, a straightforward enough, albeit unpleasant, procedure. I called into one of the many corner-shop clinics that offered the test at seven thirty and had my monthly inoculation done at the same time. Then I grabbed another Autocar to make my nine a.m. meeting at ProLabs. My plan was to arrive early as, from experience, I knew they were an overly punctual bunch. Then I would have more time to make it to the Centre.

Thankfully, it was one of those mornings that went to plan. By the time I got to ProLabs, I had received a text to say my swab test was fine, which legalised my permit. Considering the cockroach incident, I was extremely relieved.

At eight thirty, I arrived at ProLabs. The manager I needed to talk to was already in and working. The snooty receptionist scoffed as I breezed past.

'Professor Selbourne, how's your tomorrow?'

'Uncertain, Professor Harold. And you?'

'As always. Follow me. You're a little early. I've just got some emails to send and then I'll be with you.'

I was ushered around the outside of the main lab, wincing at the sound of my ostentatious footwear, though I doubted Harold either cared or noticed.

The lab blinds clicked shut before I could see anything inside. As expected, secrecy was well adhered to. I arrived at a corridor of offices and sat on the sort of low plastic chair usually reserved for children. A multi billion-pound lab should have better chairs for their guests, I thought.

Harold's office blinds were askew and his door slightly ajar. Careless? Or purposeful, maybe, to encourage my interest. Perhaps he wanted to show off about something. I refused to let his persuasion work and stared at my e-pad instead. My article should be in the news, but I had no time to read it, as at that moment Harold called me through. His office was somewhat disorganised: beakers where they needn't be, a disused computer screen lying flat with paperwork haphazardly balanced on top. It had the hallmark of a man with too much on his plate. Marcus would have had his work cut out here.

'Sorry about that, emails just don't stop.' He kept his eyes on the floor or his computer screen, never looking at me. 'Apologies about the temperature, too. The air con either goes full blast or doesn't work at all.'

'It's fine, my office is similar,' I lied. I took a tissue from my handbag and wiped sweat from my forehead.

Harold grunted in acknowledgement. 'This new vitamin infusion, then?'

'Yes. I have some samples.' I took some packs of the colourless liquid from my bag and handed them to him. 'Our preliminary results show this formulation increases absorption by forty percent and does not lose potency when infused with food. We're awaiting the final results, but you said you wanted preliminary samples. The computerised modelling we've done for the testing is state-of-the art, as you know. Human testing results are due in over the next few days, which I will forward to you. We expect the results to be similar or better.'

He lifted the vials and held them up to the light, scrutinising the liquid over the top of his glasses. His chin hung low, pulling the corners of his mouth with it. 'Well, that all sounds very impressive and just what we've been looking for.' His tone was tired, his breathy voice revealing interest, yet lacking energy. 'Here, try this new snack food. It's modelled from something called chickpeas. It's what they ate a century ago.'

He handed me a bag of crunchy morsels, and I obliged. They

were a unique texture and flavour, not instantly agreeable, perhaps the sort of thing that would take some getting used to. Very salty, too, which reminded me of The Raft's edge. I made the required noises that implied I was impressed.

'We create the best proteins here, as you know,' Harold said, his face expressionless except for occasionally biting his lower lip with the few teeth he had left. 'Excellent textures and flavours. But I agree with your latest scientific paper. The way things are in the world, more vitamin enhancement is what we need. My nephew won't touch synth veg. He only wants protein and carbohydrates.'

'Like many children, I'm sure.'

'Sneaking some vitamins into the proteins would be wonderful for the fussy kids. Are you in talks with the carbohydrate labs?'

'We make our own carbohydrates, as well as synth veg and fibre,' I said, smiling through my clenched jaw to hide my annoyance at his error.

'Of course you do, my mistake.' Harold was unshaven and looked unrested. Work must be stressful, I surmised. If ProLabs were so stingy with the guest furniture, they must keep their staff under a lot of sales-performance pressure. 'Actually, I heard you engineered some new roast potatoes?'

'I can't lie. They are the best roast potatoes ever created.'

'I can't wait to try them.' He gave me a smile that seemed false on his sagging face. His unpleasantness was the same as ever, and I was well used to the indifference of fellow scientists. Congratulating each other only served to highlight one's own stunted career. Overworked, unappreciated, I tried to have patience for Harold despite his attitude, as I suspected mine was often similar. Although his lifetime of work was longer than mine, he had failed to achieve even a fraction of my success, although my signature on BioLabs' packaging was the only reward I had been given. That and the functioning air con in my office. Some acknowledgement is better than none, I concluded.

'I'll take these samples and check them over with the data, and get back to you in a week or so. Sound okay?'

'Perfect, Professor.'

'Let me give you a tour of some of our other new flavours while you're here, to show you that your vitamin infusion will be in the best hands.'

I glanced at my watch. 'So sorry, I really don't have the time. I'm off to the Centre today.'

'The Centre?' His eyebrows rose almost to his hairline. 'Well, we are going up in the world, aren't we?'

I cringed at my brag. I didn't have time to mince my words. 'It's just for work.'

'Well, I won't keep you. Thank you for sparing us this time.' I couldn't tell if he was being sarcastic, so I responded as if he were genuine, said my goodbyes, and was back in the Autocar by nine a.m. I was off to the Centre.

14

Chapter 13

It was a two-hour Autocar ride from ProLabs to the Centre, and then another hour to the parliamentary office. The entire way there, my palms were sweating so much that keeping hold of my e-pad was difficult. I gave up and spent the time trying to meditate and practise breathing exercises. I felt calmer and relatively unruffled when I arrived at the inspection gates.

Huge, iron fences surrounded the Centre, five storeys high at least, solid at the bottom and topped with long, malicious spikes. Each panel was inscribed with the Blue Liberation Party's slogan: '*With Sterility Comes Liberty.*' There were engravings showing hands, lots of them with thick fingers, doing the air-shake greeting commonly seen among Centre people. Other pictures were of the sun, moon, snowflakes and raindrops: the elements we were at the mercy of. A mural to the elements that challenged and threatened us seemed odd. I guessed some paganism or ancient religion still existed where people could afford the luxury of hope. It was an antiquated mindset for the Perimeter. There was no point in us praying to anyone, our voices were too small.

Outside the fence were shoddily built blocks of pale rendered brick with no windows, and a line of tall air-filter chimneys. I knew what these were. Everyone had heard the rumours. They contained rows of barren cells, each sealed off from one another and the outside world. I watched as some staff in full hazmat gear exited with empty food trays. Quarantine cells. A jail for the people who tried to cross into the Centre without the relevant paperwork. No one could enter those gates without being endorsed as one hundred percent healthy, non-contagious, and fully approved. Such measures had spared the Centre from the last two pandemics, its precious inhabitants shielded from the filth we had to endure.

'Permit,' a guard demanded, his hand hovering over his taser. I handed him my e-pad. 'Proof of being contagion-free,' stated the on-screen permit. I tried to steady my breathing as he checked through my documents, took an additional finger-prick blood sample, and measured my temperature. He then walked off for some time with another guard, inspecting my documents, studying computer screens and sporadically glancing up to stare at me. When it felt like I had drenched my clothes in sweat, they waved me through and lifted the barrier for the Autocar.

I exhaled and sunk into my seat. My hands were trembling and my heart felt as though it would erupt out of my chest. I breathed gently, counting each breath in and out as I willed my heart to slow.

We passed the fence and straight away the Autocar pulled into a carwash. Robotic arms reached into every crevice of the vehicle and scrubbed. It took twenty minutes to spray and polish the vehicle. By the time they had disinfected the car, my trembling had stopped and my sweat dried. I could then allow a brief pang of excitement to come over me, as I reminded myself that I was in the Centre!

The hastily built Perimeter roads with all their jumps and jolts were replaced by an even surface, expertly constructed. The Autocar drove effortlessly, like oil on water, just like Archie had said. Either side of the road was row upon row of SolaArbs, all the latest models. They were immense, with layer upon layer of tiny, paper-thin solar cells piled over larger ones, spanning metres, sucking up every watt of solar available. The panels were the blackest black, surrounded by the shiniest reflectors. The stunning, gleaming constructions shone with efficiency in the sunlight. And there was plenty of sunlight in the Centre. The ring of pollution surrounding The Raft never made it this far inland. We in the Perimeter suffocated long before the smog even made a mark on the Centre.

The air was cleared further with the help of the highly advanced ArbAir forests I could see in an adjacent field. In the Perimeter, our ArbAir trees choked from the strain of cleaning the filthy air. Their filters were frequently changed, but the task was too great. Space was too limited for the number of trees needed. The smog thickened and stuck in gloopy entrails to every surface, dripping off the ArbAirs as if they were weeping. The latest models in Centre, though, displayed in all their magnificence, had a superior surface area, thicker trunks that could clean a larger volume of air, as well as more proficient filters. I could just imagine how much cleaner our air would be if they moved these trees to The Raft's edge! My thoughts of what could and should be were pointless, I knew. A lifetime of waiting in line is what we expected in the Perimeter. But the sight of the technology, of what the engineers had achieved, was awe-inspiring. I couldn't help but feel hopeful that, by protecting the Centre, its success would one day trickle down to us too.

As the Autocar passed the forests, the Centre buildings came into view, and they were everything I had imagined. Towering structures of chrome and gold, blazing in the sun with their buffed surfaces and crystal-clear glass. Not a patch of rough grey render in sight. Architectural genius was displayed in their size and shape, soaring higher than anything in the Perimeter. They were not the standard box designs I was used to seeing, either. Instead, these were gravity-defying creations with angles and curves that swooped into the sky in a grandiose display of engineering. And with the clean air, I could see all the way to the top. The streets were also huge, with wide polished surfaces you could see your reflection in. How did they get them to shine like that? I wondered as I watched the autonomous street cleaners. The discreet little things patrolled with silent suction brushes, furbishing rollers, and driers (no wet feet from street sprayers here!). Streams of Autocars followed them, rolling along, all filled with people, no one apparently concerned by the cost of transport.

The lighting was controlled at street level so as not to dazzle, soft awnings giving shade where buildings did not. Tables with tall umbrellas were dotted around, inviting people to sit and mingle; and they obliged. Those not in Autocars were on the street, walking and talking in groups. I struggled to think of the last time I saw groups of people walking together, besides Alternates. Here they were out in droves, walking with confident strides, their heads up and uncovered, smiles blinding with their whiter-than-white teeth. I could see people sat at tables with friends, chatting and laughing, sitting close, their exposed skins almost touching. Even babies were wheeled around, or cradled and carried, on display for all to see, and for anything to infect. This must be the hubbub my parents missed so much. The noise, the clamour and the busyness of the streets. Outdoor life hadn't died out, it had just been cordoned off, ring-fenced for the Centre.

The brazen disregard for caution made me gape with astonishment. 'Everyone is safe now,' that's what they said. So these people, with their social practices, their nonchalant attitude to sterility and their disregard for microbes—apparently they were safe. Content in their bubble of buffered protection with the Perimeter soaking up the impurities and contagions like some philanthropic sponge. Keeping everyone safe in the Perimeter meant staying indoors; in the Centre, it meant this. Of course, there were no rules forbidding us from congregating on the streets in the Perimeter. There was just no desire to do so. Who'd want to take the risk just to parade through smog down bleak, claustrophobic streets, littered with holes and enclosed by stark grey tower blocks? I stared through the Autocar window at the elegance of it, the opulence. It was a different planet.

The billboards still cut through the buildings, but the LED quality looked clearer with the lack of smog. I squinted at the brightness, my eyes unaccustomed to such clarity. The headlines were different to the Perimeter's.

Prime Minister Polling on the Rise Again as Perimeter Shows Support. With Sterility Comes Liberty! Rogueless Water Co. Bumps BioLabs up Companies Rich List! Progress is Paramount! Famines Across Europe, The Raft Food Supply is Protected. Everyone Is Safe Now!

Unlike the Perimeter, the safety alert was reassuring, and showed microbe and particulate matter air samples as reading zero percent. At the end of each rotation came an upbeat message that changed with each round.

You Look Great Today! The MindSpa Works Wonders on You! Feel Healthy, You Deserve It!

The staffed Selfie Stations were no myth, just like Archie had said. There was several per street, well-stocked, with beauticians on hand to take care of every freckle, every blemish. Not a strand of hair would be out of place here, everyone was pampered with every step. A MindSpa was on each corner, lights above them showing if they had vacancies, their steamy windows adding enticing mystery to their interiors.

Fashion houses dotted the streets selling brand-new garments, where you could actually visit to look at them before buying. I remembered my parents telling me about this, when in the days of their childhood people would go to shops to buy clothes, before they all shut down. The fabrics were advertised as being made by recycling 'only the best' fabrics. The Autocar slowed down as it cruised along the high street, affording me the chance to peer into the shop windows. Display after display of dresses and shirts, non-functional designs and decorative pieces. Some fabrics looked so cutting edge they must be new. Where would they get brand-new fabric from? The sheer abundance baffled and astonished me. Such excesses and extravagances were unknown in the Perimeter.

The Autocar rounded the Grand Central, past the ornate building that I knew was the school. Flanked by statues, it had been meticulously preserved after being moved from the old museums. The pieces used to educate visitors about past civilisations, an education now branded as redundant. So instead of educating, the golden statues pilfered from all corners of the former globe now stood hauntingly in their gilded gold, illustrating the dominance of the school they enclosed. It was the only non-virtual school left on The Raft, and its legend had crossed the lips of every inhabitant. The school of politics, where face-to-face meetings and the relationships they formed were as important as the lessons they taught. Less of a school, more a club for the elite. The who's who in wealth and dominance sent their offspring here, aspiring for the notoriety and perks it promised. Such an immense structure, accommodating just a couple of hundred students, costing a fortune in fees, where every single graduate was guaranteed a place in Parliament.

The Autocar eased to a stop near the Parliament building and chimed its familiar tune to say that I had arrived at my destination. That was stating the obvious: I could hardly miss it. The new building was crafted from ancient bricks, sanded until it was flawless and rounded off to create a great orb, smoothed and painted in gold leaf. The tower jutted out of the roof at an angle, pointing to the sky to symbolise our missed loved ones. Inscribed somewhere were the words '*We Have Learned From Their Loss*', but it was lost among the scale of the building. The once-famous bell now stood on top of a great plinth, broken in half lengthways. The plaque underneath read: '*The Broken Old World Gave Birth to the New.*'

A moat surrounded the golden orb, like we were still in the Middle Ages. It was supposed to symbolise the floating Raft, not aimlessly, as we felt it was. Their message was that we were floating above the carnage. The water gave us safety; that's what they taught us at school. The grimy ocean protected us from any wayward invaders and stopped us from exploring the rest of the desolate planet, where diseases lurked uncontrolled. Of course, the twinkling moat that surrounded the Parliament building was not at all like the thick sludge of sea that surrounded The Raft. Not that the Centre folk would know the difference. I'd bet a month's wages that none of them had ever even seen the sea. A few bits of immortal plastic, some fish bones and the smell of sulphur would make it a bit more realistic.

The Autocar prompted me to exit, and I made a beeline for the nearest Selfie Station. I had my hair spruced up, and the attendant actually managed to give it some volume by moving my parting and spraying it with what I could only assume was magic. She then gave it a few snips to even it out in its altered style. My makeup was touched up, or pretty much redone, as my beauty skills were rather poor, and my eyes were delicately lined. She shaped my brows and made my cheeks look silky and healthy. The roughness of my skin was disguised, its pallor camouflaged under a thick layer of high-quality rouge. The dark circles under my eyes disappeared, and I looked awake and a decade younger, even without a filter. I was sprayed with perfume, its scent nothing less than divine. After a quick photo uploaded to my social media (Wow! I looked gorgeous!), I entered the building, pinching myself, disbelieving what was before my eyes. I was in the Parliament buildings. So few people from the Perimeter had ever made it past the fence, let alone into the Parliament buildings. But here I was, and they had invited me!

Chapter 14

'Good morning, ma'am. How can I help you?' The receptionist smiled at me, his face radiant with enthusiasm. I smiled back, keeping my mouth closed. My yellow, uneven teeth seemed like the most out-of-place thing here. His desk was in the middle of the vast entrance hall, the gold-and-white chequerboard design seeming to go on forever.

'Professor Savannah Selbourne, here to see the Minister of Impartiality,' I said, trying to add clarity to my voice to hide my gravelly Perimeter tone.

After joyously inputting my name into his computer, the receptionist marched me across the entrance hall and up a staircase. Behind us and all around were a team of cleaners wiping down the floor after every step, so it constantly gleamed. Not a speck of dust anywhere. The disinfectant smell was subtle, not barraging the senses like I was used to. My lungs felt the least irritated they ever had.

The staircase snaked round the edge of the entrance hall, the marble steps surrounded by what looked like a real wood banister, each baton thick like it was made of a whole real tree. The handrail was engraved ornately in a swirling pattern and the slogan '*With Sterility Comes Liberty*' repeated in elaborate calligraphy over and over. I did not dare touch the banister, fearful I would mark it, even though it shone with thick varnish. Other people passed on the stairs with no such concerns for the furnishings. Accustomed to abundance, they barely even glanced at the adornments. The vast ceilings echoed our footsteps. I felt noisy and intrusive in my clicking heels and wished I could silence them. I tiptoed as much as my stride would allow, which was difficult as my legs were shorter than those of the elegant receptionist.

At the top of the stairs, we made our way along a capacious corridor. Benches sat along the edges, mostly made of the same heavily varnished wood as the banister, though some were crafted from curved iron and padded with cushions. The wood had to run out sometime, I thought.

The corridor was empty except for the benches. I presumed they were there for contemplation. Some people may have wished to sit and gaze upon our great rulers. The walls were lined with ancient paintings on canvas, protected by glass. I had never seen a real painting before. Even through the glass, I could make out the rough texture, the brushstrokes and the grain of the canvas. Fascinating that people once had the time to sit and pose, and even to paint these images. The efficiency of the modern age would have seemed as alien to them as their sluggishness did to me. Each painting must have wasted hours! They would have been saved when the old buildings were demolished as the computerised posters of the more recent Prime Ministers had begun forty years earlier. Face after face of wealthy, pale-faced rulers, each with the same foreboding brow, high cheekbones and dark eyes, implying that they were of the same bloodline. Their smiles were a mixture of sinister and commanding, their white teeth peeking out from their stern mouths. The Blue Liberation symbol was on each lapel. So few women, I realised, as I walked past image after image of smug and pompous men. The twenty-second century, and still so few women leaders. Some old habits were hard to break.

I arrived at a large door, a vast dark iron structure similar to the Centre fence. A magisterial fortification, impressive in its substantial use of materials, stately in its design, set in a heavy, solid frame. The receptionist opened it with a laborious push and gestured for me to enter.

I was in the main office where public announcements were filmed. I had seen photographs and footage many times, but experiencing its lavish scale and portrayal of prosperity was something else entirely. What a successful country we must be to have somewhere like this! The fortune spent on its ornamentation could buy a whole tower block in the Perimeter. The amount of real wood was astonishing. It shone like oil under tiered lacquer but was still richly lined with grain, appearing like veins through its limbs. Heavy and imposing, the colossal desk stood ominously at one end of the room in front of a bookcase housing shelves of real paper books behind glass. It seemed like a morgue for the carcasses of shredded trees displayed as a dead woodland; just as useless and infinitely more dangerous. The vast number of microbes an old book could shelter was well documented, and I knew it well since I harboured such an item, carefully stowed away, but still unlicensed. But it was just one book, well-treated and kept away from the interfering public. Here there were hundreds of them. Computer modelling demonstrated how a whole new pandemic could arise from one book, if inadequately cared for. Such a bookcase would have been illegal anywhere else. Almost every known book had been burnt or thrown out to sea long before. Yet here they were, audaciously displayed. An insolent smirk at the vigilance we displayed in the Perimeter.

On top of the glass cabinet were photo frames of the Prime Minister air-shaking with other politicians, several advisors, the Minister of Impartiality included, looking elegant and sophisticated. The epitome of modern power.

I turned and saw the view of the office they didn't show on broadcasts. The room was long, the far end like a museum. More sealed glass cabinets, this time accommodating animal heads mounted on wooden plinths. Awful, savage-looking creatures covered in fur, some supporting great jagged struc-tures I knew were called antlers. Their deader-than-dead eyes looked like glassy orbs of vengeance, rubbernecking me as I inspected them.

'Fascinating, aren't they?'

I jumped at her voice as it cut through the room. The light caught the red dress stretched around her substantial frame, displaying her well-fuelled strength.

'Good afternoon, Minister,' I said and managed a sort of awkward curtsey. Her height cast a shadow, and I strained my neck to look up at her. I had seen her before but hadn't noticed her individual stature. Her sturdy legs thumped the floor with every step, the jewellery that dripped off her rattling as she walked, like a warning. Her large nostrils glared down at me angrily. I didn't dare look up to face them and kept my head humbly low.

'Relics of our savage past, reminding us that if we live among animals, we will become mere animals,' she said as she raised her chin higher and paraded around the room. The scraped-back bun on her head like a golden orb. 'My family killed all of these, some of the last to roam this country. Like Saint George, my family slayed the last of the vermin.'

'Impressive, ma'am,' I said. I was sure there were contractors back then, hired to kill and eradicate the filth. Her wealthy ancestors must have killed for pleasure, not practicalities. I wondered what such people took delight in, now there were no beasts left to slaughter.

'Can you believe that, despite the disease rates, there were some who campaigned to save these feckless creatures? They'd rather the country lived in grime and squalor forever, germ-ridden and festering in filth, rather than modernising and defeating our enemy. For we were at war, in those years of pandemics. At war with viruses and bacteria. And through science, as I am sure you know, we won.'

'A marvellous achievement, ma'am.' I tried a curtsey again, even though she did not look my way.

'Indeed. An outstanding achievement. But we did not sign a peace treaty. Our war against the evils of Mother Nature continues. Now we must battle the heat and the cold. We are at the mercy of the sea, and with all other land lost to wildfires, the planet has become a desert. We are the survivors and, I think you will agree, we are thriving.'

I nodded in agreement. The photo frames clinked as she continued to stomp out her speech.

'We live in a remarkable age where everyone has enough. The famines are over, disease is rare, we have protocols and medicines to deal with invaders. The entire population of The Raft is protected efficiently. I'm sure even the Perimeter feel safe and cared for by our efficiency and policy-making. Even today there are some who do not recognise the hard work and sacrifices that have gone into making this country safe. Our independence, our freedom, our liberty and sterility, the very principals that are the foundations of this Raft, are constantly questioned. Those that question have the best intentions, I'm sure. Nostalgia is strong, progress is still scorned by some. Do you understand what I mean?'

'I'm not sure, ma'am.'

'Come, sit, Professor Selbourne.'

I felt rather taken aback to hear her say my name, but I dutifully sat where she indicated, on a stiff cushioned chair dotted with gold studs. Was it real leather? I had seen pictures. Surely this couldn't be one? I almost gagged at the thought of sitting on something so revolting. She sat opposite and I could finally meet her eye. Her complexion was smooth and her features angular. The large precious stones in her earrings and necklaces danced glitterball light across her skin. The effect was far too cheery for someone so overbearing. She was not unattractive but had a formidable look, wilful and judicious. I did not want to cross her.

'This desk is quite something, isn't it?' She ran her hands over the wood.

'Magnificent, ma'am.'

'It was bought by my great-great-grandfather and passed down through the generations. It's a shining example of how filth and nature can be beaten by greatness. All the bacteria that this desk could house, yet humankind has contained it and stopped it leaking into our lives. When our country's muscles flex, the bacteria and climate cower. The Great Sterilisation Project rid us of the chaos. You remember the headlines back then, when we rid ourselves of our anchors to the mainland? Those headlines empowered the population. "*Another Breakthrough!*" "*Sterility Is Strength!*" "*We Are Stronger Than Ever!*"' She held her clasped hands together, almost in prayer.

'This desk,' she said, 'has been cleaned and waxed and varnished over the years, hours of labour dedicated to nurturing it, to make it stand the test of time. Humankind giving it strength and sterility. And here it is today, stronger than ever. Now what do you think would happen if everyone wanted a bit of this desk?'

I swallowed and searched my mind for answers. 'I don't know.'

Her dark eyes glared straight at me, almost through me, less than pleased with my response. 'Well, it would be cut up into pieces, and then no one would have a desk, would they? They would have fragments. The antibacterial varnish would be compromised, and most likely some dormant disease inside the wood would leach out.'

'I guess.'

'Do you know what caused the pandemics?'

'The first was a virus that—'

'Wrong!' She slammed a fist on the desk and I jumped. 'What caused the pandemics, all of them, was the idea of a collective culture, the entitlement that goes with the notion that everyone can have anything they want. Sharing. People thought it was best to give, to share, to distribute wealth and products, germs, even themselves. They believed the very land beneath their feet was for sharing, like the planet was a communal resource, that they could step where they wished, touch what they liked. There was no ownership. Every atom of the planet was on loan to anyone who wanted it. And at a cheap price, too. Even the air they breathed was passed around from lung to lung. But if the population kept what was theirs and their family's alone, and nurtured that, then they would have something magnificent and strong, like this desk. Instead of pandemics.'

I nodded, unsure whether her point was accurate.

'Now, during the first pandemic, many people died. The second pandemic killed a lot more, and untreatable bacterial infections killed thousands, as you well know. By the third pandemic, when that evil bird landed on our shores and coughed its pathogen at our people, do you know what killed more people than the illness itself?'

'Maybe famine, ma'am.'

'Wrong again.' She waggled a long finger at me. 'Suicide. Suicide killed more than famine and the disease combined. I appreciate they don't teach these things in your education establishments. Such things we learn in politics school. Believe me, by the third pandemic, suicide killed twice as many people as the plague itself.'

'Gosh, that's tragic.' I remembered my parents' mental decline with a pang.

'Exactly. Now, someone in your role would like to claim that it was famine, and that would mean that your role carries a far more important role in society. And you would be right. People killed themselves out of fear. Fear of famine, of disease. Fear is the single biggest killer of humankind. So, knowing what fear can do, what do you think would be the biggest saviour?'

'Hope?'

'You may think so, but no. Hope is almost as deadly.' She'd softened her tone now, with a practised, pained expression.

'With hope comes disappointment. In the old world, the continuous race to the top was actually a race to the bottom. People the world over strove on in desperation, in hope, to attain more than they required, to promise themselves they could have more! More! More! To be more powerful, to have bigger things, fancier things, to accumulate needless niceties to pamper their egos. And now our oceans are choked with medications that were designed to make people falsely happy, to give false comfort so they could continue their journey to mental destruction. No, that is not the way we make people content. Hoping for the unachievable does not bring happiness. The saviour of humankind is stability. There is safety in that. With stability comes self-control, understanding, realistic achievement. Happiness is knowing you are safe. Gambling your future on whims is not safety. It's a rollercoaster of instability leading to despair.'

She paused and looked at me for a response, but I had no words. I glanced around the room and its richness, its immeasurable display of 'More! More! More!' It was clear that 'realistic achievement' meant something quite different for the Centre than for the Perimeter.

'This education wasn't meant to make your job seem any less important,' she said. 'Quite the opposite. Fear is the biggest killer, so we need stability. Reliable and nutritious food is crucial to that. You may remember the lootings that came with the last famine. The riots? They caused a great deal of instability. Fear of famine, hope of finding food. Food availability is one of the fundamental aspects of a civilised, stable country. And if I search online for an expert in synthesised nutrition, in health, in palatable food, in the vitamin demands of the modern age, do you know whose name comes up time and time again?'

'No, ma'am,' I said.

'Yours. Ha! Surprising, I know. We have experts here in the Centre with excellent education, yet it's your name that the public searches for when they want confidence in their food. Your name makes a particular brand sell almost four times more. Did you know that?'

'My boss doesn't give me that much feedback, ma'am.' My little voice sounded so feeble. I should have been more confident, considering what she was telling me. Yet I felt shrivelled and small in her presence.

'Greg? He's a bloody fool. Can't see potential past a pair of tits.' I stifled a laugh at this. The Minister didn't seem to notice. 'Your skills and notoriety are something we can really harness. As I said, there are some who still... distrust us, here in Parliament. And there are some who say we in the Centre are out of touch with the needs of the Perimeter. And of course, we mustn't be seen to be out of touch with the Perimeter, as even those people get a vote. Your name on press articles, to do with the sciencey things, you understand?'

'Sciencey things, ma'am?'

'Yes, food and disease and whatnot. Your name gives those articles a stamp of approval for the Perimeter. For some reason, they trust you more than those with the superior breeding here.'

'I see.'

'So, we need to make sure that your articles hit the right note, and shine the correct light. Help the Perimeter see we are only doing what is best for them. Since fear is such a big killer, we must not feed it. The public must be assured that they are safe to reinforce stability in the Perimeter population.

As the Minister of Impartiality, I have done a lot of research on the subject. If your articles can emphasise stability, they will help us save lives.'

'I'm honoured, ma'am.' I smiled, remembering to keep my mouth closed.

'And you should be.' She displayed a wide smile of her own for a few seconds. 'Now, for example, the article you wrote about the protests at the docks. We obviously had to edit that a bit. We need the public on our side, after all. We can't have them all jacked up on fish oil, or whatever it is they're doing there. They need to understand that medicines are available for everyone, as long as they contribute appropriately in return.'

'I see, ma'am. I think. Like I said in the article, a lot of the problem is the lack of patient confidentiality.'

'We should have nothing to hide from each other. Honesty and transparency are the hallmarks of any working relationship, don't you agree?'

'Of course, but—'

'Excellent. Impartiality only works when scrutinised. People must be open to guidance. And you will be rewarded in return, of course.' She smiled again. 'I understand you've been on the fertility waiting list for quite some time?'

My eyes widened. 'Yes, ma'am.'

'People with the correct mindset like yours deserve a family. To have a child to nurture. So we have an understanding?'

'I... I think so, ma'am.'

'Wonderful talking to you, Professor.' She stood up and air-shook my hand. 'Fantastic to meet such an inspiration.'

My fumbling attempt to reciprocate her air-shake made my cheeks blush. 'Likewise, Minister. It's been an honour.'

'I'm sure it has.' She smiled that wide smile again and

pressed a buzzer. A second later, the receptionist reappeared to escort me from the office, my heels clip-clopping down the corridor all the way.

Chapter 15

As I was about to leave the Parliament building, the receptionist presented me with an e-pad with '*How was your visit?*' written across it, and a photograph of the Minister of Impartiality in the top right corner. I tapped the green 'thumbs up' symbol and got into the Autocar that was waiting for me.

It was only then that I took a proper breath. My stomach was in knots, and as I unwound, my whole body started trembling. I had been there, in that famous office, talking with a Minister. As the Autocar pulled away, I felt dazed and foggy as I tried to process the enormity of it. I wish I had taken notes. My incessant nodding must have made me look crazy. I should have looked more professional and I should have spoken more instead of just sitting there, bewildered by her and the surroundings, unable to find my words. I tried to replay what she had said. She had complimented me, said my role was important, that my branding carried weight. I felt a swell of pride bubble through the trembling and relaxed into my seat.

The car rolled past the gates out of the Centre. There was

no car cleaning, no health paperwork needed on the way out. The guards waved the Autocar through and ushered me out as quickly as they could, like they were shooing away a pest.

The Minister had mentioned the fertility list, and it was the most exciting news. Grace would be ecstatic. I replayed the conversation again and again. 'Great minds like yours deserve a family, to nurture a child,' that was what she had said. As long as I reported favourably, didn't scare the Perimeter, we could have a baby. That was easy. All the news articles did that. I just had to make sure mine blended in. I checked the news app for my article on the protest. It wasn't online yet, but the editor had emailed me and copied in Greg:

Savannah. We will publish the finished piece this afternoon. See attached for the slightly edited, final version.
  Regards
  Peter

I clicked the link and read, then read again, in utter disbelief. The edited version was like a whole different article. I had tried to tell the tale of both sides, the reasons why people couldn't get medication, using inclusive language and giving both sides dignity. My unbiased article had been turned into anything but. My compassionate language had been replaced with prose designed to vex and provoke. *'Invasive.'* *'Vermin.'* *'Invading.'* *'Foreign.'* *'Treachery.'* *'Betrayal.'* *'Swarms.'* *'Extraneous.'* I had never used such words, had painstakingly avoided hateful terms, to sound approachable and compassionate. I had tried to be understanding, to speak up for the Perimeter and the challenges some face. They had left in the context of the piece, the worries about confidentiality and people being unable to

161

source medication if their professions excluded them from free treatment. The bare bones were there, but the change in terminology undermined any unity the article was meant to show. '*Junkies.*' '*Illiterate.*' '*Mob.*' '*Beggars.*'

This new article was designed to propel hate. How could it be the tone they wanted? I was shocked and mortified that it would be attributed to my name. Someone like me, born and bred in the Perimeter, someone trusted, who tops search engines! I would be seen as using such provocative terms against my neighbours. It felt wrong. It wasn't even that I disagreed with the sentiment, as all those words have been in my thoughts before, and 'fish junkie' was a common term. To see my name accredited to such vile terms in print, however, was shameful. I felt like I had betrayed the Perimeter. I felt we deserved a voice, some sort of representation and solidarity, and it had been sabotaged.

I rang Peter, the editor. No answer. I reprogrammed the Autocar to turn around and made my way to the news offices on the very edge of the Centre. The guards were confused when I returned, but my permit was still valid and so, after a short deliberation, they allowed me through.

Even the Centre had a poorer part of town and the Press Office was in it, a drab building right up against the fence. There was no receptionist, just an open-plan office with several plastic desks sectioned off by floor-to-ceiling Perspex barriers. At the far end was an office door that read '*Editor*' on a small plaque underneath his name, Peter Melrose. The photograph hanging on the door revealed his Perimeter status—he was smiling with a closed mouth. No one from the Centre would hide their teeth like that. The Photoshop blurred his likely skin imperfections but hadn't bothered to alter his hairline. I guessed there were some truths not worth hiding. Why would someone from the Perimeter write such a defamatory piece? I wanted answers.

I knocked. No answer, and the door was locked. Microbes! I peered in through the windows at a sparse room with a metal desk, a couple of computers, and a swivel chair. There were bottled samples of various new foods, some I recognised from BioLabs. The press gave reviews of most new products, and the editor was clearly the one who got to enjoy the samples. The reviews had all been favourable, I remembered. '*Refreshing and flavoursome*' was how he described the last batch of IcyCrema we had sent in for review. I'd liked his comments. Now I felt he was as disgusting as that cockroach.

The walls were decorated childishly with posters from a century earlier, pop-culture things mainly. Likely all collectables and worth quite a sum, but in an office setting they looked gaudy and unprofessional. Some sculptures adorned a corner table. By the looks of the surrounding mess, the editor was restoring the old junk. Glue pots and paints had splattered the cloth underneath, adding to the effect of it being like a child's room. The most prominent poster displayed a picture of a handsome man with messy hair next to a marijuana leaf, a rebellious print from a century earlier at least. A throwback from the days when weed was grown illegally in dirt, before they synthesised it and marketed it correctly.

'Can I help you?' A rather shrill voice from behind startled me. I span around to see a frumpy middle-aged woman with slicked-back hair, wearing an overly tight dress and badly applied lipstick.

'I'm looking for the editor, Peter.'

'Well, he's not here, obviously,' she said, emphasising every syllable.

'He's not answering his phone. How can I reach him?'

'You can't. He's taken the afternoon off, gone to check out some newly discovered collectables, I believe. He'll probably respond to an email tomorrow.' She pointed a finger, as if gesturing towards the next day.

'It's important,' I said. She shrugged a reply and made a sarcastic sad face at me. It was maddening. 'I write for the news, my article about the protests at the docks—'

'Oh, great article!' Her piercing shriek hurt my ears. 'And I totally agree. Junkies, the lot of them. All they have to do is find a useful job and get their meds like everyone else. So selfish.' She folded her arms and shook her head.

'The article has some mistakes in it. I'd really like to speak to Peter.'

'Like I said, he's not here, and since he checked it over before it went to print, it will be fine.'

Then she escorted me from the building, and I quickly found myself outside breathing clean Centre air once more. 'Microbes!' I muttered to myself as I left.

* * *

By the time I got home, Grace had finished work and was sitting facing the window, legs crossed, arms by her sides, her hand weakly clasping a crumpled tissue.

'Grace?' She didn't turn to greet me. Her silence told me everything. She had read the article. I had texted to tell her not to on my way back, but clearly I had been too late.

'Grace, please. It wasn't me. I didn't write it, not in that way.'

'Grace? Don't you mean "junkie"? Or "beggar"?' She spat those words through tight lips and stifled tears.

'They twisted it all.'

'So that's what you think of them? Of me? That I'm "vermin", some "invasive filth"?' She made air quotes with her hands.

My article, my words. Each demeaning expletive had stabbed her like a dagger. It seemed there weren't enough fish guts in the freezer to soften the blow. It was a personal attack for her, that she was the subject of my intolerance and had spurred such hatred.

'That's what you think of me, that I'm disgusting, undeserving. Me. Your wife!' She wiped her eyes but still couldn't look at me. 'And all those other people, desperate, marginalised, you've made them sound so hateful, so undeserving. Cruel, that's what that article is. Cruel. Those words are more toxic than any fish.'

I shook my head and went over to her. I held her shoulders and looked at her. 'Those words aren't mine, Grace. I did not write them. You know me, you know I wouldn't.'

'Yes, I do know you.' Her eyes bore deeply into mine and saw the truth I was trying to deny. She realised the extent of my prejudices, a character trait I was failing to keep under lock and key. Grace had always been the more tolerant one of us, always the more open-minded. That night, trying to justify myself, I realised that though I hadn't written those words, I had certainly thought them.

'I would never say such things. They twisted everything. Let me show you the article I wrote. Here.' I took my e-pad from

165

my bag and opened it, showing Grace my real article. 'I would never be so condemnatory of anyone. You were desperate, and I know you are hurting. You are none of those horrible words. I would never, ever write such things.'

She took the e-pad from me to read, sobbing as she did. 'I know I was upset with what you did, but I understand,' I said. 'Really. Anyone could find themselves in such a situation. I understand why you did it. And it helped, didn't it? It really helped. I know it did.'

She nodded and cried some more.

'Oh, Grace. Please know that I didn't write that.' My disgust at her habit was still raw. The thought of her ingesting that filth still made me shudder, but I understood. My Grace, my poor Grace.

'Everyone will think you did. Everyone we know will see your name on that article.'

'Sod them. I don't care about any of them, I only care about you.' I held up her chin to meet her gaze, but her head sagged weakly. Her damp eyes were red. My heart broke with hers. 'The system is all wrong. It's wrong that anyone has to resort to going to the docks. It's not fair. I know it isn't.' She leaned in and put her head on my shoulder. I felt the weight of her sadness on me, the sorrow in every breath, her tears staining my shirt. 'But you know what? The Minister today, she said if my articles say what they want them to say, they're going to bump us up the fertility list.'

'Really? She actually said that?' Grace lifted her head, and I felt her heart lift with it.

'Yes, she really did. I don't want to write such things, but I care about you and having a baby more than what anyone out there thinks of me.'

She almost smiled, and I hugged her tight. I hadn't meant to tell her. I didn't want to believe it myself until it actually happened. But Grace seemed pacified by the news, which worried me. Hope, I remembered, was a dangerous thing.

That night I fretted in my sleep, torn. I thought about what the Minister had said and how I felt pressured into agreeing with her, into obeying. Even so, wasn't she right? The world was cleaner now, the fish docks were dangerous, transparency is usually the best way. Usually. If my words could persuade people to be professional, to contribute in a meaningful way, wasn't that better than scavenging for rotten scraps? Maybe she did have the Perimeter's best interests at heart. Perhaps underneath her extreme facade of overindulgence in finery, beneath the excesses of gold and rare objects, there existed a considerate soul, barricaded by the pressure of family values and enforced entitlement. The pretence of privilege could be a powerful tool, I thought as I lay awake.

Chapter 16

Excuse my musings on my old friend's love life. The awkward conversations of a man so out of practice distract me from the niggling sadness I can't escape. The way his smile changed to a wonky gape, his eyes unfocused on the here and now, the mind fog that goes with those initial encounters. All the signs were there for me to see, but of course, at the time, I had no idea. I'd laugh at myself later. How could I not have realised? My cluelessness seems absurd now. I'll chuck it in the bucket of ignorance to mingle with everything else.

He told me how debonair he was, how articulate and cool in his conversation. But Archie, my dear friend, I knew you too well.

'Excuse me, sir, might I ask some questions?' Amalyn stood at Archie's door, leaning one hip against the frame.

'Sure, intern seven, come on in.' The volume of Archie's voice destroyed its intended discretion.

Amalyn entered and closed the door behind her, then kissed him fully on the mouth.

'Woah.' He pushed her away. 'Not at work, yeah?' His face reddened despite his air con having a rare moment of normal functioning.

'I just can't help myself,' she said, biting her bottom lip. 'When can we meet up again?'

'We can talk online tonight?'

She laughed. 'Properly meet, I mean.'

'Hmm.' Archie stalled, aware he had no plans at all and didn't want to seem too keen. 'Friday again?'

'Great.' She beamed. Then she walked over to his desk, sat down between monitors, and eyed his screens. 'What's this you're doing? Looks important.'

Satellite images showed other lands and the cloud patterns overhead. But he wasn't zoomed into the clouds nor observing the weather patterns on all of them. He was looking at the land. A vast red expanse, featureless except for dust devils spinning in the smouldering sand.

'Just looking at the land we're closest to, and how screwed it is. And checking for storms, trying to figure out where we're going to go.'

'What place is that?' She pointed at some orange wasteland on the screen.

'Not entirely sure. I think it was once called Gabon.'

'Looks like a desert now.'

'That's pretty much it. This place used to all be forests.' He pointed to another area. 'It burnt down, like everywhere else.'

'No people there?'

'None in Africa that I know of. It's way too hot to repopulate. Pandemics, wildfires and famine wiped out the continent.'

'Like everywhere, I suppose.' She shrugged.

'Pretty much.'

169

'I'll bet you can see other countries, though. Places where people still live that haven't burnt to a crisp?' She leaned in and let her hand graze his inner thigh.

'Erm,' he coughed, 'yeah, sure, some of Europe still seems to be fine. Well, not fine. There are habitable places in northern Europe. Paris, I think, is the most southerly place we've seen where significant populations still live.'

'Paris. That was France, right?'

'Well done,' he said, impressed that she'd even heard of Paris, let alone knew the right country.

She frowned. 'I thought all of Europe was wiped out in the pandemics and famines? That's what science history taught us.'

'Well, they suffered, for sure. Floods wiped out a lot of land too, but there are still cities and they are recovering. Actually, the third plague barely affected them at all. When the bridges blew up, we took it with us.'

'Really? That's so interesting. My memory of science education must be patchy.'

Archie laughed. 'Maybe. They haven't got our food technology, so they're slower to recover. Plus, they lost a lot of land to floods. Some countries have totally gone. Satellite images looked quite different a few years ago.'

Amalyn's face lit up, and she clasped her hands together. 'Oh, I'd love to see some old images.'

'That's kind of... not allowed,' he replied. 'I mean, it's definitely not allowed. You need special clearance for such things.'

'Oh, I get it. They don't permit the sullied hands of scientists to glimpse any of the commotion beyond the lab.' She rolled her eyes and kissed his cheek. 'I don't want you getting in trouble.' She sighed a wistful sigh. 'I bet the world looked great in those golden fifty years.'

'Golden fifty?'

'Like my tattoo?' She pushed up her sleeve to show him the swirling gold-leaf design with the '50'. 'There was this time, about fifty years from the end of the twentieth century into the twenty-first, when people could travel freely, and for the most part, could afford it. They say there was even a sort of "middle class", it wasn't just the billionaires and the rest of us. They used to just get a boat, or even a plane, and go somewhere. There were obviously wars and diseases, but not like the pandemics. People weren't constantly afraid. The climate was manageable. It was fifty golden years.'

Archie raised his eyebrows, feigning surprise at the mention of the strange group, not wanting to let on that he'd been researching it. 'If they knew then what we know now, those fifty years wouldn't have caused so many problems.'

'Yes, but they didn't have our technology,' she said smugly. 'They used to burn stuff for power, like cavemen. They didn't have such good solar or nuclear or vaccines or supercharged vitamins. And now we have all these things. So why don't we travel, explore, see more than our own neighbourhood?'

'New diseases happen all the time. Power isn't sufficient for the population's housing, let alone travel. The weather is crazy... should I go on?'

'No,' Amalyn said with a laugh. 'I think it would have been a magical time to be alive. An entire planet to explore.' She squeezed his thigh, making Archie squirm.

'You're probably right,' he said. 'As long as you survived it, I guess.'

'Such the pessimist.'

171

'I remember a bit further back than you do.'

'I guess so, my old man!'

'Hey, no need for that.' He pulled her closer, close enough to kiss. She smelled clean and fresh. He could feel her breath on his neck.

She looked at him coyly. 'I was wondering,' she said as she brushed some flyaway hair behind her ear. 'Could you check something for me? Since you're the best hacker around.'

Archie pulled back, his eyes narrowed. 'How illegal is this?'

'Oh, silly.' She sat forward on the desk and opened her legs, dragging him in closer. 'It's not illegal. Well, not really.' She bit her bottom lip again. 'There's just this name that keeps popping up here and there, me and some friends—'

'Friends with the same tattoo?'

'Yes.' She smiled and rubbed his chest. 'Just, this name—we think it's a bad person, trying to hurt people.'

'Fine,' he said, 'what's the name?'

'We know him as the Poison Maker.'

'Sounds like a proper villain.'

She kissed his cheek and hopped off the desk. 'Thanks, sweetie. See you Friday.' And with a wink, she left.

18

Chapter 17

When I arrived at work on Tuesday, the lab was disappointingly quiet. It was a little early to be losing interns. It was still a week or so until that familiar stage of the programme when they started dropping out, unable to handle the workload or too stressed with the thought of failure. The fallout rate was always high, but not this early.

Marcus was running around keeping things in order, only with fewer interns to oversee. 'It's the news, Professor,' he said when I quizzed him. His glasses were thick and heavy, serving to improve his one seeing eye, the other lost to vitamin A deficiency in childhood. This impairment spurred his passion for nutrition, he had said in his interview. Idealistic and proud of the lab, he was yet to run into the wall of discontent as I had. 'The bird, you see. And then, with the protest at the weekend, all the germs that could have spread. And it hasn't finished yet, so some don't want to leave their homes at the moment.'

I groaned with frustration. 'That's simply ridiculous. They

can't just come and go as they please.'

'It's only a couple of them, Professor. And I've given them work they can get on with at home. They should be back in a day or two, once the protest has properly dispersed.'

He looked so upset about making me cross. Usually that would wind me up even more, but I was feeling gracious that day, plus slightly guilty: perhaps my article had stoked some fire in the protestors. Such demonstrations never normally lasted that long, especially in the heat.

'Fine. This is their one and only warning. There has been no official advice to stay at home, so they should bloody well be here.'

'I'll pass it on, Professor. Thank you.'

The interns staying at home doubled my workload for a couple of days. It meant I was disproportionately irritable with the ones who had bothered to show up, which I knew was unfair to them. As much as I tried to view them as individuals, I still regarded them as one insidious being, causing me more hassle than it was worth. Penny chastised me for my lack of sympathy while Marcus attempted to stop the interns from bothering me. I wished my office had a deadlock and an electric fence.

'Have you even looked through their files?' Penny shrieked one morning, treating me to a view of the lipstick on her teeth.

'Of course I have, and they're as predictable as ever.'

'I would hardly call agoraphobia "predictable". For most, these are likely their first ever non-virtual interactions.'

'Which is why agoraphobia is predictable.'

'Mysophobia is also listed highly,' she said as her thin eyebrows reached as high as her hairline. 'You may think a fear of germs is nothing less than sensible but, with the bird and the wave, the poor youngsters won't even be sleeping.' She held her chest as she spoke, like the meagre troubles of the interns were giving her a heart attack.

I rubbed my eyes. 'They can't just not come to work because they're scared or tired. There is always something to be afraid of.'

'Well, a little more sympathy from you would go a long way.'

'I'm not here to hold their hands, Penny.'

'I should hope not!' she said. 'Hands are filthy, as you well know. Imagine even suggesting such a thing. With language like that, no wonder the interns are all afraid.'

I faced my computer and began reading through some emails, allowing her to become nothing more than white noise.

The level of anxiety young people felt always baffled me. They knew nothing of vermin, of bombings, of disease. They had a clean, paved world. They'd never had to share their planet with filth, so they knew nothing of the putrid crawlers that used to invade our space, or the archaic desire to preserve dirt. I bet they'd never even seen a bug. They never had to battle such old-world thinking that was so abundant when the Great Sterilisation Project was in its infancy. Those ancient ideals sunk beneath the waves when the anchors blew.

I was on the verge of firing all the lab staff when an email from the housing department came through. Grace and I were invited to view some two-bed apartments in a new high-rise being built a little way from our current home. It wasn't the development I had been to look at the week before, but in a part of town I was unfamiliar with. It was still more Perimeter, though, much to Grace's displeasure.

I had no doubt why this sudden hint of progress had occurred. At least the defamatory article hadn't been for nothing. Finally, my life's work was paying off. Having my signature on every BioLab product was giving me some credibility. To receive this invite was without doubt a reward from the Centre. I couldn't help smiling. A bit of hope, just a little.

I read the email several times, and that evening, collected the required documents. I had to bring a government letter from Greg naming me as the key science writer for the Perimeter, endorsed by the Minister of Impartiality, along with various character references, my marriage certificate, and a letter of intent from Grace saying we were intending to renew our vows. Our vaccination records and fertility clinic application were also needed, along with our latest swab-test results, as well as payslips, our credit-check score and clean criminal records. We had been in our current apartment for ten years. A lifetime had passed since then. I couldn't remember the procedure. I definitely couldn't remember needing so much paperwork for a viewing. Two-beds were so much more sought after, I reasoned. And now, finally, it was our turn.

Grace expressed concerns that the apartments weren't in the best part of town, which were well-founded. I looked at a map and satellite images to locate the development and, although there were a few streets between the new high-rise and the coast, it was certainly much closer to the edge than our current block. Living in an area I had just criticised so publicly didn't sit too well with me. What if the estate agent knew? Or our neighbours? But opportunities like this didn't come around often, so we had no choice. At least there was no risk of erosion there. The coast appeared well-fortified, and the crime rate was relatively low for the outskirts. Still, Grace fretted.

'It would feel like moving backwards, not forwards,' she said.

'Just because it's further out, doesn't mean it's necessarily worse.'

'The postcode looks worse, though. We'll be judged.'

'The neighbourhood is safe. Some coastal areas are bad, but that bit is okay. There's no access to the sea, so less you-know-what around. We can hopefully move closer to the Centre one day.'

'The air will be filthy.'

'We'll get better masks. And they're likely to install new ArbAirs soon.'

It was too hot to debate it for long. The thermostat hadn't dropped below forty degrees in several days, and The Raft's power supply was stretched to its maximum as fans and air con bled every watt available. Three times that week our apartment block's power had gone off completely. The official advice was to save air con for night-time to aid sleep, but the heat was relentless all day long.

Grace was irritable, working in her little IC. Her pupils were being cantankerous little monsters as they too suffered with the heat, adding to her frustrations. With water prices still sky high, a lot of the kids were thirsty. Grace and I had spent a fortnight's wages on bottled water, while the news refused to say when the tap water would be safe again, so prices kept on increasing. Greg's ten percent off barely made a difference.

The lab had power priority from the grid and was kept below thirty degrees, so it was bearable for the most part. My walks to work were slow, and twenty minutes twice a day was all I had to endure. Grace was at home, sweltering and aggravated. She needed a break. I suggested she go to the MindSpa, but she had not bothered yet. Sapped of motivation by the relentless heat, she preferred to just lie still and melt into the sofa.

177

Because Grace was teaching, I would have to attend the apartment viewing alone. I had seen the look on her face as I left. There really were no other two-bed options around, not within our means. Even if we thought we could scale back on a few things, we wouldn't pass the credit checks with our current wages. Perhaps if my journalism did well, we could move closer to the Centre one day, I told her. Grace smiled weakly at my efforts for reassurance, her rosy face wearied and fatigued. The heat had also drained her of the will to argue.

'Whatever you think is best,' is all she said.

I kissed her goodbye and went out.

There is a cycle I think almost everyone goes through with their career. At least, I assume I'm normal in this regard. I began full of aspirations and was excited to take on the world. I progressed, but at some point I got a bit too comfortable, hit a wall and stopped advancing. It's not that I got worse at my job, it's that it takes a lot more effort to make even a small impact. The idealism of youth dissipated and I came to realise that the difference I thought I could make, that feeling I had when I was younger that I could change the world, improve lives, be rich, have notoriety, all of those heartfelt ambitions were a few steps ahead on a treadmill turning the wrong way. With every laborious step, it became ever harder to make smaller and smaller gains. The ocean's current span The Raft too quickly. I couldn't keep up. It was either run, burn out, or sit down and think, *What's the point?* But the point presented itself to me that day. An apartment was within our grasp. Finally, we were making progress.

Chapter 18

I had to get through a morning at work before the viewing. I was delighted to note that efficiency had returned. The lab was tidy, and the interns were all present, flushed from their commutes yet busy with their tasks. My recent absences had made no impact on functionality, Marcus had it all under control. On my desk was a note from him to say the blood-test results for the vitamin infusion were in. I logged on to my computer and sifted through the spam to find what I needed. Fifty thousand human test subjects had taken part in the trials and the results showed, compared to the old vitamin infusion, that the new formula increased absorption by only ten percent.

Microbes! Why such little improvement? I was hoping for closer to forty. I read and reread the results, searching for a mistake somewhere, some anomaly, but found none. The results were thorough and accurate, the interns had checked and double-checked them.

The reputation I had built for myself in my early career days had waned significantly over the years, my early successes becoming something of a distant memory. My signature on the packaging was like an archaic mark, noting the brand's historical significance rather than its modern functionality. The Minister of Impartiality's statement about my notoriety had been a surprise. I assumed someone would have overtaken me by then. When I racked my brains, though, I could think of no one. I could recall several big names in the pharmacy world who had developed medications to treat the symptoms of vitamin deficiencies, but no one working on nutrition. Protein labs hadn't made the headlines in years and none of the other carbohydrate labs seemed to be even trying. They were concentrating on textures and confectionery rather than nutrition. I needed to do better. I felt the burden of the entire country bearing down on me. The people needed to be healthier. This formula was meant to do more than just an extra ten percent absorption.

I heard Marcus's feeble knock at my door.

'What?' I shouted back.

He inched the door open ridiculously slowly and poked his head in. 'Sorry, Professor, I just wanted to check you were okay with the results?' He looked as pale as ever, dark circles under his eyes, his thinning hair thickly oiled, and his clothes tatty. His heavy glasses slipped down his peeling nose and were so smudged I could hardly tell which was his blind eye.

'Obviously, the results are not okay, Marcus. I will have to let Professor Harold know of the minimal improvement. Greg will be furious.' Disappointing Greg was a terrifying prospect. I imagined his massive face, red with rage, those whiter-than-white teeth bearing down on me.

'I could email him for you, Professor.' Marcus almost squeaked his offer.

'No, that would seem extremely unprofessional. I'll tell him myself.' At least I could avoid Greg's voice and face with an email. It was only words on a page then, much less forbidding.

'Excellent idea, Professor.' He lingered in my doorway, not retreating as he usually would. I ignored him for as long as I could while I emailed Greg and Harold, but he was still there, like a bad smell.

'What else do you want, Marcus?' I sighed.

'I was reading some of your papers, Professor.' He continued to intrude, he really was becoming a bit more brazen. 'Well, rereading. Your Masters on vitamin-enrichment techniques, and your PhD on increasing vitamin A levels in children.'

'What about the ten papers I've published since then, on vitamin absorption, on increasing concentrations, about digestive barriers and making the right compounds for effective absorption?' I snapped at him. I was being cruel. I knew it. It was easier to be unkind than considerate sometimes.

'Well, I've read them all over the years. And I really believe, if you can't figure it out, no one can.'

His grovelling face irked me often but now he looked so genuine, his weak little frame giving every ounce of its fortitude to supporting me, I tried to soften my tone. 'The repugnant truth is, we are working against millions of years of evolution. Mother Nature solved this problem millennia ago, that much we know. And now Mother Nature is angry.' Marcus blushed at the mention of nature. 'Technology takes time to solve problems, but it's quicker than evolution, I'm convinced of that. Mother Nature's mission to eradicate us is not going to prevail without a fight.'

I saw Marcus's face light up and his scrawny chest swell slightly with pride. 'There are other papers, too, I'm sure you're aware?'

I made no effort to hide my groan. 'Listen, Marcus, there are many theories and papers written on vitamin issues in the modern world. The lack of sunshine, as most of the population barely leave their homes and the smog blocks a lot of the UV. Some studies have shown weak evidence that the altered immune systems after the pandemic years hindered vitamin uptake. Depression and endorphin issues, stress and genetic factors have all been blamed. Over the years, I've written off all such ideas. No one reason alone is enough to account for the high levels of deficiency, and even collectively the data is ambiguous.'

What I didn't say was that such theories were bad for business. BioLabs made its money from food and vitamin compounds, not lifestyle changes. There was no funding to research such areas.

'Of course, Professor. You know best.' His lips twitched into a grin.

I should have been kinder to Marcus. I should have thanked him for his efforts. He was such an integral part of the lab, a quiet and dependable worker who grafted without complaint, yet he was also part of the furniture. I saw him more as an office desk than a human. Something to dump my workload on and push out the way if it suited me.

'I just cannot understand why the modelling versus human trials could be so different. The lab results showed so much more promise than the human trials,' I said.

I put my hands on my head, racking my brains for reasons. An error in the modelling software? Improbable. Mistakes in recording information? Impossible, I'd checked them all. Tampering with the results? I brushed away that idea before even pondering it.

Marcus gave a little cough. 'Just to reassure you, Professor, the lab does seem to be working effectively.'

'I've gone over the results. I can't see any mistakes, so I'm sure it's not that.' I glanced up at him. His face looked so clueless, beads of sweat dripping through his hairline as he wrinkled his nose to stop his glasses from slipping off completely. He stared at me blankly, my ramblings lost on him. 'Well, maybe I could request funds to study environmental factors, instead of just upping concentrations of infusions. Perhaps one of the old, small-scale studies was on to something?' I offered.

'Would you like me to draft a proposal?'

I paused before answering. During his initial interview, Marcus surprised me with good knowledge, despite the lack of exam grades to back it up. Such job opportunities were rare for those without the certified education, and so he was incredibly dedicated. However, drafting proposals was outside of his expertise. Before I had time to tell him that, my computer pinged. I had a reply from Greg:

Ten percent is better than nothing. It will have to do, and gives us more room for improvement for the next one.

'Well, Greg isn't throwing his toys out of the pram just yet,' I said, surprised.

'Excellent news, Professor.' And with that, Marcus finally left my office.

I breathed a huge sigh of relief. Greg wasn't writing me off. And he was right, really. The new formula was still set to make him a lot of money, and I doubt he even knew what percentage I wanted. Perhaps I had been aiming too high. I tried to stay motivated by mentally listing the tasks ahead. There was plenty more work to do. I emailed Greg, asking if we could investigate environmental factors, stating our focus would have to shift to make improvements. We would have to rework the formula and figure out why absorption was less than expected.

The email from Professor Harold was also notably more positive than I imagined it would be. His simple response read:

It's a step in the right direction. Still the best infusion around. Send me more samples ASAP.

Another relief. Yet still I couldn't shift my disappointment. I was in search of a masterpiece and had delivered a mediocre version of what I wanted. My expectations of myself were too high, I concluded. I wanted the unachievable. Harold was more conservative, but also more realistic. It was still a notable improvement, I assured myself.

Only a couple of minutes later, Greg hit back with his next reply:

Environmental changes don't make a profit. Make the formula better.

So that was that, fairly predictable, Greg only cared about the balance sheets and didn't care a jot for the science. His email continued:

Blood test the worst absorbing candidates. Look for patterns.

Maybe we can combine this with some endorphins or similar. Get pharma labs on board. Mega bucks then!

Well, it was better than nothing. Greg's qualifications to run the lab were a big unknown. He inherited the business from his parents and their parents, and seemed to have little passion for helping people, only his pockets. His reputation and relation-ships with those in power were more important to him than anything. The Prime Minister needed a healthy population to secure votes, Greg needed the power and privilege that came with delivering it, along with the women. Such symbiosis in the Centre population was common. The recognition and reward did not often filter down towards the Perimeter, and my recent cavorting in that circle was such a rarity.

My opportunity with the National Press had occurred due to my scientific success, and if my results didn't keep up with expectations, I feared my chance would slip away. My chance at prosperity, to provide a better home with better opportu-nities for Grace and me. I was hoping to make headlines and earn esteem for making such a breakthrough. But my hot new product was lukewarm at best. Work was needed to find out why the mismatch had occurred. As Greg said, there was room for improvement.

As I was feeling a little more upbeat and motivated, Marcus's flimsy knock tapped on my door again. I grumbled, exasper-ated. 'Yes, Marcus, come in.'

His meek face peered round my door. 'Sorry to disturb you, Professor. It's about the interns.'

'Yes? What is it this time?'

'You remember Mabel?'

'Who?'

'Intern four, who asked about ancient nutrition?'

'Oh yes, intern four. Is she causing trouble?'

'Not at all. She's very bright and dedicated. It's just...' He searched for the right words. '...a number of other interns have approached me with the same idea.'

'Growing food in dirt? The need for pathogens in digestion?'

'Yes, along those lines.'

'So, she's broken her confidentiality agreement. Have Archie check her communication records,' I replied matter-of-factly.

'I've already done that, Professor, and she hasn't spoken to anyone. She really is very astute. It seems that the other interns came to the same hypothesis independently.'

'Really? How odd.' Puzzled, I sat and thought for a while. The interns had seemed like a more intuitive bunch than normal, and the years of filth were becoming a more and more distant memory. Certainly, their generation had never known dirt and pathogens. The thought for them was perhaps not as scary, as they hadn't seen the effects for themselves. The smell of infection, the sight of viral asphyxiation—it was all too abstract for them, and as such, their thinking was all wrong.

'How would you suggest I manage this?' Marcus asked, his snivelling voice barely more than a whisper.

I sighed. 'Gather the interns together. I'll make an announcement. Five minutes.'

Best get this over and done with, I thought. Such rebellious ideas were unusual, although they did show a degree of independent thought. I had hoped for fresh ideas from the intern programme. I should have been careful what I wished for. To disrespect the Great Sterilisation Project was libellous and a waste of company resources. It had to be addressed and, as I entered the lab, I saw to my relief that Penny was nowhere in sight.

'Interns, please all sit at a desk.' The interns obeyed, sending equipment clattering in their haste. Their faces gazed at me, bewildered and alert. 'There is something we need to go over. Intern one, that seat will be fine where it is. No need to drag it halfway across the lab. If someone could please turn off that alarm and move that beaker from the burner. Thank you.'

They all sat still, their dazed little faces reddening with worry. 'Now, it has not escaped some of your eager young minds that vitamin absorption is not as high as we would like with the new formula. Welcome to science research, where we are often disappointed. There are still problems that need solving, and that is what we are here to do. I have heard whispers that some of you have begun to theorise that the absorption of vitamins was higher when humankind ingested organic filth.' An exhalation of gasps spread throughout the room. 'Calm down, calm down. No one is in trouble. You are scientists, and as scientists, sometimes we have to work with our minds in the gutter. Those who have pondered this... well, you're right. It's well known among scientists. Looking at some of your reactions, this is a big surprise. Intern five, please look out for intern six next to you. He looks rather faint. Now, if you could all please compose yourselves, there is more that needs to be said. Intern six, are you alright if I continue? No? Please make your way to the wellbeing manager's room. I'll have this talk emailed to you, and you can read it when you're mentally prepared.

'We have always known that, in the old world of filth, before the Great Sterilisation Project, humankind utilised bacteria to aid digestion. We had bacteria living inside of us. Intern nine,

187

are you okay? Good. If you need to vomit, please leave the lab and make your way to the recovery room.

'As I was saying, we know that some microbes aided nutrition in the past. This is no longer the case. Our mission now is to replicate those benefits without reintroducing hazards. Regressing to the days of dirt is simply not an option. We will not return to squalor and, believe me, if we reintroduce bacteria, squalor is what we'll be left with. Bacteria are pathogens. Nothing more. If some don't cause disease, give them time and they will, eventually. The old filthy ways evolved over millennia, and then, quickly, bacteria turned from symbiote to menace. What the planet did over millennia, we must achieve quicker. We must progress, not regress. Progress is paramount. The Great Sterilisation Project is the very reason you are all standing here living and breathing today. Any mention of bringing back microbes is simply insinuating a desire to design biological warfare, as that is what the outcome will be. Such thoughts are dangerous for the whole of humankind, as well as for you as individuals. Do you all understand the seriousness of this?'

They all nodded.

'I'm not chastising young minds that are curious and want to achieve. I'm merely instructing you to exercise caution when viewing the science of the modern age as somehow inferior to the filthy ways of the past. What we must do is find ways of synthesising the benefits that those microbes delivered without reintroducing the pathogens. I applaud you for thinking outside the box. It's great to hear such initiative, but please channel your minds to acceptable topics of research. Everyone is safe now. That is what we must remember. Dismissed. Carry on.'

I left the lab of visibly shaken interns and retreated to my office. It was almost time for them to start dropping out, and my speech would likely hurry some of the more squeamish ones out the door.

I set out to brainstorm my plan for research topics. I would retest the subjects for unusual hormone levels, as Greg said, though that was the area of research I thought least likely to yield results. It had to be more environmental than that. Hormone imbalances had existed since forever: it was the environment that had changed. I knew it was risky, but I decided to check water supplies for pollutants. Greg would shut down the idea immediately, no way would he want his neck on the line for a whim. I sought Archie's help and found him a little distracted.

'Archie?' Instead of staring at his monitors, he was gazing out of his tiny window. His room was as hot as always, but he didn't seem to notice. Several bowls of IcyCrema were abandoned and melting on his desk. 'Archie?'

'Oh sorry, Sav, I was miles away.'

'You okay?'

'Just tired.' He had a look of carelessness, more so than usual, with creased trousers and his shirt buttoned wrong. His hair wasn't parted on either side, just a messy muddle, and his mouth was frozen in a half-smile. His eyes looked not weary, but vacant.

'You seem weird. You not sleeping well or something?'

'What? No, of course not,' he said, swivelling his chair to face me and giving an animated thumbs up. 'I'm fine. What can I do you for?'

'I need a little favour. Can you access water readings? I'm looking for any tests on drinking water. I'm wondering if

189

there's some old pesticide or something that's built up.'

His alertness returned, and he grimaced at me. 'Careful, Sav. Searching for that kind of intel raises a lot of eyebrows.'

'I know, but it's important.'

'It's a specialist government department, only checked by the Centre. There's no way I can get access to those systems. I'd be in deep shit if I tried. Especially with the recent contamination.'

'Please, Archie, I'm sure there's a back door you can get through.'

'I need to start charging commission for hacking. There's good money for this on the black market.'

I stepped closer to him. 'What else are you hacking?' I whispered.

'Nothing, really,' he said. 'Just a friend asked me to search for someone who goes by the name of the Poison Maker.'

'Sounds like some super villain.'

'That's what I said!' We both laughed. 'Some think it's someone trying to harm the Perimeter, not really sure. The information everywhere is quite vague. I need to search a little deeper.'

'Sounds fun,' I said, not hiding my sarcasm.

'Read your article, by the way.'

'They weren't my words, you know.'

'I know, I figured as much.'

'I even went to the editor's office to try and stop them from publishing it. Did you know the National Press editor, some guy called Peter, is Perimeter?'

'Doesn't surprise me,' Archie said. 'When you have nothing, you're easier to manipulate. Anyone from the Centre would want to put their own mark on things. A Perimeter editor would just do what they were told. You want me to research the guy? See what I can dig up?'

'Nah, it's fine. You've got enough to do,' I said. 'It's brutal, having to kiss ass and look after your own. I feel awful about it. Grace was distraught. She thinks I'm some narrow-minded person, hateful, having a go at our neighbours and desperate people.'

'The Centre always wins. You're doing what you can for her. It's just the way things are. Hierarchy, you know. Prestige is rationed. Would you rather scavenge for scraps at the bottom, or feast at the top?'

'I feel like I'm feasting on others' misery.'

'Hey, don't take on extra guilt. You know, years ago, we had this saying: it's a dog-eat-dog world.'

'Gross.' I mimed a gag. 'Did you actually eat dogs?'

He laughed and shook his head. 'It just means you've got to do what you've got to do.'

It was the first time I'd heard that name, the Poison Maker. I instantly dismissed it as just some scare story from the unregulated press. The Alternates trying to spread fear, some nut job with too much time on their hands. It seems so stupid to have scorned it like that, to have laughed, even. But if I hadn't, if I'd panicked and figured it out, what would have changed? Nothing. Most likely, the course of action I took would have stayed exactly the same, the only difference being that I would have been aware of the consequences of my actions for longer. The blissful ignorance I once had would have eroded quicker, and the despondency would have set in sooner. Maybe that would have helped my transition, given me some extra time for processing it. It makes me think that, in the not-too-distant future, I will feel content. The impossibility of that is clear, that itch will never be scratched. So no, I shouldn't berate myself over this. The wheel started turning long before that conversation with Archie. It powers itself. There was nothing I could have done. Nothing I would have done.

And Archie was right, I knew it. I couldn't worry about the entire world. My research and Grace were all I should have concerned myself with.

So, I concentrated on the press write-up for the new formula. It had been much anticipated; the public and the scientific community would want the data. I chose my words carefully, singing its praises without promising too much. Then I left the lab to look at the new apartment block.

* * *

I waited at the entrance to the construction site as instructed. There was some shade from the adjacent buildings, so I hovered there as much as I could. The concrete outlines of the new buildings were all that existed so far; no details yet, just the bare bones. The square footage looked acceptable. I could see the bedrooms and IC areas. I walked around the perimeter of the development, skirting the shade, and noted the area was as I expected. Salty air, but nothing alarming in the neighbourhood. No fish junkies or Alternates walking around. The quantum cables had been laid and, as was often the case, the road hadn't been filled in. Street sprayers were busy dampening the ground, which meant it was still at least two blocks to the coast. It wasn't perfect, as Grace said. We'd be judged by the postcode. But it wasn't awful and would allow us space for a baby. So, I waited. I scouted the perimeter again and waited more. After thirty long, scorching and wasted minutes, I phoned the estate agent.

An exceptionally cheery voice answered the phone, the sort of tone that is so falsely merry it's instantly irritating. The words the jovial woman said were even more irksome. 'Apologies, Professor Selbourne, you are not on our list for this development.'

'But I made an appointment just yesterday.'

'I'm sorry, there's nothing I can do. Goodbye.' She hung up before I had a chance to argue. How can someone have such a chirpy voice when delivering bad news? *Dammit! Dammit, dammit.* What about my Parliamentary approval? What use was that? I emailed the agent a copy of my letter from Greg and received an instant autoreply back:

Thank you for your enquiry. We have no availability currently, check the website for updates.

I called the agent's number again. It went straight to voicemail with the same message. So that was that. My first almost chance at getting a bigger apartment: over. How could there be no availability already? According to the website, this wasn't the only development in that postcode. It was impossible. There were just too many people. Invisible people, unseen, unsociable recluses. Faceless, nameless people ahead of us every time. Some unidentifiable rogue jumping in front of me at every opportunity. And that's just what I felt was taken from me: opportunity. I knew why. The agent would have done a quick scan of my name, seen my career success, but also my family history. My parents and their degrees in useless careers, the news articles about my father and his insects and the diseases they caused. They would have assumed I was an Alternate or, at the very least, had inherited my father's interests. I never even had a chance to show them my paperwork. The barrel was full of people from better backgrounds. Why bother scooping out the dregs?

The Minister of Impartiality's words rang in my ears: if I wrote appropriate articles, I could get boosted up the list. Just how many and how appropriate must they be? I had gained notoriety throughout my career. Now I needed fame, and to fuel the Centre's propaganda to the Perimeter. It was possible this tease was orchestrated by the powers at the Centre. I had done well enough to get a sniff of a viewing, now I must do more to actually secure an apartment. The Minister was snapping her fingers at me, dangling the prize just out of reach. My treadmill was still at full speed backwards.

Still, there was hope. That deadliest of things. Grace was researching a grandmother for adoption. Having a babysitter, a property to inherit—perhaps there was a chance. I was disheartened, but I was not quitting just yet.

Chapter 19

Grace had been searching adverts for hours, the dark web proving a treasure trove of adverts from lonely elderly people. 'Grandparents without grandchildren' was how they described themselves. Many were asking for company, as the AI programs just didn't offer the right interaction. There's no substitute for a human hug, it seemed. Some were located too far away, a few lived even closer to The Raft's edge, where the smog was worse and Alternates even more plentiful. Grace's criteria were strict: she wanted the perfect grandparent at the perfect location.

I had encouraged her investigations, keeping her mind busy and, dangerously, offering her hope. She searched every moment she had free. Some evenings I watched as she waded through the pages, feeling more and more reassured that it would work for us. It seemed commonplace, she said, and was annoyed she hadn't thought of it before. We could have had a baby already. But how best to approach someone without seeming like we wanted their money? She worried about that, turning it over in her mind. She was wretched with apprehensions about portraying herself as a pauper, a gold-digger, a conformist.

She had never known her own grandparents, and imagined her baby in the arms of that kind of figure, having that relationship. Even if the grandparent didn't help our application, they would still be a blessing. One more person to love our baby. One more person to know. Grace missed her parents terribly. Losing both as a teenager had been horrific. The flu had wiped out so many. As much as Grace's arms longed for a baby, it made her doubt her abilities to be strong for a child. If another disease hit, could she maintain hope? Her parents had battled through the previous two pandemics, and their parents had fought through the first two. Grace had been lucky: her family's strength had saved her.

The devastation of the last flu was still a vivid memory. The fear and the heartbreak and the hopelessness of it all. Her mother coughing herself to death, her father's cries as he watched her last breath, his own asphyxiating cough taking his life shortly after. Their faces went blue before they died. Swollen and suffocated, their eyes bulging out, red and desperate. 'Never again' was the promise. The Great Sterilisation Project had been swift and effective. Now, after all the years living in a clean world, Grace could not take that for granted. 'Everyone is safe now.' For now. But if it happened again, could she be strong? Could she protect a baby? My reassurances fell on deaf ears. Her confidence needed fortifying in ways words could not provide.

Her desire for a baby dwarfed any doubts, but they were still there, lingering in the back of her thoughts. On her lowest days, they would niggle and fill her with uncertainty. Was it right to bring a child into a world where their prospects were limited by who their parents were and where they lived? Was it fair to raise children in constant isolation? Grace remembered, somewhat distantly, playing outdoor games with other children. She had memories of holding hands, consoling a friend with a hug, even playing in the dirt like it was harmless. She remembered being fascinated by cows and finding sheep adorable, eating real blackberries from a bush, and being scared of spiders and bees. Rare as they were, their sporadic appearance was all the more terrifying. All these were relics of her childhood, when some green still existed, before everything non-human was wiped out and the world was painted grey. 'Everyone is safe now.' Grace understood the mantra. We were safe, we were alive. But were we living?

Yet, despite her concerns, I knew her arms felt heavy with emptiness, and her heart was not whole. 'The world will improve,' she would often say, in those rare moments of optimism when hope eroded fear. It justified her yearning.

The hours searching the dark web for grandparents had turned up all sorts of profiles. The most abundant were the simply lonely. Some sounded angry, some overly hopeful. One stood out as more than just lonely and seemed to have a desire to help. At a hundred and twelve years old, she looked surprisingly well from her profile, and her advert was solemn yet witty:

Old lady seeks young folk. I've no grandchildren of my own, and now I'm ancient, and I'll be damned if the crooks that run the country are taking my home for their own gain. I think I'd be a good grandma. My sweetie tin is always full and I love a natter. Happy to babysit, of course, if the kiddo is happy to get up to mischief with

an old lady.
  Maisie.

Her light-hearted profile called out to Grace, reminding her of the days when she used to be fun and laugh more than she cried. When she read it to me, she giggled and her face lit up.

Through a series of emails, Grace arranged to meet at Maisie's house. She was delighted with the address as it was several postcodes closer to the Centre, a quiet part of town away from rivers and other pollutants. There was a field of ArbAirs just half a mile away, so the air would be cleaner. The apartment had three bedrooms. Three! There was no IC, but that could be added.

Besides her trip to the docks, it would be the first time Grace had left the apartment in years. She had weakened, inactivity causing her once-toned legs to waste away. Childhood scurvy and rickets had been dealt with, but the aftereffects had crept back in, and the aches were now a daily annoyance. On the journey to the docks, her legs cramped for most of the walk and continued to do so for days afterwards. The street sprayers and salty air made her skin flake. Pollution particles from the smog had lodged themselves in her clean lungs, and she had coughed every morning since. The thought of leaving the safety of her apartment again was daunting.

'Just go, you'll be fine. It'll do you good,' I said to her that morning.

School finished early on Fridays, so she would head there in the afternoon. It would be good for her, I rationalised. And she had an aura of optimism I had not seen in years. Yet still her eyes stared at the door, deep pools, devoid of courage. I kissed her forehead and left for work.

When she told me later how she got an Autocar all by herself and went to visit Maisie, I was delighted for her. Taking some control in the eternal hopelessness had given her strength. She had faced her fears and made me so proud. She attributed it to her 'maternal instinct', the drive of motherhood propelling her out the door. When she told me the story of her encounter with the old woman, she spoke with an animation I hadn't seen in years. Revived, reinvigorated, with renewed hope and optimism, she told me about her day as she looked at me—not out the window or at the floor, but straight at me.

The walk from the apartment to the Autocar was not too terrifying, Grace realised. The vehicle was clean and the air con efficient. She barely worked up a sweat on the short walk to the pickup point. The drive was about an hour and the air got cleaner and cleaner the whole way. Buildings that had been hidden behind haze came into view, their render looking cleaner, the sky turning from grey-blue to azure. It was a part of town Grace had never ventured to before, a sleepy region with a more gently fragranced disinfectant. SolaArbs lined the streets, making it look like an old-style avenue. The buildings were shorter and painted in a softer grey. Quantum-cable connectors were visible, but the streets had also been repaired. It felt homely.

The low-rise building where Maisie lived was white-washed and clean with shining, smog-free windows. The buzzer was loud in such a peaceful block. After calming her nerves with a breath, Grace took the lift to the fifth floor, where Maisie greeted her with a warm smile and a comforting handshake. A real contact handshake, not an air-shake. If Grace flinched at this, she hid it well. Despite Maisie's warmth, her hand felt brittle and cold, like glass. She was stable on her feet for someone of her age, and her voice shook a little, but maintained a mellifluent quality that was soothing and heartening. Life had left its smudges in the form of yellow and purple blotches, translucent marks over her skin that looked so delicate, like crumpled paper.

She ushered Grace into the living room, which was busy with furniture and ornaments. Grace liked it immediately. Not of a tidy nature herself, she enjoyed a room that appeared lived in, like it housed life and stories.

The lighting was bright, the lower housing blocks allowing more visible sky, and the sun beamed through the large windows. Grace sat down at a table opposite Maisie. The brilliance of the room highlighted Maisie's face, and Grace could see the thousands of lines that criss-crossed her skin like shattered china.

Maisie served up mugs of MimikTea in porcelain cups painted with a floral design. Grace did her best not to flinch at the sight of the flowers and took the cup from her. Maisie held up her teacup with a fragile hand.

'Cheers, dear.'

'Cheers?'

'It's what we used to say before drinking. Bad luck not to.'

Grace smiled. 'Cheers.'

Maisie smiled back at her, the lines on her face seeming to tug her lips upwards, revealing long yellow teeth. Her lower eyelids hung in red semicircles, but she didn't look tired. Her furrowed skin was bronzed and bright and her glazed eyes bore intensely into Grace, their hazy centres deep in contemplation.

'So, tell me about yourself, dear.'

Grace sipped her MimikTea, then took a deep breath. It was all a bit overwhelming. Being away from home, the journey, in a total stranger's apartment, drinking tea. It felt like something from an old film.

'Sorry, I'm just a little nervous. Meeting a new person face to face... it's not common, you know?' Maisie nodded. 'Well, my wife, Savannah—'

'Savannah, what a lovely name! The African plains,' Maisie said, her grey eyes focusing on something far away.

'Yes, her dad was... well, he was a bit of a renegade, I'm afraid.'

'Ha! The world could do with a few more of them, I think.'

Grace laughed and relaxed. Maisie emitted such warmth. It was hard to stay tense. She seemed odd, which was disconcerting. That was all, though. Just a bit odd. 'I'm a teacher and Sav is a food scientist. We've been on the fertility list for nine years. We're running out of time.'

'And you think an association with an old coot like me might help?'

Grace beamed and shrugged. 'It couldn't hurt.'

Grace watched Maisie as she talked; the astuteness in those lines, the kindness in the vibrato of her voice, the ease with which she spoke compared to Grace's awkward stuttering. It was like going to the MindSpa used to be for her. She felt her worries dissolve.

'You are a pretty thing,' said Maisie. 'You remind me a lot of my granddaughter. She was terrified of the authorities. Such a good girl. Never put a foot wrong.'

'I didn't know you had a family.'

'They made it out, across the last anchor before it blew. I was too old to follow, so we said our goodbyes. Her and my great-grandson, and his dad, of course. He was Polish, so they wanted to get to the mainland...' For a moment, she was lost in contemplation. 'I wish we had some communication, just a phone call. Not knowing is the worst thing. You'd think with all these satellites whizzing around, we'd be able to get a call or an email. They tell us The Raft moves too much, and we can't get a signal. In this day and age! Surely, just a phone call...' Her voice trailed off, hitching a ride with her sadness.

'You know, we mined every last bit of rock, turned the sea to acid, and no one thought to check the very land under our feet. A finite resource. Who saw that coming?' She chuckled to herself. 'Who would've imagined such a thing? Disregard, that's what it was. Neglect. Our solid foundation perished. Do you understand what I'm saying, dear?'

Grace nodded.

'It's like a family, see? Without strong foundations, the bonds wither away.' Maisie sipped her tea. 'You and your wife, yours is a good marriage?'

'We have our ups and downs, like any couple. But yes, we love each other very much.'

'Relationships can creak and buckle under the stress, just like the land did,' Maisie said. 'Those bridges they built were too little too late. But it was better than the current situation, don't get me wrong. Those anchors were like a saving embrace. The haters burnt them, though. Every hateful word spoken needs ten kind ones to cancel it out. Did you know that?'

Grace shook her head.

'There was no undoing it. Those words, the nasty headlines back then. What was said was said. Those headlines caused as much damage as the mining. Even when they started concreting the land to keep communities in place, they continued to blast the rocks underneath, and kept telling us it was okay and necessary. Scavenging for every bit of ore their greedy hands could get hold of. Just so they could bulldoze homes and build tiny apartments. But without solid foundations, of course, it was never going to work.' She narrowed her eyes to analyse Grace's face. 'I can see you're not like that. Your kindness runs deep.'

Grace smiled. For all Maisie's sadness and resentment, Grace could feel her warmth.

'I had a son once, but he died in a pandemic. Is that how you lost your parents?'

'Yes, all our parents died in a pandemic or famine. Sav had a brother who made it across the bridge.'

'You know what baffles me?' Maisie put down her teacup and sat back in her chair. 'We're still sending people to the moon and Mars, but we won't send people to another country. And we can't even talk to the rest of the world.'

'I think they're building a holiday retreat on Mars for the richest people. I guess it does seem daft when you put it like that.'

'Savannah. I've remembered where I know that name from. The press, am I right? She wrote that piece about the docks.'

'Yes. But she didn't actually write it. They don't print what she writes, they just say what they want and add her name to it.' Grace shocked herself with her bluntness. That was too forthright. She didn't even know this woman.

'I don't doubt it at all, my dear,' Maisie said. 'The powerful ones up top don't want the little voices out here being heard. She's very brave to try. Excuse me a moment.' Maisie got to her feet and shuffled out to the kitchen. Grace stared around the room again and took in the array of artefacts cluttering the place. It was like walking back through time to her childhood. Paintings of trees, real trees, and flowers, and children playing.

Photographs of people with their arms around each other. Some with animals, a dog, a cat, even wild animals. Grace couldn't recall their names: one had a long neck, another was stripy. She noticed the smell of the place, too: musty. Not at all like bleach. She liked it.

Maisie came back with some VitaBiscuits. 'You must like children a lot then, being a teacher.'

'Oh yes, very much! A child of my own is all I've ever wanted. I preferred teaching when we were actually at the school, when I could see the children, not just in the IC.' Again, Grace shocked herself with her candidness. Her yearning made it difficult to keep honesty at bay. 'Though I suppose it's for the best,' she said. 'Everyone is safe now.'

'Yes, yes, safety, very important.' Maisie frowned as she dunked a biscuit in her MimikTea. 'They're knocking down my old school. The last relic of my childhood. They dug up all our old pictures and now they're bulldozing the lot.'

'Progress is paramount,' said Grace.

'Mm.' Maisie took a bite out of her biscuit, some crumbs falling onto her lap. 'Seems like a strange world to me, a lonely one to bring a child into. Not enough laughter these days.'

Grace flinched a little at this. It was slanderous to belittle progress. 'Everyone is safe now, though,' she said again. 'And our child would have the most loving parents in the world.'

'I can see that.' Maisie smiled at Grace. 'I suppose when the dangers are invisible, priorities change. This new world is full of invisible dangers. I fear that sometimes the Centre prioritises the wrong ones. Or at least tells us to.'

It was difficult to read someone in the flesh, Grace realised. After years shut indoors, she wished she could do a quick internet search on this person. Maisie's scepticism could be a test. It wasn't that Grace didn't share her views, but speaking freely to a stranger? That felt precarious. An invisible danger, like Maisie had said. Had that been a warning? Grace stayed quiet and waited to see.

Maisie chatted about her upbringing, explaining the photos around her house, reminding Grace what animals they were, what countries she had visited. It was hard to stay dubious for long in her company. The talk of the creatures and travel turned Grace's stomach slightly, but Maisie spoke with such warming nostalgia. She was a great storyteller. Her voice rose in pitch when she got excited and tears came to her eyes when she mentioned her family, while her tone flattened when she spoke of resolving to live with the way things were now.

'It seems so odd, don't you think? That a lovely, capable and caring couple needs a reference from an old woman like me to have a baby. All those hormones and god knows what that made everyone infertile. Doesn't seem fair. You know what some people say? It's the universe rebalancing things, taking back control. But the universe doesn't take back control, it just hands it to the people with power. It's not Mother Nature or some god. It's Centre people, bred into power, who hold all the cards. They decide who lives where and who can have what.'

Grace only gasped in reply. Maisie spoke with a gleam in her eye and a half-smile. She twinkled with insight, an educator in a way Grace could never be.

'Well... I think it's also so they know there's the option of childcare,' Grace said. 'We'd put no pressure on you, obviously.'

'I'm not going along with it unless I get to spend some time with the little one! The streets are so quiet these days. I miss the sound of children. I suspect I even have great-grandchildren now, somewhere. Hopefully.'

Grace's eyes fell to the floor, feeling the weight of Maisie's loss. 'Of course, a grandparent is such a lovely person in a child's life.' Grace swallowed and played with the corner of a napkin. 'I think they'd also like to know that one day, not soon or anything, just one day, we'd have more space for a child.'

'Don't mince your words with me, dear!' Maisie said, then immediately laughed. 'I know I'm not going to be around forever, and I'd die happier knowing a wonderful young family was going to take this house. So many of us oldies live such long lives, there seem to be no houses freeing up for young families.'

She rattled off again, talking of her old school, her teachers, the work she and her husband had done. Grace listened and eventually concluded that there wasn't a sinister cell in this old woman. She spoke her mind, that was all. She was frank and opinionated and wholly disappointed with the modern world. Grace felt her trust blossom. Maisie had some strange ideas: an ancient take on the country so different from the one she grew up in had instilled more than a degree of cynicism. Her melancholy was evident, and justified: she had lost her family, after all. The modern world denied her access to her daughter, and her son had died. Grace could think of nothing worse. *The world is safer now*, she reminded herself. Her baby would stay close.

'Here I am, talking your ear off, and you probably have a lot to tell me, and a whole heap of questions,' said Maisie.

'What else are grandmothers for?' Grace smiled.

They chatted all day, drank MimikTea and polished off half of Maisie's sweetie tin. Since her parents died, Grace had barely spoken to anyone face to face. Certainly, she had never had a conversation with someone like Maisie, who had lived a life so different from her own. She loved the sound of the woman's voice, so articulate, so much enthusiasm for a long-lost world.

As they munched their way through a final VitaBiscuit, Maisie leant in a little closer and cleared her throat. 'I believe there is someone doing this country more damage than anyone. Have you ever heard of the Poison Maker?'

'No. Never,' Grace said. 'Who is it?'

'I just think something bad is going on, something this Poison Maker can account for.'

Grace fidgeted. The world was meant to be safe for her future baby. It had to be. 'How bad? Like birds again?'

'There are much worse things in the world than a few birds,' said Maisie.

'You mean,' Grace swallowed, 'bugs?'

Maisie shook her head. 'It isn't old Mother Nature I'm concerned about. Flies and bacteria.' She flapped her hand over her head like she was swatting them away. 'I'm worried about the people, the powerful ones. So many people on this Raft, yet I can't remember the last time I saw someone walk past my block.'

'Well, that's good. People are being careful.'

'Hmm.' Maisie's eyebrows knitted together. 'I mean, a lovely young couple like you can't get a bigger house, even though there are loads of blocks. And do you ever see anyone moving in?' She clicked her tongue and shook her head. 'Something is wrong, something toxic, but is that truth or lies? The press certainly isn't being very forthcoming. We're all locked away at the sight of a single bird, no contact with the outside world. It just doesn't seem right to me. It doesn't

207

feel like liberty.'

Grace gasped once again. The Great Sterilisation Project may have changed the world Maisie had known, but what had the alternative been? Progress is paramount. That's how things were. She tried to understand, to appreciate that Maisie's life was now so unrecognisable. She was bound to be sentimental, as her past life sounded adventurous. Filthy, but carefree.

'I suppose. I don't know, really, it just is how it is.'

'Would you do an old lady a favour? I suspect you have friends who have their ears to the ground more than me. Can you see what you can dig up on this Poison Maker? There's so much nonsense online, but that name really stuck with me, and it seems whatever I read disappears a moment later. I think it needs research from someone a bit more with it than me. Your wife might be able to find something, though, being in journalism.'

'Of course.'

They said their goodbyes and Grace left, with a promise to return every week. Even going back to the smog couldn't spoil her mood, and she barely noticed the murky shadows creeping in. She felt more hopeful than she had in years. As soon as she got home, she updated our fertility clinic application to include Maisie as a reference, along with her postcode and a description of her apartment. And she hoped, she really hoped.

When we spoke that evening, Grace told me how well it had all gone. She painted a vivid picture of the neighbourhood and apartment, and Maisie's kindness and demeanour. She didn't mention Maisie's outdated views or scepticism. It was only months later, when I finally met Maisie myself, that it became apparent. I suppose Grace had been trying to shield me, had been worried about associating with someone too much like my parents. Maisie wasn't an Alternate, but she was hardly a conformist either. Her outdated way of thinking was a testament to her age, the way old people always hanker for the life they had in their younger years. The pains of old age clouding any benefits the modern ways present. The wisdom they have is limited to their own experiences, and her experiences were plentiful. Grace knew to pay attention to her, to heed her warning, that her wisdom outshone ours combined.

Maisie gave Grace a peek at the danger, and ever since, I have had to convince Grace otherwise. There was no joy in knowing, no benefit for Grace at all. So, I attempted to shelter her from her own curiosities and life's realities. To keep her in the dark, where happiness was visible under softer lighting. The glare of enlightenment was blinding.

When we eventually met, months later, I recognised Maisie instantly as the elderly woman I had seen at the old school the day the Prime Minister had opened the time capsule. One of her pictures had been inside. She had been there to say a goodbye.

'It was the last of it, everything I had known. When they knocked down that old school, that was the last remnant of the old world, my old world.' Her voice disappeared after a breath, lost in remembrance. She absentmindedly took a sweetie from the tin and sucked on it silently.

Grace had been worried I'd find Maisie too different, too old-world, too close to an Alternate. Maybe she would have been right at one time. When I finally met her, after learning so much about her, I saw her as less a relic and more a mentor. Those gaudy, childish pictures were the last messages of hope, the voices of children pleading to save the world they knew.

Forgotten words from a generation now buried under concrete and chrome.

Chapter 20

'You're looking dapper today. Hot date tonight?' I said as I entered Archie's office. He looked more well-groomed than usual. Even his shirt was ironed.

'A gentleman never tells,' said Archie, grinning from ear to ear and avoiding eye contact.

'You do have a date! No way. Who is it?' He mimed zipping his mouth shut, and I scowled. 'That's why you were so weird the other day. Daydreaming about your date. I'm right, aren't I?' I poked him in the arm. He shook his head and mimed the zip again. 'Well, screw you and your silence. You'd better tell me the gossip next week.'

'Maybe,' he said. 'Too busy to gossip today, anyway. Want to see the crazy trajectory we're headed on now?'

'You mean this heat is going to get worse?'

'No, quite the opposite. The Gulf Stream. Look.' He turned a monitor to face me. The screen showed a map of the sea with lots of circles and lines that meant absolutely nothing to me. I didn't know if I was looking at the Gulf Stream or someone's fingerprint. I could see The Raft, though, a weather-beaten shape bobbing around near the middle of the ocean.

'Where is the Gulf Stream?'

'Exactly,' he said, wide-eyed and gesticulating at the screen. 'It's gone nuts. That looks nothing like the Gulf Stream, which means there are some pretty crazy currents in the South Atlantic. It's all upside down. I've run it through my modelling software loads of times, and every time it comes up the same. We're headed straight for the Falklands.'

'The Falklands?'

'Yep. The Falklands.'

I shook my head. 'Never heard of them.'

He laughed loudly. 'You scientists. So smart, yet you know nothing. They're a group of islands in the south, far south. British-owned. Still British-owned.'

'You mean we could anchor?'

'It's possible,' he said. 'The government's trajectory models are all wrong. They show us heading to South Africa and back up again, so I'll bet they haven't spotted the Gulf Stream change.'

'Gosh. Sounds like a possibility. That far south would be a good anchor point too, I guess. Less hot?'

'Yeah, the climate there is still fine. A lot of rain but that's no bad thing. With the amount of money desalinating and cleaning the water costs and all the space it takes up, a bit of fresh rainwater would be a useful alternative. And their population is so low I can't imagine there's any issue with disease. Who knows, though, nowadays? That'll take some research. They've lost land over the past century with sea levels rising, but there seems to be enough for an anchor. The granite looks stable,' he said and nodded, pleased with himself.

'I'll email the government department. I'm sure my modelling is right.'

'So, this heat will come to an end. That's good to know.' It seemed unimaginable at that moment, sat in Archie's stuffy office, that it could be anything but sweltering. I tried to remember the last time the air con was off at home. Years, it must have been, besides when the power shorted out. Any respite from the heat would be very welcome. The forty-degree average all year was getting tiresome.

'Winter food, how exciting is that? Hearty, warm comfort food. You going to tell the factory to start with casseroles and discontinue IcyCrema production pretty soon?' I asked.

'Definitely. It should start cooling down in a few weeks, then nosedive shortly after.'

'My new Syntho roast potatoes should be in production right on time.' I had fond childhood memories of the odd cooler month, the smell of the kitchen, the calming and consoling effect a bowl of warm soup could bring. Archie's air con spluttered to a stop, as ineffective as usual.

'It's hard to imagine a more suitable spot,' he said as the room immediately started to heat up.

'Best not get our hopes up, Archie.'

'Drifting was always meant to be temporary, so they say, until a good anchor spot came up. This could be it.'

'Your optimism is weird,' I said, and frowned. 'Must be the effects of your hot date.'

He rolled his eyes at me. 'I'm not excited about the prospect of anchoring. It was pretty scary last time. Our close call did nothing but irritate an old wound. Who knows if the politicians on either side even spoke? Our drift was taken as a sign of aggression. It could be the same this time.'

'We blew the bridges. I guess those ties can't be rebuilt so easily.'

'Exactly. They saw us as nothing but pirates.'

'An old empire reclaiming its turf,' I said. 'I wondered about my brother. Would he be there? Is there anyone left?'

'Who knows?' Archie shrugged. 'But our army was under orders to invade. Before they attacked us, anyway.'

'Really? You'd think they'd be more cautious. There could have been savages living on the mainland. I'll bet they were still eating filth then.'

'The idea was to give them the knowledge of sterility, spreading our sanitary sermon.' He held his arms up in a mock holy pose. 'We were to concrete what was left of their land and wean them onto our food and recycled air. Glorify ourselves by spreading like the viruses we had eradicated.'

'That would have been reckless. I mean, cross the anchor, sure, but doing it straight away would have exposed everyone.'

'I never heard about it directly. The whispers were loud, though. Imperialism now comes vacuum packed and microbe-free.'

I leaned back in my chair. 'When the blasts stopped, I went outside to watch. Loads of people did. That's the last time I remember seeing big groups outside at the Perimeter. The last time we saw the mainland, just drifting out of sight. So strange to think we might see land again.'

'We never got close enough to make out people. The faces of the bombers were unrecognisable...' Archie trailed off. Talking about those days pained him. His lost comrades were strong in his memory.

We had been isolated for so long. The short-term drift spanned two decades, and over the years, through the diseases and famines and climate, we had all learned not to get excited about anything. Anchoring or a change in the weather had only limited interest. Positive thoughts would lead to disappointment, of that I was sure. *How's your tomorrow? Uncertain.* The mantra of the Perimeter population reflected our eternal pessimism. Stability, as the Minister of Impartiality had put it. Our pessimism was certainly stable. No peaks and troughs in our outlook, just an eternal shuffle in the ditch.

'How's the hunt for the supervillain going?' I said, bringing Archie's thoughts back to the here and now.

'Who?'

'The poison guy.'

'The Poison Maker. It's interesting, actually.' He folded his arms and sat back in his chair. 'There's a lot of traffic looking for him. And whenever I find anything on the dark web, the site is shut down before I've even finished reading it.'

'Shit, you're not looking on your work computer, are you?'

'Don't be daft. I'm a professional, you know,' he said and winked. 'Anyway, there are lots of stories about how this person is making us less healthy somehow. It's just so hard to track it properly and fact check when sites shut down so quickly. I need to find a back door to get a better look before I'm detected. It makes it seem more legit, though, how they're taken down so quickly. Normally, whoever patrols this stuff just lets the rumours carry on. Deleting it all kind of stokes the fire, you know?'

'Weird,' I said. But I wasn't really interested, despite Archie's enthusiasm. 'Anyway, the real reason I came in here, besides being denied knowledge of your sex life and hearing about the unregulated press, is to ask about the water-pollution results. Any info?'

'Nope, afraid not. The tests were done recently, I can say that much, which means all the charts are being updated and the old ones are temporarily down. I've even been super nice and called an old friend with higher clearance than me to have a dig around. He said to wait a few days.'

'Great, thanks.'

'I'm trying to think of ways to get you to pay me back for the favour.'

'Maybe by making you and the world healthier?' I said.

'Hmm, I'm thinking something a bit more personal.' He grinned and passed me his empty cup.

'You want hot tea while sitting in this sauna?'

'It's my one joy in life.' He sighed a theatrical sigh.

'Just the one joy? What about your date, whoever she is?' I paused and thought for a moment. 'She?'

'Yes, she.' He laughed.

'Hey, I've never known you date anyone in real life. I had no idea!'

As I made the MimikTea, Archie's words rolled around in my head. An anchor point: that was huge news. I remembered when we drifted close to the mainland years ago. People gathered at the usually deserted coast to have a look. Those who lived on the top floors close by had their blinds open. We all watched the land with bated breath, its great rocky mass getting closer and closer. But with change came rumours. Whispers of re-anchoring spread. Relief and concern rippled through communities. Headlines added to the fuel. Social media was flooded with theories and opinions: '*Why would we want to re-anchor? We've been doing fine!*' '*We're liberated from the mainland! There's disease there.*' And the counterarguments: '*Let's get some stability back!*' '*We have family there.*

If they are suffering, we can help.' '*We are overpopulated, more land means more space for us!*' '*Let's stop by briefly, we might as well explore!*'

Now the possibility was on the horizon again, with a better climate. I pushed it out of my thoughts, though, too busy for the unease it caused. *Everyone is safe now*, I reminded myself.

* * *

Archie was still in the lab when I left that day, as he usually was. An intern lurked in the far corner, waiting for him to finish. They'd deliberately avoided each other all day, no stolen glances, no sneaky whispers. If my best friend and an intern could be so devious, how easy it must be for the powerful to deceive.

Amalyn met Archie round the corner from his building. She smiled demurely as he approached but they avoided eye contact, not daring to say a word in such an indiscreet setting. (He actually used that word when he described this night to me: 'demurely'. Who knew he was such a poet?) He glanced at her as they walked, the evening sun casting her complexion in a favourable light. She looked less pale. Perhaps she was blushing, like he was.

In the lab, she had tied her hair back. Now she looked more unkempt, less restrained. Her hair was loose, making her look brashly spontaneous as untamed wisps blew around. She had untucked her blouse and held a scuffed handbag with a fraying zip and fading pattern that was larger than her work bag. Archie suspected it was for overnight. He sweated more than usual on his walk home. Eager to impress, he untucked his own shirt in a show of contrived unity. The increased air circulation gave some relief from the heat, though his cheeks stayed flushed.

They arrived at his door in moments. Archie wished they'd had longer. He'd had all day to prepare himself. Now the actuality of having a real-life woman enter his home was a certainty that hit him hard. He suddenly felt unimpressive, a mediocre man totally unworthy of company, let alone hers. But here they were. He could hardly run away.

That morning he had swept through his apartment, clearing away junk-food cartons, deleting search histories and making his bed look rather more inviting than the mismatched un-washed sheets that usually adorned it. The night before, he'd replaced blown light bulbs, put all his laundry away and taken out the rubbish. It smelled okay, he thought. To be sure, he had liberally sprayed antiviral spray with floral additives and wiped every surface with scented disinfectant.

The front door to his building was scuffed with rusty fittings. There were smudges on the window and junk mail littering the edges of the lobby. A couple of discarded food wrappers were on the floor. He had cleaned his apartment, but hadn't even noticed the mess of the lobby. He decided to ignore it and just ushered her through, and she politely followed him to his apartment.

'It's nothing fancy, but it suits me fine,' he said as he opened the door. He was relieved to find that the place didn't smell too musty. With his history of service and pay grade, he could definitely get a better apartment. A proper window would be a bonus. The thin slits in the ceiling allowed only a little light in and virtually no heat out.

'It's everything a bachelor pad should be,' said Amalyn, and she circled the living area in mock scrutiny. 'Tidier than I imagined.'

'I'm quite a tidy person,' he lied, and poured her a glass of water.

'Aren't you organised. You filled those bottles before the wave, I assume?'

'I knew it was coming. Shame the government didn't listen.'

She nodded and walked around the living room, inspecting his sparse belongings. On the wall hung a print of The Raft, an old aerial shot from when the anchors were still in place.

'Wow! I've never seen a picture like this before.'

'Hardly any around, that's why. They're quite rare.'

'Check you out! Hoarding old-world images like some antiques dealer.'

He laughed. 'I just like the beauty of it. Look.' He pointed at the bridges. 'We were tethered so delicately. Like a kite on a string.'

'Kite?'

'It was an old kind of toy.'

She smiled. 'I think it's weird that the land used to be connected. Seems odd to think that we were joined to the rest of the world by dirt. You ever go across the bridges?'

'Me? No. Those bridges were burnt long before the anchors blew.'

She continued to walk around his apartment, moving with such ease as Archie stood still and rigid. A framed photograph of his family rested on a desk. It showed him as a little boy sitting on his mother's knee, his younger sister on their father's. Archie was a true mixture of both parents. He had his father's mouth and forehead, his mother's eyes and nose. All were smiling the same cheeky grin.

'They still alive?'

'No, sadly.'

'I'm sorry,' she said, moving closer to stroke his arm. 'Did they live near here?'

'This block was built where our old house was.' He felt awkward talking about himself and personal matters. Work, The Raft and other people were much more comfortable topics. No one his age talked about family; not so openly, anyway. Not that it was a secret, more that everyone was hurting. Those wounds hadn't healed.

'Did you get an apartment when they took your house?'

'Yep. Would have preferred the house, but at least I'm in the same spot, I guess. I'm standing where they stood. The views are all different, too. It's not really the same, but it's the closest I have.'

'Can't imagine how hard it must have been for you and so many who lost their families. I mean, mine drive me crazy, they can be a total nightmare. But if they weren't there, I'd miss them.'

'That's basically it.'

'I'm sorry. I didn't mean to bum you out. I just want to get to know you.' She squeezed his shoulder.

He grinned at her and sat on the sofa, his nerves dissipating. He patted the empty seat next to him. She obliged and rested her head against him. He could feel her warmth and his hairs tingled.

'At least you've got your own place. I can't imagine ever being able to move out.'

'Still with your parents?'

'I put my name on the list for graduate apartments, but no

luck yet. From what I've read, the waiting list is years.'

'Really? That sucks.'

'I'm in no hurry right now, but when the internship is finished and I get a proper job—*if* I get a proper job—then I'll really want a place of my own. Thought I'd be organised and get on the list early, but it barely made a dent in the schedule. It's so annoying. High-rises everywhere, more being built all the time, and they're full straight away.'

'Seems harsh. I think it's a common story, though.'

'I think it's a lie,' she said. 'They tell us they're full, so we live with our parents for longer. The councils don't want people with independence until they're too old and boring to get up to any mischief.'

'Old and boring?' Archie's eyebrows rose in mock offence.

'Well, you're not old and boring, obviously.' She pulled him close. 'I guess things were different when you were my age.'

'Yeah, fewer apartments, and they were easier to get.'

'Maybe a superb reference from my employer would help my application?' said Amalyn.

'Probably would, but that's not me, unless you want to retrain in computer engineering?'

'Ha! No chance, I'm not that kind of geek.' She poked him in the chest and laughed. 'But maybe you could use your hacking skills and bump me up a few places?'

'Second date and you're asking me to commit that level of crime!' he said, assuming she was joking.

'Maybe I'll ask again on our fifth date?' Amalyn tilted her head and looked up at him, biting her bottom lip.

'You're trouble, I'm sure.' He kissed her. 'Unfortunately, those lists are stored offline. You need a burglar instead of a hacker.'

'A burglar. Now that sounds like the kind of badass man I could get along with.'

'Bit more exciting than a computer geek, I guess.' Archie feigned disappointment.

'Oh, don't look so sulky,' she said. 'I'm sure I can still find ways to make use of you.' She moved closer. 'Have you had a look for the Poison Maker? Find anything interesting?'

'Ah, yes, mild hacking. The criminal activity you asked me to do on our first date.'

'What can I say? There are so many ways to impress me.'

He told her what he'd found, how the sites got shut down quickly, that he was working on it.

'What a resourceful man you are.' She smiled and kissed him. 'Lucky me.'

Chapter 21

My weekend was a rarity in that it was quite pleasant. I had no work to do, at least nothing that couldn't wait, so I visited the MindSpa twice. Grace had been more cheerful since her meeting with Maisie, but didn't want to come. She had once loved the MindSpa but, when she started to stay indoors, she had called it 'false', accusing it of igniting dormant parts of the brain with fakery, like the breeze and rustling noises were somehow twisting our thoughts instead of untwisting them. I didn't work in the field of mind therapy and hypno-medicine but I knew it wasn't some subliminal whatnot. It was just pure relaxation. Why a rustling sound worked so well was a secret only the hypno-medics understood, but to me, it was something innate and natural. It made me feel at peace in a way our unwelcoming world of sharp angles and grey just couldn't touch. One visit to the MindSpa on a weekend was a necessity; two, a rare treat. I felt renewed.

When I was home with Grace, we watched old movies, drank too much wine, laughed and looked through old photographs of our early days when we socialised, our brief honeymoon and our families. I managed to push work out of my mind for two whole days, and the nothingness it left me with was blissful.

Monday started with me feeling refreshed and motivated for the week ahead. The walk to work was usually accompanied by the gentle hum of air con and street sprayers, a noise that had become a kind of tinnitus; just a permanent feature ringing in my brain every moment I spent outside, and one annoyance the MindSpa couldn't unravel. That day, though, there was a much more intrusive noise, a buzzing and whirring drowning out the hum. At first, I couldn't locate the source. It seemed to come from all directions. When I looked up at the narrow strip of sky between the buildings, I saw several drones circling and searching up and down the streets, inspecting the tops of buildings. Some even got close to windows and hovered by the glass in snoop mode.

I picked up my pace, and it quickly became clear that there were hundreds of them, thousands even, sweeping through the empty streets. Their presence was designed to intimidate and annoy, buzzing us into subservience. But who was even around to pay attention? My walk to work was as lonely as ever. Police drones hadn't employed such tactics in years. In fact, they were barely used at all by that time. Even rescue drones were left idle since so few people ventured outside. I struggled to remember any drone patrols since we drifted close to Portugal. Before that, the riots. Both famine and anchor riots resulted in drone patrols. My first thought that morning was that we had drifted much more quickly along Archie's projected course than he'd predicted and were close to the Falklands. But knowing that Archie would not have miscalculated, I assumed the fish riots were to blame, even though so many drones for a few fish junkies seemed extreme.

I caught sight of the strip billboards that cut through the buildings, and stopped dead in my tracks as I read the sort of message that fills everyone with fear:

New Disease Outbreak in South America Confirmed.

The public-emergency announcement pinged on my phone, displaying the same headline.

South America was far enough away. Surely we didn't need to worry. Another new strain of zoonotic bird flu, though. *Another* new strain. *How are there enough birds left to cause a flu?*

The drones were out looking for invaders, checking for filth invading our shores. Thousands of them swooped through The Raft, looking for signs of land parasites poised to compete with us for air and precious resources. The vermin would be eradicated swiftly, the article reassured us. They believed the flu was limited to penguins, a flightless bird from the South America area, so it was unlikely to reach us here. *Flightless birds*, I laughed to myself. *How is that even a bird?* I shrugged it off, not allowing myself to worry about some stagnant creature miles away. Then I read on and glanced over the map. My geographical knowledge was poor. It hadn't been taught at school, and such studies had no place in most professions. I zoomed in, searching the red zone, and saw that the epicentre of the outbreak was the Falkland Islands.

'You reading this, Sav?' Archie appeared in my doorway. He looked concerned yet more well-rested than usual.

My mouth was hanging open in disbelief. I gestured for him to come in and shut the door. 'Do they know? Do they know that's where we're headed?'

'I sent the government department all my modelling trajectories on Friday. I'll email to remind them, but their news sources are still saying we're headed for South Africa. They're wrong. I've checked it all again and I know they're wrong.'

'Shit.' I pondered this for a moment, disbelief giving way to concern. 'This could be really bad.'

'It certainly could. And they've no samples on The Raft, so we can't even make a vaccine. They're saying it could be worse than the last bird flu.'

'Another pandemic. I don't think I can cope with this.' I held my head in my hands. Years of health control, concreting everything, eradicating everything. All this time we had been so clean, it was hard to get my head around such a leap backwards.

'Hey relax, Prof.' Archie lightened his tone. I could hear its falseness. 'We're still miles away. We've got at least a month before we're in penguin territory. They'll think of something.'

'I hope so. Shit, Archie, I really hope so. A month isn't long.'

'I mean it, Sav, don't worry. You know how quickly they can develop medicines now, and there'll be plans in place to divert us, if needed. The drones are on it. And look on the bright side: a pandemic should free up some housing for you.'

I gasped. 'Oh, that's seriously bad taste, Archie.'

He smiled and shrugged, and I tried to laugh along with him. We still had time, like he said, no need to panic yet. I put my concerns to one side for the time being.

'Let's talk about more pressing matters,' I said.

'What can I do for you? More hacking?'

'No. You can tell me how your date was.'

'Ah. No,' he said, but he couldn't hide his smile. He beamed.

'Still not telling. Except to say I had a lovely weekend.'

'A whole weekend? Wow, sounds serious.'

'Taking it slow, you know how it is.'

'Not too slow, I hope, you're not getting any younger.'

'Hey! I'm in my prime.'

'And her?'

'She definitely is.' He grinned.

At that moment, a new public service announcement pinged up. The drones had detected and disposed of an insect on The Raft. So it wasn't just one cockroach, then! Also, a bird had been seen on the water not too far away. It had been shot, and no contamination issues were expected. The drones and army were all on high alert.

'Wonder if the interns will turn up today with this news?'

'Take a look.' He pointed out my office window. 'Most are just arriving. They're a good bunch this year.'

'Oh man, imagine if they had an inkling of how bad it could be.'

'I think a lot have an idea. It's just a bit abstract, like when your folks told you about how they used to play with ropes or something weird. It just doesn't register.'

'Play with ropes?' I had to chuckle.

'I dunno. It's all I could think of. Parents said weird stuff, anyway.'

'Seriously, Archie, you have no idea. My dad actually liked vermin, remember?'

'Yeah, sorry, must be weird for you when stuff like this comes up in the news.'

I shook my head. 'It's like he's haunting me. If he were still alive, he'd be out looking for the filth to bring it home.'

'Crazy. I can't imagine.'

'Seemed normal when I was a kid,' I said. 'It's only as I grew up that I realised how disturbed he was. He wasn't a bad man, just unable to adapt.'

'Well, let's hope these interns can.'

'Definitely. Although if they all went home, I wouldn't be too disappointed. One actually cried when the scales wouldn't turn on the other day.'

'Blimey,' said Archie, 'They've got some growing up to do.'

'Same every year. They seem to be a bit more self-motivated than usual, though. I don't think any have even wet themselves yet.'

Archie went to his office to contact whoever he could about The Raft's trajectory. It niggled at me, but wasn't worth worrying about yet. As Archie said, we had weeks, and I had enough to do.

I looked through the news to find my vitamin press release, only to discover it wasn't there. After rifling through emails, I realised I had never sent it. *Microbes!* Greg would be furious if he found out. Luckily, with these headlines, it was quite plausible that they wouldn't publish until tomorrow, anyway. I read through it again and spotted a couple of mistakes. Pleased I'd had time to perfect it, I sent it off.

Work was frustrating; I felt directionless and was unsure what research to pursue. I didn't want to nag Archie about the water-pollution reports. I knew he wouldn't forget, it was just a waiting game until he could get hold of the information. However, I felt stuck without it. If that showed up something, it would be the obvious direction for research. Without it, anything else seemed like a waste of time. My gut instinct was that it would show something, but scientific research needs more than a feeling.

So, I spent the morning walking the lab and talking with the interns and Marcus. Intern four, Mabel, had continued her initiative research and concluded nothing of use so far, but was focusing on hormone levels and vitamin absorption. *Not a total waste of time*, I thought. The other interns were all data-inputting, the mind-numbing work I could never face doing. I had a few words with the interns, looking over their shoulders and inspecting their work, peering at their monitors in exaggerated fashion to look for mistakes.

On these patrols I liked to walk slowly, purposefully, with louder footsteps than usual. I loved how rigid and sweaty they all became as I loitered to observe their efforts. The tension, a little ripple of panic as they dropped something, their voices reduced to a stutter. Everyone loves feeling powerful once in a while, even those who are totally powerless. The average human is a weak and feeble creature, breakable in every sense. But before we break, we bend. Sometimes it's nice to feel like I'm the one putting the pressure on. Lurking in that moment before the buckle and break. I like to watch them squirm and crumple. The sweat pooling in their hairline, the bottom lip quivering, hands shaking. I'm unkind, I know. We all get our kicks somewhere. It's the best way to weed out the weak ones. There's no room for fragility in this line of work. The pressure is on, always. Results are required. There is too much competition from a thousand other competent young scientists. Academia is cheap, a backbone is not.

After this unproductive yet satisfying day, I left work early.

I walked home to the same buzzing as my morning commute. The drones were still circling, the ferocity of a thousand propellors shaking windowpanes and making the smoke from the long chimney swirl, its orange marbling against the

229

darkening sky, more foreboding than comforting. The buzz was a deafening threat.

I arrived home to find Grace panic-stricken with the news, like the buzzing and rattling had shaken her bones. She held her hands to her ears every time a drone passed. A particularly loud one dawdled at our window, its glassy eye assuming filth was lurking everywhere. It made my skin crawl, making me think of buzzing insects invading our home.

I comforted Grace and told her not to worry, that the sheer abundance of surveillance should be reassuring. The drones were merely being thorough.

'It's a good thing,' I said. 'They'll find every invasive scrap of non-human life this way. We're safe.'

I didn't dare tell her about The Raft's trajectory. Her shoulders relaxed as I spoke, only slightly, and she blinked away some tears. We sat on the sofa, her in my arms as I stroked her hair. 'We're fine, we're safe,' I said. 'It's all precautionary.' I couldn't tell her what I knew. She was better off in the dark.

The invasiveness of the searches, the looming presence of drone cameras, looking into every window, watching us as if we were the filth, was alarming, and Grace's fretting was understandable. I hid my concerns. This level of alert was way beyond what we would expect for a single bird or bug. The machines should have been blasting the birds away from the Falklands; it seemed an overreaction to patrol our own sanitised shores so thoroughly. The press releases were uplifting, commending the military for their swift response. No corner left unsearched. Every crevice and crack would be scrubbed and rid of filth. Every inch of The Raft watched. The street sprayers upped their dosage and the treatment hubs would be open around the clock to dish out any required therapies. Anyone eligible could get their happy-pill prescription fast-tracked. We were safe, they said. *Everyone is safe now.*

That evening Grace told me she'd been researching the Poison Maker. With shaking breaths and trembling voice, she told me she had been searching for information only to find it all deleted as quickly as it was written, just like Archie. She hushed her voice as a drone came to the window. The soulless spy lurked there for longer than felt comfortable. She said she'd read something that implied the Poison Maker was behind the bird flu, or that they had some birds somewhere that they released to cause panic and attempt to spread disease. All hearsay, the sort of thing you could read anywhere if you searched the depths of the internet for long enough, I was sure of that. Several articles backed up this theory, she said, but of course they had disappeared by the time I was home.

She noted my lack of surprise when she mentioned the name.

'It's well known, the name,' I said.

'So it's true?'

'Just gossip, people wanting to scare others. Archie is looking into it.'

'Archie?' Her worry lines softened.

'Only out of curiosity, we're not worried. Not at all. It's all nonsense, but he always follows leads. You know how good Archie is, how thorough. If there's any truth to it, he'll find it.'

I saw the tension in her face ease when I mentioned his name. If anyone could figure it out, Archie could. 'You'll tell me whatever you find out? You'll let me know?' she said.

The maps Archie had shown me were vivid in my mind, that red zone we were headed straight for. I knew I couldn't tell her. She was too delicate, her mental state prone to shattering. I had to keep her in the dark, protect her for as long as possible. 'Of course I will,' I lied.

A drone passed our window again, a little further away, so the rattle was less severe. 'At least they're responding,' she said.

I wished I could turn off the news, to stop her reading or investigating by herself. I wished I could put some old recording on repeat and fool her into thinking everything was going to be okay. But she read the headlines, and searched the articles every hour. My words of reassurance were a whisper against the screams of the National Press.

23

Chapter 22

I awoke at sunrise the next morning to the continued whirring of the drones, and my walk to work was once again escorted by their relentless percussive buzz. If people didn't panic at the news, the incessant noise would make sure of it.

The headlines said that someone had spotted another bird offshore and it had been shot. My skin crawled to think that so many creatures still existed. The useless beings consuming our air, their biomass leeching off the planet, spreading their diseases. The news even showed a picture of one. It was even more disgusting than the cockroach. I remembered the months when the birds went crazy and tore at human skin. The last few scavengers on our shores went mad and turned on any other living thing they could find. They attacked people outside, flew through open windows, pecking out eyes and ripping away flesh, their last onslaught on humankind. Driven by starvation or simple derangement? Watching them bash their bloodied heads against the window made me believe the latter. Those beaks looked like nothing more than weapons.

The one in the picture was called a gull. It had evil eyes and a pointed beak like a machete. To think millions of them used to fly around our lands. Huge, obscene creatures, shitting wherever they liked, intimidating, mutated webbed feet strutting around. 'Kill the lot of them,' I whispered when I saw the photo. 'Every last one.'

I scrolled and found my press release for the vitamin infusion. They had printed a picture of me, the selfie I had taken when I went to the Centre. I looked polished and professional. My skin looked smooth, healthy, and my voluminous hair shone. The editor had decided on the headline himself.

Breakthrough Vitamin Formula Will Solve the Nation's Health Problems.

The hyperbole made me cringe. That wasn't a statement I had made, and the article was full of such remarks. Where I had written 'modest improvement', they had changed it to 'marked improvement'. It contained exaggerated claims about fighting deficiencies. There were no outright lies, but instead of changing my data percentages, they simply omitted them. The scientific paper would be out the next month with a breakdown of the data. The inflation in the article would become apparent soon enough. I just hoped it would be forgotten by then. This sort of language might be okay for the general public, especially when the nation needed good news. The scientific community preferred accuracy, however. I rubbed my temples, embarrassment and anger giving me a headache. Twisting my words made me look like a charlatan, like I was marketing beauty products rather than a scientific formula.

When I got to the office, I emailed Greg and the editor Peter to air my annoyance. I received their replies quickly:

The article is great. We felt this version was a more accurate representation of what this means to the public.
   Peter

Looks fine to me.
   Greg

Simple as that. My concerns were not legitimate, it seemed. No one was concerned about the extravagant language, so long as it made for better reading. The newspaper preferred gossip over facts.

As I read the rest of the news, I started to doubt everything: the bird threat, the government's actions, the level of sterility. I tried to shake the feeling, but all of it, I realised, could be inflated, exaggerated, downgraded or brushed aside. It was like Grace had said: 'those words are more toxic than the fish'.

It's regulated, I told myself. *The Minister of Impartiality does her job well.* This wasn't some dark-web rag reporting on the likes of the Poison Maker. This was the National Press. It was normal to add a bit of hyperbole, I concluded. The facts remained the same.

* * *

Archie arrived late that morning, running into the lab and straight to my office. Breathless, he closed the door behind him.

'You remember my friend?'

'Morning, Archie.'

'Yes, morning, this is important. My friend?' he said, panting and wiping sweat from his brow.

'How's your tomorrow?'

'Uncertain. Come on, Sav, I've run all the way here! Stop with the formalities. This is important. So, my friend—'

'I thought I was your only friend. Or are you talking about your mystery woman?'

'No.' He held his chest and caught his breath. 'Just listen! I got some data from my friend about the water pollution.'

'Oh, that friend. Great, what have you got?' Time to stop winding him up.

'I couldn't send you the email, had to delete it sharpish. It's high-clearance stuff. Would have taken a lot of dodgy backdoor snooping for me to get this myself. I printed it. Look.'

He handed me sheets of paper. I took them and skimmed the printed details. In red were the cadmium levels.

'Cadmium? How is that so high?' I asked, alarmed. It seemed so strange. 'It's not like we're burning anything anymore.'

'But we are. There are chimneys, and the filters might not be working as well as we're told. And that's not all. Look.'

'Perfluoroalkyl and polyfluoroalkyl substances. PFAS. Okay, I'll need to put this into a search engine.'

'I've done that already. They're chemicals made in some manufacturing. Not so many processes these days, but lots before—and when they get in the water, they stay there. They seem to have been getting more concentrated over the years. And look, even the sulphur dioxide levels are higher than is safe.'

'This is crazy.' I scowled at the data. 'How can this not be public knowledge? Is nothing being done about it?'

'It's being monitored. Every three months they get more data. As far as treatments, I can't find anything. Desalination plants are being built all the time, but I can't find what they're dealing with besides salt.'

I flicked through the pages again. 'How can that be? This is a massive public health issue. A bird being shot miles off the coast is all over the news and we have dangers like these in our own water. How are we meant to make the nation healthy when they're ingesting these pollutants?'

'Seems weird, doesn't it? This should be top priority. This is way more important than the penguins. Maybe it is being addressed, and the action is so top secret I can't find it. But since the levels are getting stronger, that seems unlikely.' He sat on the corner of my desk and leaned in. 'You know, some of these pollutants can seriously affect fertility, too.'

My jaw dropped. 'That explains a lot. No amount of hormone therapy can punch through that contamination.' I was stunned. 'Do you think the Centre are doing this? I mean, levels are increasing, they say the population is high. Are they making us infertile?'

'Woah, Prof.' He held up his hands. 'That's a level of cynicism way beyond even me.'

I nodded and frowned. 'Archie, I don't know what to do with this.'

'Nothing. Absolutely nothing,' he replied, shaking his head. 'This is way over your head and way over my clearance level. We're in deep shit if they know we've even got this information. Use it for your research, but otherwise sit on it.'

'Maybe I'll try to get a news article written on this. I'll say I have a theory and want to investigate water pollution. It seems like something the public should know about.'

'Be careful, for both our sakes. Say you're curious but not that you know anything at all. We'd get more than a slap on the wrist for this.'

He was right, as always. I knew he was, that damned gift of his. Stumbling across high-clearance government data would not be explainable to someone from the Centre. Saying I had a hunch based on research, maybe that would get me access to the data in a legitimate way. Either way, I'd try to make the research and vitamin formula fit these figures. I felt a degree of elation knowing that my infusion wasn't bad. It just had some other variables to contend with. But the high levels, secrecy, and inaction were baffling. At least I had some direction and explanation for my results so far. The ground was shaky. I had to tread carefully.

I took intern four and two of the more resourceful interns to one side and asked them to focus their research on modelling vitamin absorption with the pollutants. Except I didn't call them pollutants. I just named the chemicals and said to increase absorption in their presence. They seemed happy to have some more direction, and delighted to be singled out. If they were concerned, they didn't show it. I updated their non-disclosure agreements accordingly. They couldn't speak to anyone, not even Greg, about their lines of research. They hid their discomfort with that, if they felt any. These three had barely quivered when I stood over their shoulders. Harder-to-intimidate interns were more likely to stick to their NDA, I rationalised. They could hold their nerve. They wouldn't break under pressure to reveal what they knew. It wouldn't take a genius to figure out why I wanted them to direct their research towards ancient pollutants, and if they didn't know what that implied, then they soon would. Their discretion was crucial.

I spent the rest of the day writing the article. It was not a long piece, only highlighting the potential issues, being careful not to disclose Archie or any actual evidence I had to hand. Speculative, inviting, implying suspicion, no hysteria: just an educated guess and a request for further information since, after the recent water contamination risk with the wave, the public may have wanted to know more. If the public got behind the theory, the people at the top would have to let us study it. They couldn't brush a public outcry under the carpet. I searched online government resources and found no mention of water pollution, only that they were monitored as part of the Great Sterilisation Project. This highlighted a legitimate question next to the results. It was only natural a scientist would want that blank page filled. Then I had an idea, and searched for both water pollutants and the Poison Maker. It came up blank. Whatever the stories were about this villain, infecting the water supply had yet to become one of them.

Mid-afternoon, I sent the article to Greg and Peter, citing my own initiative and public interest. I received no reply. *Got to be a good thing*, I told myself. Maybe they were actually reading what I'd written instead of morphing my words to reflect their own ideals.

'Any news from the boss?' Archie enquired, armed with a cup of MimikTea.

'Nothing yet. I guess no news is good news?'

'Maybe he's just in awe of your genius.'

I laughed. 'Perhaps.'

'Another bird, though. That's three in two days. But at least the water is okay. Did you see that bottled water was back to normal price and the tap stuff is fine to drink? The factory can start making the infusion instead. Just in time for the launch.'

'I have enough water stashed in my apartment for weeks. Spent a fortune on it.'

'Keep it for the next time,' said Archie.

'Next time! Are rogue waves going to be a frequent thing?'

'Unlikely. Maybe birds are, though, looking at the news.'

A cold chill inched up my spine. I had been so busy writing the article all morning that I hadn't looked at the press. Its constant, irremovable stream across the bottom of my computer had just become part of the background. I could shut out that noise when I needed to. 'Scary stuff. It's weird there's so many. You'd think we had eradicated all of them.'

'Well, it was only The Raft that killed them all. I guess other countries didn't bother. So there are still populations out there.'

'You check the satellite images, right? You've never mentioned seeing any.'

'Never have, that's why.' He shrugged. 'They're small, tiny on a satellite image. I'd have to zoom in loads and scan every square metre. I guess if there were a few all grouped together, they'd be easier to spot, but I haven't seen any. Which means it's unlikely there are masses of them, just the odd one here and there.'

'I suppose these are from Africa? Or southern Europe?'

'Maybe. When there were loads of them, they migrated.'

'Migrated?'

'Yeah, they flew across the world all the time. They didn't stay on a particular continent.'

'No wonder the plagues spread so much, with germs hitching

a ride on vermin birds. How did anyone survive for so long?'

'Just got used to it, I guess,' he said. 'It could just be that, right now, we're on some old migration route and the ones that are left are passing through. Like us.'

'Like us? Don't make me retch!' I feigned a gag. Being compared to a bird: what could be worse?

Archie rolled his eyes. 'Moving around, stuck in a current, like us.'

'What about the Falklands? Have you looked there?'

'Not close-up footage.' He sipped his MimikTea and made his thinking face, one eyebrow raised and his eyes following upwards, like he was searching his brain. 'Shall we have a peek at the satellite footage?'

'Yes, please!' I jumped to my feet, excited at the distraction. 'Marcus, I'm not to be disturbed,' I shouted across the lab as we walked through.

We sat in Archie's office, where the dripping air con seemed to have worn itself out completely. He logged on to the satellite software and zoomed in. The islands appeared, looking barren.

I let out a breath. 'Well, besides some greenery, they seem nicely desolate.'

He screwed his eyes up as he peered close to the monitor. 'That's a relief... wait.' He pointed at the screen. 'That's not right.'

'How so?'

'That part of the island isn't supposed to be there. It was lost to the sea decades ago,' he said.

'So sea levels have dropped?'

'Don't be daft. Impossible.'

'An old image, then?'

'Let me see.' He moved over to another monitor. 'I'll have

to get into the army systems.'

'Wow, Mr Super Hacker,' I mocked.

It took some time, but he typed his way through various firewalls, and the image reloaded. The live stream came through and, as Archie suspected, the islands looked smaller.

'That's weird,' he said, and leaned in closer to the screen. 'Why would the second-degree clearance cameras be so out of date? They must be decades old.'

'Oversight?'

'No way. Look at the old images. This little blur here. If I zoom in to it... see? To me, that could be a group of birds. None are flying, and since penguins can't fly, that could be penguins.'

I grimaced, but curiosity dwarfed my disgust. 'And on the live stream?'

'I'm looking, I'm looking.' He searched for a few moments. 'None. Not a single bird. I mean, I can keep watching this for a few hours before getting kicked out of the system, but look at the rocks, they're not the same colour. Penguin crap on the old images. On the new ones, it's been washed away.'

'Maybe they've moved? Relocated to mainland South America?'

'Maybe. I'll search, but it'll take a while.'

He searched, and gestured me towards the monitor so I could do it while he rubbed his strained eyes. Then we took a monitor each and searched some more. Several interns knocked asking for help, despite me telling Marcus I was not to be disturbed. I shouted at them to find Marcus or figure it out for themselves. Our search continued but, after many hours, we found not one single penguin.

'We need to tell someone,' Archie said, echoing my thoughts.

'They're panicking about a flu that probably isn't from penguins at all. They're fighting this all wrong. I mean, look here on the new images. There are no big towns, but there is a small population in a few dwellings here, some people outside there. If there was a sickness, everyone would be indoors.'

'Maybe they don't know, or they have to work outside. They might not have a choice. Or the sickness isn't too bad.' I was trying to rationalise, although I knew it sounded all wrong.

'It doesn't add up. It feels like their intel is out of date or just plain wrong. If there's a flu, there's a good chance it's not from birds this time.'

'*If* there's a flu? You think maybe there isn't?'

'I don't know,' Archie said. 'It seems odd that I can't find any penguins. And if we're headed for the Falklands, it's a good way to shut up the pro-anchor people.'

'But drifting was always meant to be temporary.'

Archie smiled at me. 'The most powerful Centres are the ones who wanted the anchors blown up in the first place. You think they've changed their mind and are keen to build new bridges? Nah. They'll say anything to stop that happening. This flu seems way too convenient, if you ask me.'

I rolled my eyes. 'You're getting more cynical by the day. Who's filling your little head with such suspicious thoughts?'

He cleared his throat, ignoring my remark. 'You heard back from Greg or your editor guy yet?'

'No, nothing. Oh microbes! Look at the time.' How was it so late? It was gone five, and I'd done nothing except search satellite images with Archie all afternoon, and had missed several messages from Grace.

'Go home,' he said. 'I'll email someone about this. Not sure who. I don't really want to tell anyone I've been hacking the army's satellites.'

'Okay,' I replied as I made for the door. 'Be careful. I'll see you tomorrow.'

I felt stressed leaving the lab. I craved the sound of rustling paper at the MindSpa, the feeling of a breeze on my face. There was something about the scents they used, a wholesome smell you couldn't find anywhere else. Almost damp and mouldy, in a clean way. Impossible to describe. I think it reminded me of my father and his insect hotel. The bugs gave me the creeps, but the smell was just cosy. And the sounds of the MindSpa, the strange clicks and cheeps, didn't exist anywhere. I think that's why they were so soothing. They took my mind away to another place.

But I had no time. I had to get home to Grace. The headlines had hit her hard and I needed to be there to comfort her, to protect her from her fears.

* * *

The apartment had been scrubbed when I got back. Pine scent was Grace's favourite, manufactured to smell like trees when no one could remember what an actual tree smelled like. Dirty, I imagined. The pine scent, though, was sweet and clean. There's no way a germ-ridden pole sprouting out of some dirt could smell like anything but filth. The scent was still called pine, some homage to the old world and its wasteful biomass. For as long as I could remember, life had had the constant reek of disinfectant, jazzed up with the scents of bygone fruits and leaves.

Grace was pacing the living room. From the state of her, it looked like she'd been doing it all day. She was unkempt, dishevelled, her eyes wet and wide, her socks slipping off her feet and trailing underneath her. Her legs were shaking, exhaustion and worry rippling through her whole body. A mug of MimikTea was cold and abandoned on the table, spillage around it.

'I'm so tired, Sav. I've scrubbed the whole place.' Looking around, I suspected that pouring disinfectant over everything and cleaning wasn't the same. 'This Poison Maker thing, Sav, I think it's really dodgy.' She was gesticulating frantically. 'I can't shake the feeling. It's in my gut, you know, I can't shake it. It's real, I just know it is. And this bird, these birds, this flu—I think it's all connected.' She wiped nervous tears from her eyes. 'There's loads of information about it. I was looking on the dark web, but stuff pops up on regular searches as well. For a moment, anyway. I think he's doing it, or she, them, whoever. They're going to poison us all. That must be what they're planning with the birds. It's not just coincidence.'

Her panic was palpable. 'Careful what you're looking for,' I said. 'You're not using your work computer, are you?' I tried to nudge the subject in another direction.

'No, of course not. Of course not. But look. Look. I took photos of the sites before they got taken down.'

She handed me her phone. I took it and sat down to read. Pages and pages on the unregulated press detailed what they believed the Poison Maker was up to. 'Clever girl.' I kissed her cheek.

'Loads of people are linking this poison thing to the flu, that it's actually a plot to cull us all. And the water—'

'Did you see the news? The water's fine now, the rogue wave

didn't affect it. And everything else is just hearsay. There's nothing in the National Press.' I hoped my casual tone would calm her down.

'I knew you'd say that. I knew it. I don't want to say bad things about your new job, but the press is owned by Blue Liberation, you know. All of it. Maybe not directly, but they own the companies that own the press. Look.' She scrolled to a photo on her phone, an article that showed the hierarchy of the press. It was likely to be true and no great surprise. Blue Liberation owned everything.

'It's how it's always been. I mean, they own the ArbAirs, the bloody air we breathe. I'm not saying it's right, but it's nothing new. And it doesn't mean they're the Poison Maker, if that's what you're getting at. They're not going to just stand back and watch us die or kill us. It's not in their interests.'

'What if they are trying to kill us? The Perimeter?'

'That would be daft. They're not that stupid. Who would make their food and medicines? Think about it logically.' I stood and hugged her. Her rigid frame was damp with perspiration. She pushed me away and started pacing again. 'I think there's something in this Poison Maker thing, I really do,' I said. 'But I think it has to be someone less scrupulous than the government. Archie is looking into it. I promise, we'll find out what's going on. And in the meantime, we're safe.' I went to her again and took hold of her. This time she relaxed into my embrace, her tired arms flopping over me, and I led her to the sofa. She nuzzled into my neck.

'It just seems scary, you know? Like it's all going to start up again. I can't lose anyone else. I can't lose you,' Grace said.

I held her tight. 'It's fine. We're going to be fine.' I kissed her forehead. 'Where on earth did you come across this Poison

Maker thing, anyway?'

'It just popped up somewhere. Nowhere specific.'

Neither of us could eat much that night. I had too much going through my mind and Grace, exhausted as she was, was still visibly fretting. I had calmed her slightly, and she trusted me to take care of her. But it was the future she worried about. The future for the child we hadn't even conceived yet, the world it would be born into. About our abilities as parents if it turned bad again.

Her eyes twitched restlessly and her brow furrowed with apprehension. But there was an exquisiteness to her unease. The years had been kind to her face, her features still soft, her golden hair shiny, her skin serene. Her inner candle burnt tentatively, though, and right then it seemed close to extinguished.

We put the telly on and curled up together. I knew her so well, I sometimes felt I could read her thoughts. Even when she said she wasn't worried, if she was trying to hide it, I knew it. She'd wrap a ringlet of hair round her little finger and tug on it, or bite the inside of her cheek. She wasn't one to make eye contact often, but when her emotions were at their extremes, she looked directly into my eyes. I wondered if she was as perceptive about me; she knew me so well, after all. I hoped she wasn't. I think I was better at hiding my worries than her, and with everything Archie and I had read that day, I was worried.

Chapter 23

The following morning, Greg sent a reply about the article I wanted to write:

What the hell is that meant to mean? No, you can't write an article telling the whole Raft the water is polluted. My company will not be the source of a Raft-wide panic. I'll tell you when you can write a story.
   Greg

Well, that was fairly predictable. I was angry at myself for asking him. I should have just written it and sent it off. By the time I got to work, I had decided that was exactly what I would do. Irritated by Greg's reply, and the heat, and the drones, I had little patience left. I decided to tip off the papers anonymously and hope they'd do their own investigating. It could end my career, I knew that. But it could also make it, if I could investigate freely and find a miracle infusion to work around the problem.

On my walk to work, the strip billboards gave our safety score as three out of five. Bird-flu updates were the main feature. One more bird had been shot, with the flu currently contained in South America. Every billboard told the same story until they flashed to reveal a breaking news article:

Raft Trajectory Updated. We Are Headed for the Falkland Islands, South America.

They must have seen Archie's research and known he was right. To announce it like this, though, among all the bird-flu stuff? The panic would be a lot worse than my story about the water, I was sure of it. I ran the final few blocks to work, as fast as I could manage, with burning lungs and sweat dripping from me. For the first time in my career, I didn't even stop by the Selfie Station. My one-hundred-percent loyalty score would have to suffer.

Archie was already in when I got there. In fact, he looked like he hadn't been home.

'You seeing this?' I asked. He didn't turn around to greet me. 'Your research must have caught someone's eye.'

'It's not mine,' he said.

'What?'

'The trajectory doesn't match my modelling, and I traced the email I sent. It didn't go anywhere. I mean, it was read and dismissed, but not forwarded. They never listen to me. This is someone else's work. It's not even correct. My modelling says we'll get there in two months. This has it down much sooner, only that's impossible.' He was scratching his head. On the desk next to him were several mugs of undrunk MimikTea.

'So, who leaked it?'

'Honestly, no idea. I'm trying to find out. I need to tell them they're wrong. It's most likely the military, but their security was rerouted overnight.'

'You think they know you were looking?'

'Probably,' he said and shrugged. 'They won't know it was me, only that someone got in.' He finally turned to face me. His eyes were puffy, his face drawn with sleeplessness. 'You hear from the big man yet?'

'Greg? Yep. Told me to shut up, basically.'

'He always is so articulate.'

'I'm thinking I'll write the article anyway, anonymously. Not a whole article, just tip off the press. Hopefully, they'll do their own research.'

'Are you mad?' His eyebrows rose so high they lifted the bags under his eyes. 'If they find out it's you, your career is over. Your family is over.'

'It needs to be known. Researching this could save the nation's health problems. It's crazy that this is going on and no one is saying it.'

'Sav, seriously.' He held up his hands. 'You're not going to change the world, you're only going to screw yourself. The Centre will close ranks and you'll be on the outside, branded as some anarchist, and before you know it, you'll be living in a squat somewhere, starving to death.' I rolled my eyes at his drama. Archie saw it and said, 'Remember what happened to your dad?'

'Don't bring my dad into this. That was totally different.' It was. He would never have understood. He would have saved that hideous cockroach.

'The powerless are even more so now. Things have got worse, not better. Your dad didn't toe the line, so he was out. His career never recovered and your mum starved to death.'

'Shut it, Archie, seriously.' How dare he compare me to my father!

'I'm serious. If you want to go against instructions from the Centre, question their safety standards publicly, you'll learn very quickly that the likes of you and I are nothing to them. They'll spit you out and you'll be destitute.'

'My dad was fighting for a crap cause.' My voice was a little too loud. 'What I'm researching is important. I'm nothing like him and this is so much more important than the bugs he was obsessed with. I'm a scientist, he was pretty much an Alternate.'

'He was respected in his field once.' Archie sighed. 'Look, use the info to improve your work in the lab. That's how you can make a difference. Trust me.'

I said nothing in reply and stormed out, slamming the door behind me. Two interns dropped some glassware in shock. *Idiots!* I stomped into my office, grinding my teeth, and kicked my desk. How dare he bring up my father, and liken me to him, of all things? My dad's ideals were archaic, filthy nonsense. He wasn't trying to help anyone, just his own interests. Trying to save bugs and creepers rather than help the world. My work was totally different. I was trying to help people, not stupid bugs and their filth.

Archie meant well, and by the time I'd cooled off, I felt bad for storming out and not listening to him. I dropped by his office a while later with a cup of MimikTea and some VitaBiscuits as an apology, but he'd gone.

I didn't write to the press. Instead, I wrote what I wanted to say, then just saved it. I couldn't bring myself to click send. Archie was right, I knew that. Grace had to be my priority, and such actions could destroy her. I looked over the paperwork he had given me. I trawled through the data again. Some levels were so high. How was this not being addressed? There were no reports on the previous year, so maybe it was new. It would certainly explain my vitamin research's suboptimal results. Maybe Grace was right, and it was the Poison Maker leaking all this junk into the water. That seemed unlikely, surely it was just remnants of the old world, their filth lingering in ways we hadn't yet thought of.

The interns had thinned out, as expected. Maybe half were left now. The news, my patrolling the lab, the tedium of what a lot of the job actually entailed, their panicked parents. It was always the same, every year. I felt no remorse for them. I wasn't there to sugar coat life and wrap them in cotton wool. The ones who remained appeared busy and engaged with their tasks. The clinking of glass, the soft whirr of the burners, the odd timer beeping, all telling me that work was being done and results were possible. These were always the better candidates. Strength, resilience, and determination were the characteristics we needed. The weak ones could go work in the protein labs.

I had an email from Penny that I deleted before even reading it. The last thing I needed was moaning from her. It wasn't long before I heard Marcus's tame knock at my door. I sighed and told him to come in.

'Sorry to disturb you, Professor. Just to let you know that the ones who aren't in today... well, they're not coming back.'

'As expected, Marcus. Thank you for letting me know.'

'Also... one more thing.'

'Yes?'

'The task you gave some of the interns, to look into cadmium and other... chemicals, I suppose, is the best word.' He cleared his throat. 'It's caused a bit of worry, you see. They're quite upset about what that may mean.'

'Is it hindering them from completing their work?' I barked. My impatience was on autopilot.

'No, no, they're very good workers. It's just, perhaps a bit more clarity would help?'

'Fine,' I said through gritted teeth. 'What it means is, we need to investigate all possible reasons as to why absorption is suboptimal, and that is one area of research I think would be sensible to pursue. Let's not leave any stone unturned. Apologies for the filthy metaphor.'

'Okay, Professor, thank you.' He turned to leave.

'Marcus,' I called after him. 'Tell them they're all doing a great job, or something to that effect.'

I felt frustrated that I couldn't share what I knew, but it was best to keep the interns motivated rather than scare them. Maybe we'd think of something to combat this and we could make a real difference. As Archie had said, that was my skill set, that was my job. That was where I should concentrate my efforts. I did not want to be the cause of any panic. Imagine if The Raft refused to drink the water en masse. The short-term expense of Rogueless Water was bad enough. There was enough fear among people right now.

Over lunch, the lab emptied more than usual. It seemed overly quiet in its abandoned state. Perhaps it was just Archie's presence I missed. He never left the lab during the day. I'd never known him go out for lunch and I was worried he was mad at me. He arrived back early afternoon, smiling a lot more than in the morning. He greeted me with no animosity at all.

'Afternoon, Prof, you're looking a little lost.'

'Where did you go?'

'Just out for lunch.' His tone was particularly breezy.

'You never go out for lunch,' I said with a scowl. He shrugged, still smiling. 'Oh, my god!' My jaw dropped. 'You went on a lunch date!'

'Shh. Nothing wrong with that,' he said as he glanced over his shoulder, his cheeks flushed with... what was that? Guilt? Secrecy?

'Oh man.' I slapped my forehead as I realised. 'You're shagging someone here! It's not Penny, is it?' He grimaced. 'Tell me it's not an intern.'

'What? N-no. I mean no, of course not.' His cheeks were ablaze.

'You are! How red is your face? Bloody hell, Archie, that's a bit dodgy isn't it? Which one is it?'

'I-I'm not.' He stumbled over his words.

'You bloody liar. Well, if you don't tell me, I'll have to make my assumptions. I reckon it's that one with missing front teeth. Intern eight.'

'It's not her.'

'Ah ha!' I pointed my finger at him. 'So it is one of them. Spill!'

'Alright, alright. But please don't say anything,' he said and I nodded. 'Intern seven.'

'Seven? The blond beauty?' I gasped, unable to hide my surprise. 'Very nice. She's produced some good writeups, too.'

'Yup. Beauty and brains.'

'I'm actually impressed. With you, not with her, I mean... what is she thinking?'

'Quite how I got so lucky I've no idea. I guess she likes a proper gentleman, a man with experience.'

I laughed. 'If she wants experience, I suppose she is most interested in your right hand?' He feigned offence. 'Okay, I'm making tea and you're going to tell me everything.'

And he did: about their date in the bar, their conversations and how cool and calm he was (yeah, right!), about the crazy drinks, and her tattoo. I got through two cups of MimikTea listening to him. His reports were inflamed with testosterone and self-worth. Even the likes of Archie were led by their hormones.

'How did that organisation not come up in her background check?' I asked.

'They meet in person. In bars. They talk face to face, never online. They're not anarchists or anything.'

'But it's her who told you about the Poison Maker?'

'Yeah.'

'That reassures me it's nonsense, at least. Some illicit anti-government protest group idea, that's all.'

'Hey, she's not daft, or some radical,' he said. 'They're just nostalgic, I guess. They want a bit more freedom.'

'Nostalgic for something from before they were even born? Unlikely. They're just too young to remember the bad old days caused by the good old days. Well, if one good thing comes out of this bird-flu scare, it'll be that it wakes them up a bit.'

'Maybe,' he said.

I thought for a moment. 'So, this young free-thinker has bagged herself a man with high internet clearance, one of the best hackers on The Raft.' I mimicked Archie's thinking face.

'Lucky her.'

'Just be careful, Archie. I don't want you getting hurt.'

'I've got nothing to lose and everything to gain,' he said.

'Even Grace is upset about the Poison Maker thing. It seems

like someone is trying to incite hysteria.'

'Shit, you told her?'

'No, she told me,' I said. 'Last night she took photos of all these websites before they got shut down.'

'Clever girl.'

'That's what I said.' I grinned. 'Loads of people are saying this Poison Maker caused the bird flu. They'll probably claim it's the Poison Maker who made The Raft head for the Falklands next.'

'That would be a bit far-fetched,' Archie said.

'You told anyone it's wrong yet?'

'Emailed the same desk as before. There's not much more I can do.'

'You told them about the satellite images?'

'I'm not suicidal. Hopefully someone else will spot it. I can't be the only one with a brain on The Raft.' He swallowed hard. 'You haven't emailed anyone about the water pollution, have you?'

'No. And I'm sorry I was cross. You're right, it would be suicide.' It felt good to apologise, even though Archie never held a grudge.

'I'm sorry too,' he said. 'I shouldn't have said that about your family.'

'It's the truth. Not eloquent, but the truth.'

'I'm glad you've had second thoughts, anyway. It'd be crap around here without you.'

'Don't be daft. You've got intern seven to keep you amused.' We laughed.

* * *

Grace sent a few messages over the rest of the day, their length and frequency showing me how worried she was. The trajectory news was terrifying for her and everyone. My promises to keep her safe seemed redundant when the news was full of such peril. Classes finished early that day and she got an Autocar to visit Maisie. I was pleased that she was out of the house and had someone else to talk to. She seemed so much more content after their last meeting, and they'd been emailing in the meantime. The relationship seemed good for her. The grandmother idea had given her a new lease of life, a glimmer of light in her otherwise desolate thoughts. There was no news from the fertility clinic, though. I replied to Grace, reminding her it had only been a few days since she added Maisie's referral to our application. I doubted anyone had even looked at the updates yet. Give it a couple of weeks, I assured her. She messaged with an address, saying a new development was going up that she'd just seen from the Autocar, further from the edge. It might be worth checking out, just in case.

It was then that my email pinged with a message from Greg:

New development being built, address below. Go write about what great progress this is. The Raft needs good news.
  Greg

This fortunate coincidence meant I could leave the lab early. I considered going all the way to Maisie's first, to meet up with her and Grace, but decided against it. Grace needed some time with her, and didn't want me intruding. I left her to it for now. I would meet Maisie some other time.

Chapter 24

The new development was sizeable and not overly picturesque in its current state of rubble and scaffolding. Being more central, the smog was thin, and the building looked clean. The dusty smell came from the building site rather than pollution. With a degree of imagination, I could visualise how the completed project would fit in. Just another boxy building to add to the long line of boxy buildings. I had my phone camera, but nothing more technical. I kicked myself for not picking up one of the proper cameras from Greg's office. Not that I knew how to use them; my photography skills started and ended with a Selfie Station. Still, I figured that if I took enough shots from different angles, one at least would be passable.

It was impossible to tell from the plans what had been there before. Through the fencing and the RenterRafts Developments posters, I could see that half of the site had been demolished and new concrete blocks had been laid. The part of the old building that remained gave me some clues. It was a low structure, just one storey, with an old-fashioned pointed roof. The windows were divided into segments by metal frames with ornate designs. The bare brick was chipped and crumbling, no trace of any cladding or render, so I assumed it had never had any. That gave me an idea as to the date. All buildings were rendered as a necessity after the anchors blew, because the air became saltier and the wind less predictable. It was a wonder this building had lasted so long.

I tried an internet search on the area but found nothing that gave me any clues. I assumed there would be a construction crew around to ask, but could see no one. The site had an eerie, deserted feeling to it, barren, like some unfinished business. I didn't write that down for the article. It would sound stupid. The staff had merely left work early that day. Scared by the headlines, probably. Not exactly newsworthy.

The half of the site with new foundations laid was already a few storeys high, the concrete outline revealing a mix of one- and two-bed apartments. I emailed the agent straight away, thinking there was a chance I could get a viewing. I mentioned I was there writing an article about the development for the National Press, just to remind them who I was. Maybe it would help. Maybe they'd think I would write more favourably if they turned up or offered me a viewing. Fat chance, but worth a shot.

There wasn't much I could write without knowing the history of the place. It's hard to write about progress when you don't know the starting point. So, after wandering around the edge of the build, getting hot and frustrated, peering through the fence and gazing up at the scaffolding, I decided to be reckless and cross the fence. Quite why, I don't know. My desire for rule-breaking with tipping off the press about the water pollution had maybe ignited some dormant, rebellious side. Still, I was nothing like my father, I reminded myself. I was on a quest for answers, for the truth. He was on a quest for self-destruction. He would have pocketed that cockroach instead of squashing it.

Metal cage fencing enclosed the development, but there was a small gap that I wriggled through. The site was more central than my apartment. There were no Alternate hangouts for miles, so the developers had little to worry about from squatters and fish junkies invading the place.

I dodged the rubble and tools, squeezing past the cement mixer in front of the main entrance and making my way up to the old walls. Some of the window frames were empty, shards of glass littering the ground. I piled up some bricks to make a step and climbed in. I was buzzing with my recklessness. Dust coated my clothes. I brushed hair out of my face with a chalky hand, and realised I must look a mess. I checked the app for the nearest Selfie Station. Not far. Good, I could hardly go home looking like that.

Once inside, I walked along a corridor until I found a door hanging off its hinges. I moved it out of the way and stepped into the room behind. Afternoon light beamed in, highlighting dancing dust particles. The room was vast, with a higher ceiling than it appeared from the outside, ornate plasterboard and detailing across it and the walls. The floor was a black-and-white tiled pattern, heavily soiled from the rubble and dust. But my pulse quickened when I saw what was inside. I was amazed. It was full of old artefacts and must have once been some old museum or gallery. There was artwork from over a century before, highly collectable objects these days. Posters of garishly dressed men and women, costumes representing fashions that had died out long before the anchors blew up. Paintings and photographs of people from those bygone years with nonsensical quotes such as, '*I Believe in Yesterday*'. A clumsily painted bright-red mouth with the words, '*Lose Your Dreams and Lose Your Mind*'. I recognised another showing the same handsome man with shaggy hair I'd seen in the editor Peter's office, which also displayed the words, '*Whoever Controls the Media Controls the Mind*'. An apt quote for the editor of the National Press office.

The items would have been worth a fortune. I suspected the developer discovered them and saw money bags in front of their eyes. I assumed the building had been abandoned and forgotten for decades, and now this half of the development had stalled while they figured out what to do. Bulldozing ancient artefacts like this wasn't illegal, but anyone with sense would know there were buyers out there. Would it mean delaying the development for a long time? It was something of a frustration.

I paced the room, keeping my grubby hands in my pockets. Blowing the dust off the images revealed more tawdry colours and flashy designs of clothing, laughing faces and a lot of flesh on show. How gaudy it all looked. The eternal grey of the Perimeter hadn't made me colour-blind, more like colour-phobic. I squinted at the visual gluttony, my overloaded head aching from the surplus. Bright designs and patterns appeared as warning signs, revealing the deadliest threats from old nature.

The walls were crumbling, the old decorative paper that used to line them peeling, broken mirrors hung at crooked angles. The flooring was chipped in places and many windows had been smashed. No way had anyone lived here for decades. A lot of the artefacts were made of old-style tree-carcass paper, uncovered and likely untreated with the required disinfectants. I backed away. This property must have been shut away since before the Great Sterilisation Project began. No one these days would be so reckless. But then, I had an old book hidden away. Worse: my father's old book. At one point, it would have been teeming with microscopic filth. I doubted hoarding these old posters could be justified with sentiment, though. There seemed nothing sentimental about such a barrage to the eyes.

I checked my phone, but the agent hadn't messaged me back, so I took some photos and went home. The Selfie Station was only a couple of minutes' walk away. It was poorly stocked, and some filter settings were not functioning. I cleaned myself up, did my end-of-day photo for work, and made my way home in the fading light.

Grace was still out when I got back. I didn't wait up or message her, not wanting to hassle her. In any case, explaining what I'd found at the development site over a message would have been tricky. After a small dinner and a sip of wine, I fell asleep quickly and deeply.

* * *

The following day, I still hadn't been able to show anyone what I had found. Grace was next to me when I woke, sound asleep. She looked peaceful for a rare change, so I didn't wake her, and slipped out of the apartment for work.

'Morning, Prof, how's your tomorrow?' Archie said, sounding even more cheerful than usual.

'Uncertain. But check it out.' I handed him my phone with all the photos of the artefacts.

'Wowsers,' he said with his eyes agape. 'Tell me this is all yours. It must be worth a mint.'

'Sadly, no, it's all at a development site I went to check out.'

'The developers let you in to show you?'

'Not exactly.'

'You bad, bad woman! Professor Selbourne, I never knew you had it in you.'

'Yeah, yeah, alright,' I said, blushing. 'It's interesting though, right? The developers must be pleased.'

'For sure, there's a huge market for this stuff. They're probably looking to sell it all. It's not contraband if it's been cleaned properly. It'll delay the development, though. They're going to have to fumigate the whole place. You didn't touch anything, did you?'

'Of course not. It was all so filthy.'

'Good. Can't imagine that building will be on schedule.' He handed my phone back to me. 'They'll make a profit, so who cares? I doubt they're in a hurry.'

'They must be, though. The waiting list for housing is never-ending.'

'That's weird, isn't it? Amalyn said the same. She's been on the list for a while.'

'Who's Amalyn?' He raised his eyebrows at me in reply. 'Oh, intern seven. Well, it's normal for interns to still live at home. They're very young, you know.' I winked at him.

'Yeah, alright, I am aware of the age gap,' he said, in a way that made me unsure if he was concerned or pleased about it. 'She applied now so that she might have a hope one day.'

'Why is that weird? There are millions of people on The

263

Raft.'

'It's just, they build so much. All the surrounding blocks on that street were built within the last two years. That's literally thousands of apartments. Amalyn reckons—'

'Oh, Amalyn this and Amalyn that.'

'Hey!' He poked me in the ribs. 'She has a head full of ideas about everything. The way she thinks, it's refreshing. Anyway, she reckons they're all just empty, and stay that way.'

'That literally makes no sense at all.'

'Being on the waiting list for a two-bed apartment when thousands are being built also makes no sense.'

'I wonder what all the people in those new blocks did to get an apartment, whose ass they're kissing?'

'Why don't you go ask them?' he said. 'Just knock on their door.' His tone was way too casual for such an unusual idea.

'That's quite intrusive.'

'They all have doorbells and buzzers, don't they?'

'But... but I don't know them,' I said. 'Just knocking on some random person's door...' I shook my head. 'That's too weird.'

'Worth a shot, I reckon.'

I frowned and considered it for a moment. Archie prodded me with his elbow. 'You paying much attention to the lab?'

'Shit, no, what's going on?'

'Nothing bad, just check out Marcus and that intern.'

'Oh, god! Those two? No way!' I held my face in my hands. 'Oh, look at his drool. And he's touching her when he reaches over! Did he learn his flirting skills from Greg?'

'It's been going on for about a week now. You really should pay more attention.'

'I read their writeups. But this?' I winced. 'Eurgh, this is more Penny's department.'

'I don't think there's any need to alert Penny. The intern seems happy. She's actually smiling.'

'That's intern four. May, Mace, Maude... something like that. He did tell me she's very astute. I mean, she doesn't cry daily and seems to have normal bladder function, so he could do worse.' I watched Marcus put his hand on the small of her back and lean in. 'Oh, gross, my father used to have a horrible bug called a leech that was all slimy and could stick to you. He looks like that. Should I say something?'

'And deny the poor guy a bit of affection? Nah, leave them be. She looks very comfortable with the extra attention. See, she's leaning in too.'

'You're on the side of all superiors shagging interns now, I suppose?'

'Just a sucker for an underdog.'

'I wouldn't be mean enough to call Marcus a dog!'

'It doesn't mean that,' said Archie, laughing. 'It just means the guy who doesn't normally win, but who might have a chance.'

'How on earth has that got anything to do with dogs?' Archie shrugged a reply. 'Well, good luck to him, I guess.'

* * *

It's only a knock at the door. Just a knock. No big deal, I said to myself. Couldn't hurt, anyway. It just seemed so indiscreet. Rude, even. I tried to think and couldn't recall ever doing it, certainly not unannounced. The only unexpected knock at the door I could think of was when the officials came to take my dad's bugs away. It was not something anyone would hear without a degree of panic, I was sure. Still, it could be the best way to get answers, and a small moment of panic was unlikely to harm anyone. I had until the end of the day to finish my article, so a return visit to the site would seem normal enough.

When I stepped out of the Autocar, it looked very different. The fence was sealed with an extra metal barrier. There were workmen there now who were patrolling wearing full hazmat gear, including goggles and breathing apparatus, and the whole structure had biohazard tape around it. *What the hell?*

One worker was carrying an e-pad. He appeared to be going through a list.

'Excuse me?'

'What?' he said curtly.

'I'm writing an article on this development for the National Press.' I showed him my press ID on my phone. 'What's going on?'

'It's sealed off for now.'

'Why?'

Despite his breathing gear, his tut was audible. 'Possible contamination, we're not sure. We need to chemically and biologically test the whole site before recommencing works.'

'Are the apartments all spoken for? Will people have their move-in dates delayed?'

'Yes, and yes. All future residents, as far as I know, have been contacted. It should only be a month's delay.'

I tried to hide my disappointment. 'Can you give me any idea of the history of the site? Anything the readers might like to know?'

'As far as I'm aware, it was an old private residence,' he said.

'Really? It's very large for a residence.'

'It's ancient, obviously.'

'Why was it not built on before?'

'Because we're not magicians and can only build so much each year. Are you saying we're not working hard enough?'

I took a step back. 'No, I'm sorry, I didn't mean to imply that.'

'It's likely that the building or the person who owned it had some historical value,' he said with a sigh.

'Who was it?'

'No idea, I'm merely speculating, as it's often the cause for delays.'

'Wait until that person is forgotten to bulldoze their house?'

'That's basically it. Now, if you're finished, I've got work to do.'

I stepped away and made some notes as he walked off.

I looked at the other buildings on the street. Past the fencing around the new development were roads of standard boxy buildings, all completed and fairly new. The air con was a modern version, the render fresh and untarnished, and they looked totally untouched by smog. The barred windows were the usual reflective glass. They could be occupied and nobody would know.

'Sod it,' I said to myself.

When the developer was out of sight, I approached one and buzzed. No answer. I tried another: still no answer. The buzzers were loud on the quiet street and felt intrusive, but I carried on. In the end, I buzzed every single door and there was no answer at all. I tried the next building and the next. All the same. Either the several hundred residents were all out at the same time, or they just didn't answer their buzzers, which seemed highly probable. I genuinely couldn't say if I would come to the door if it were me. Probably I'd use the security camera and judge from that. I checked my appearance with my phone camera. I didn't look threatening. Worthy of an intercom response, anyway. The only other reason was that they were all empty, which seemed ludicrous. My curiosity was spiked.

I checked the agent's website for other new developments completed recently that had been sold, then took an Autocar to three more sites, buzzing every door at each. Not a single answer. I tried to peer through windows and look for signs of life but, with the reflective glass, a view inside was impossible. The unstained bins outside looked new. Baffled, I took an Autocar back to the lab.

On the way, I stopped by a health-testing centre and had my bloodwork done early. If there was some contamination issue at the development, I felt I should be cautious. I was sure they were just fumigating the artefacts, which seemed logical. They could have noticed signs of my trespassing and worried about some issue arising from it. I felt well, so I wasn't worried, and I got the results as I stepped through the front door of the lab. All clear.

26

Chapter 25

Archie was in his office with Amalyn standing close, leaning in. They quickly moved apart as I walked in.

'Ah, the famous Amalyn.'

She blushed. 'Sorry, Professor, I was just checking out some internet thing.'

'"Internet thing." That's a cute nickname she has for you,' I said to Archie.

He scowled. 'How'd it go at the site?' I glanced at Amalyn, saying nothing. 'You might as well talk in front of her,' Archie said, 'she's way ahead of us on such gossip.'

'Okay.' A tingle of nerves crept up my spine as I glanced at Amalyn's face, so young and smooth. The perfect picture of innocence. *I should be cautious here*, I thought. But then, Archie trusted her, I reminded myself, and he would have done a lot of background checks. So, I told them about the development being sealed off and no one coming to the doors.

'The Golden Fifty have buzzed those doors before, several times,' said Amalyn. 'There's never any answer. I'm telling you, they're ghost apartments.'

'Ghost apartments?'

'Empty,' she said matter-of-factly. 'No one ever answers.'

I shook my head. 'That makes no sense. Maybe the residents are too old or disabled to get to the door?'

Amalyn shrugged. 'Old people don't move into new apartments. They stay put.'

I had no response. She was right. It made no sense.

'It's true,' Amalyn said. 'Thousands and thousands of empty apartments.'

'That can't be the case. Look, you're too young to remember—'

'Hey!' Archie and Amalyn protested in unison.

'I don't mean it in a condescending way,' I said, holding my hands up in defence. 'It's just that I remember when the population density exploded, and everyone migrated away from the extremes of the country before they collapsed into the sea. A lot of the land that broke away was farmland and solar fields, so that all had to move inland, too. Remember, Archie?'

He nodded. 'Yes, but the pandemics—'

'Sure, they dented the population significantly, but fertility rates were still just about okay and so numbers bounced back. The hormones from filth farming bled into the water like ruptured arteries, but hadn't made everyone infertile yet. People were grieving and, in their despair, bred like the filthy rodents that once roamed the dirt.'

Amalyn recoiled. 'Gross.'

'There's no point being squeamish about history. An entire generation of big families spawned the country. They all needed housing. And then every remaining inch was taken up with ArbAir and SolaAir trees, trying to keep The Raft habitable.'

'I understand, Professor. But then the diseases—'

'Yes,' I interrupted, 'the next pandemic spread like wildfire, as we know. The microbial jump from host to host was mere inches. And the famine was the worst yet. Thousands perished and thousands more remained with an array of disabilities. Brittle bones, blindness, rickets, chronic lung infections. Just because we never see these people, it doesn't mean they don't exist. And their health issues are catered for. You've seen the adverts for healthcare. Need a new organ? Here's a new one grown in a lab. Got cancer? Everyone gets cancer, have the treatment and continue living. Diabetic? Isn't everyone? Implant this device and your monthly blood test and injection will be every three weeks instead of four. Over one hundred years old? Make your heart-disease tests fortnightly. Your AI will check in with you daily. Everyone lives a long time. With sterility comes liberty. But with liberty comes a long life.'

'They're empty,' Amalyn repeated. 'No one ever answers.'

'Maybe they're all just too old or disabled to answer?'

'Old people don't move into new apartments. They stay put,' said Amalyn.

I had no response. I knew it didn't make sense, but nothing did.

'Hey, Sav, check this out.' Archie turned his computer monitor towards me. 'Quick, before it gets taken down.'

'Ah yes, the Poison Maker,' I said and sighed. 'Archie, I really don't think you can trust these sources.'

'Who can we trust?' Amalyn asked. I frowned.

'It says it's someone in government and the bird-flu thing is coming from them,' Archie said. 'Says they've been mixing something up for ages, something really dangerous.'

'So you think the flu is legit now, not just some lie made up to stop us anchoring?' I asked.

Archie shrugged. 'I don't know. A lot of sources seem to be concerned, but it seems way too convenient.'

I groaned, exasperated. 'Just think about this logically. If they want fewer people, if they're trying to kill us with another plague, why would they build a ton of new housing?'

'Well, something doesn't add up,' Archie said.

'I agree,' I said. 'It's definitely odd. I'll write my article. Maybe it'll make some people wake up and investigate.'

I got to work writing, saying how so many blocks were thought to be empty—a slight embellishment but worth it to provoke a reaction, I thought. I didn't mention what I'd found when I broke in, but hinted that some wealthy collector might have lived there before. Instead, I said it was suspected that old belongings were there that just needed to be cleaned, and that there was no danger to the public. *That* I did believe. I said there would be a slight delay. Everyone had been contacted, and it was great for the area to have some more multi-bedroom apartments, and maybe this one would actually have people living in it. However, it was hard to write all this in a neutral way. I couldn't stop thinking that Archie and Amalyn were right, that they were all empty. It was all just so ludicrous I couldn't understand it at all.

I submitted my article and waited.

* * *

That night I woke in a sweat, startled and trembling from my dream. I sat up and tried to shake the feeling from my mind. The sensation of being trapped, enclosed, suffocated and unable to escape. I was in a box, stuck inside with smooth transparent walls and no door. It stank of dirt and I could feel mud squelching between my toes. As I screamed, my voice echoed back at me. I hit the walls, harder and harder, the walls reverberating with every blow. Outside the walls the world looked huge, a giant's house staring back at me.

The hotel. I was in my father's insect hotel. Boxed up like some filthy crawler, ready to be examined and written up in some forbidden book.

When I managed to fight my way back awake, my mouth was parched and my head hurt. I got up to get a drink and went over to the shelf in the living room, rifling through old e-pads and clutter until I found it. Sealed in a plastic vacuum bag, I peeled away the tape and removed the back. Anxiety lodged in my gut, but I had to see it. It's no good to be afraid. Fear is for children and those with no responsibilities.

I unfurled the old pages made of tree corpse and dared myself to look at the images, to read the words my father had written years before. So many pictures of tiny beasts that he wanted to save, hideous things with the wrong number of legs, a grotesque number of eyes, misplaced skeletons and deformed mouthparts. I shivered to think the world used to be infested with these things. But he loved them. He said they were needed. He saw something important in their horrid little lives. But that was wrong. He was wrong. That's what the press said when they demonised him for harbouring the filthy creatures. Was he wrong, or just on the wrong side of power? It's like Archie said: disagree with the Centre and they'll spit you out.

I turned another page and saw the picture of the cockroach and quickly slammed the book shut. He was definitely wrong. No way could saving such an awful creature be right.

I re-wrapped the book, scrubbed my hands and the surfaces, and went back to bed.

* * *

I hadn't received a reply to my article by the next day. Instead, Greg emailed asking me to write a press release on how the new formula for vitamins could be combined with the monthly inoculations. This was news to me, as I had not been researching anything like that. However, my protests fell on deaf ears.

There's a lot of talk about the new formula. Let's keep the conversation moving, keep the momentum up.
Greg

When I replied to chase up my article about the housing, I heard nothing back. The read receipt came back but no reply. It was so frustrating. I thought about going to the Centre Press Office to speak to Peter, but sourcing a permit would be tricky. I'd never even met him, only having spoken via email. Confronting him over something so controversial didn't really appeal. Being shot down over email was a lot less distressing than a face-to-face rejection.

Instead, I busied myself looking through some data, taking notes and speaking to a few interns about making the formula compatible with the monthly inoculations. Greg hadn't given me a deadline, so a few days of research might at least make the article seem plausible. I included Amalyn in that bit of research. She was one of the few I hadn't assigned extra work to yet, and she seemed pleased to receive a bit more responsibility. I didn't smile at her, and handed her the extra work as coldly as with any other intern.

Penny had already barged into my office that day. The bird-flu news had affected some of the interns negatively.

'Why have you not responded to my email?' she asked. I had no idea how her voice could span so many octaves in a single sentence. 'You have failed in your duties by not calling a meeting with them to address their concerns.'

'Thanks for that, Penny,' I said, making no effort to disguise my sarcasm. 'Holding their hands as they read the latest news articles is not the purpose of a food-science laboratory. If they're concerned, they can discuss such unrelated worries with their families, peers, or therapist.'

'Well, their mental wellbeing is paramount to their pro-ductivity and the bird scare is a science thing. Are you not a scientist?'

The patronising crone.

She always made me so mad. Just because I put pressure on the interns and didn't wipe their tears away, that was supposed to mean I didn't care? That was ridiculous. At some point, they needed to understand how competitive and unforgiving work and life could be. I was not there to wet nurse them through every stage of life. If they were ill-prepared for the harshness of the real world, then those failings came before they had made my acquaintance. That was what I should have said. What I actually said was nothing, and instead I rolled my eyes.

The callousness of the real world taught me to put up and shut up. An altercation would have solved nothing.

Professor Harold messaged me late afternoon to ask me to go through some finer details about the vitamin infusion with him. In the hour before, I'd had one intern knock on my door and ask if the vitamin infusion would offer protection against bird flu, another came to tell me they need to see the wellbeing manager as they had just smashed a beaker, and a third that, for the fourth time that day, they were hungry and could they go on a break? Professor Harold's email was a much-needed distraction. My office felt like it was an exhibit for anyone to just waltz in and interrupt me. The noise and hassle just wouldn't stop.

Rather than the awkwardness of a video call and the constant interruptions, I opted for an Autocar to Harold's lab. As I was leaving, I heard the interns calling their little questions at me. Their chorus of moans and wants trailed off as I walked away.

The time alone made it worthwhile, away from the sounds of clinking glass and timers beeping. I didn't even read the strip billboards or look at my phone for the news. I just sat, eyes half-closed, in peace. On arrival, Harold's secretary took my name and stated that I didn't have an appointment.

'Yes, I'm aware of that. But Professor Harold will be happy to see me, I'm sure.'

'He's busy,' she said.

'I'll wait.'

'You should have booked an appointment. That would have saved you the wait.'

'I'm happy to wait,' I said.

She sighed theatrically, like I had just asked her to move the moon. After a painstakingly slow rise from her seat, she walked around her desk in a defeated manner and gestured for me to follow her. It made me wonder if our lab receptionist was as difficult. I hoped she was. I certainly wouldn't want anyone turning up unannounced, either. Appointments were bad enough.

The plastic seats in the waiting area were as cold and charmless as the receptionist. I opted to sit further down the corridor so as not to peer straight into Harold's window, which was polite, I thought, since I didn't have an appointment. The receptionist waddled away, walking the thirty paces back to her desk, clearly an arduous task. She said that she'd let him know I was waiting.

A few minutes passed where again I was able to enjoy some peace. The coolness of the corridor was refreshing, and I imagined MindSpa rustles playing in my head. All too quickly, though, I heard a door open and Harold called me through.

'Professor Selbourne, what a surprise. I would have suggested a video call to save you the journey.' His half-smile didn't reach his eyes.

'It's fine. It's good to get a change of scenery sometimes.'

His office was as messy as I remembered. Something was bubbling away in the corner, a few beakers of various colours lined up on the corner desk, spillages underneath. His air con was on full blast, and I shivered from both the cold air and the frostiness of his welcome.

'Now, let me see this contract.' He picked up some paperwork. 'It says here that we are the only protein lab that will have access to your compound for the first year, as part of our exclusivity deal.' He used his finger to underline the extract of text, the way a child reads.

'That's correct,' I said.

He continued to stare at the paperwork, not looking up, his spectacles slipping down his nose. 'Are there any other labs or bodies that use your compound?'

'Well, as you know, we make carbohydrate and fibre food at BioLabs. Your exclusivity doesn't extend to those.'

He nodded, the slowness of the gesture making me feel cautious. 'I am concerned,' he said, 'that if this compound turns up in other forms, our product would seem less attractive to our buyers. Less special.'

'I can assure you, as per the contract, that no other protein foods contain this. No other food labs besides ProLabs have even been offered the compound. And as for ingesting the compound through multiple sources—for example, if a consumer decides on a meal of protein and carbohydrate, both with the compound—that should be viewed as an excellent choice. The more sources of the infusion, the better.'

A silence lingered for a while. I felt foolish, justifying simple science to a man who, with his credentials, did not need to be spoon-fed such basics. His face hung like wet laundry, and after the silence had intruded long enough, he continued. 'I'll be honest, Professor. If I had developed such a compound, I may have been tempted to make it in tablet form, or even injectable.'

That statement hit me like a punch in the stomach. Had someone been speaking to him? Amalyn? I'd asked her to investigate those methods. Had she gone behind my back?

I gulped and composed myself. 'I won't lie, Professor. There is, of course, research into alternative vehicles for the compound. All other methods are very much in the early research phase, and certainly would not impede on your exclusivity time scale. More direct methods of ingestion are also, obviously, not protein based, so would not detract from your marketing in any case. And as I said, multiple methods of consumption should be seen as a positive.'

I was seething. Had she really disclosed such information? A job at BioLabs was the opportunity of a lifetime for an intern. Had Amalyn really just thrown it all away for some unpopular protein lab who hadn't had their own breakthrough in decades? Protein went out of fashion when the original filthy sources were found to be as germ-ridden and polluting as they are. Now these labs spent most of their budget trying to make protein look and taste like anything but. No one wants to work in protein. BioLabs was likely to buy them out and use protein powders to bulk up the carbohydrate. It was a dead-end product, yet their sales were still good enough for us to do business with them. Some old traditionalists still insisted on separate protein. It was a business model with a couple more decades in it at most. Why would she sell herself to these dinosaurs?

'Thank you for your views, Professor. I will consider this conversation carefully.'

He gestured me to his door, and we said our goodbyes. As I walked down the corridor, I heard another set of footsteps and turned around to look. There was a slim, pretty young woman, with wisps of blond hair blowing wildly about her face. I only had a side view, but it was clear who it was. I watched her walk into Harold's office. It was Amalyn.

My mouth gaped. I had half a mind to go back in there, but thought better of it and hurried away. I didn't want to make an enemy of Harold, but Amalyn. *Amalyn!* I was livid. Why on earth would she do such a thing? Sneaking out of work was bad enough, but sneaking out to visit another lab? I had a mind to sack her on the spot. Why would she do such a thing? Another job offer seemed unlikely. She wasn't that exceptional. What an utterly stupid career move for her. Well, I concluded, I could just fire her. I walked out of the building, rigid with rage. Then the realisation of her real betrayal hit me. She wasn't just betraying BioLabs, but also my best friend.

Archie.

Chapter 26

It was too late to go back to the lab by then, but I was concerned Archie would see the treacherous bitch that evening. I sent him a quick text asking what he was up to. *Hot date tonight?* He replied with:

Not tonight. How's Grace doing?

Phew. He wasn't seeing her. That conversation could wait until tomorrow.

The way home from the protein lab was long. The Autocar took me down many streets with high-rises punctuated by split billboards carrying the news, as always, on a constant loop. I'd had no time to read it that day. It seemed so odd that anyone could not be one hundred percent up to date every minute as the headlines were rammed into our consciousness by an array of media, twenty-four seven. When people went out and walked the streets, speakers shouted the headlines at us. The billboards seemed somewhat less invasive, but the constant and unavoidable pings on phones were much more so. I opted to ignore my phone most days. I kept it in my drawer, a distraction I could do without. But the headline I saw at that moment blew my mind:

Population at All-time High, One Hundred and Fifty Million Milestone Reached.

The by-line named Morris Clark as the article's author. He had returned to work, meaning I would be back to covering the science stories. His article hailed the progress. '*Progress is paramount,*' it predictably said. The last haven for humankind and the species was doing excellently. It acknowledged the progress in nutrition (crediting me by name) and medicine, how people's more cautious attitudes were paying dividends and that our great nation, The Raft of life, was a tremendous success. By keeping our country isolated, rejecting all invaders, we had flourished. It also added that fertility treatment would be scaled back since The Raft could not be overburdened at this stage and apartments were in very short supply.

I felt like the entire Raft had gone mad. If I hadn't gone door-knocking myself, I would have believed every word. It just seemed so implausible. I had not been convinced that those apartments were empty, but I was also doubtful that the population was that high. Perhaps I was wrong. Maybe people were late moving in. There would be no reason for the Centre and developers to lie. I had misunderstood something, somewhere.

As the Autocar rolled through the grey streets, it passed a fertility clinic. Its waiting room was empty, with no would-be parents inside for tests or to talk to doctors. It was a shell, like a show building, a facade, promising couples treatment that would never happen. The Centre knew natural fertility was almost non-existent, and must have known about the water pollution. Why say The Raft was full when it wasn't? The answer was so uncomplicated and obvious that I found it hard to believe. It was too simple. The Centre didn't want the Perimeter to have families. When the Prime Minister came to the time capsule, her elite lackies had said, 'Can you believe they're actually breeding?' But we weren't. Not without the Centre's explicit permission, anyway. But having babies, a family, is what humankind expects. Stability. All of it added to the illusion of stability.

Apartments being built was normal, but they were nothing but props in the theatre show of the Centre, and we were their puppets. They set the scene, and we followed their scripts. Grace and I had never had a chance.

I needed to think. I knew Grace would expect me home, but instead I opted for the MindSpa. Some relaxation might make it all click into place, or at least help me forget for a night so I could sleep and think again the next day. I didn't stay long, just a half-hour session. It felt more like a tease than a complete course of relaxation. The brief visit to serenity just showed me what my mind could be like. If only I could listen to those cheeps and rustles a little while longer, if only the breeze would stay. If only I could forget the entire day had just happened.

By the time I got home, Grace was asleep. I ate some cold leftovers, drank two large glasses of BordeuNo, and crawled into bed beside her. I tried not to think about Amalyn deceiving Archie, of how sad it would make him, of the impossible article Greg wanted me to write about the fictitious use of the formula.

Mostly, I tried not to think of the fertility clinic and how upset Grace would be. She must have seen the news. When I crawled into bed next to her, I could smell the fish on her breath.

I slept in the next day. I hadn't set my alarm and didn't care. It was the only time I had ever been late for work. When I did get up, I didn't hurry. I had slept, but felt my motivation dissipate. I had too much to think about.

Grace stirred beside me, and I gave her a kiss.

'Shouldn't you be at work?' she asked.

'I'm thinking of calling in sick,' I said, mumbling and burying my face in the pillow.

'Really?'

'Yep. I need to think and I can't do it there.'

'Maybe I'll call in sick too.' She snuggled in close to me.

I smiled. 'Did you see the news yesterday?'

'Yes,' she said, her voice etched with a sadness she could not disguise. 'I'm trying to think of it pragmatically.'

'How?'

'I don't really know. It is what it is. Be proud of me.'

'I am, always,' I said. I suspected her coping strategy was because of the fish more than anything else. I was just pleased she wasn't hysterical.

I told her about Archie and Amalyn, but couldn't bear to talk about the empty apartments and my thoughts there.

'So you don't know what this Amalyn told Harold?'

'It seems very obvious.'

'You'll have to confront her.'

'And Archie.'

She thought for a moment. 'I'd confront her first, give her a chance to explain herself. You don't want to upset Archie unnecessarily.'

'I can't imagine it will be unnecessary.'

'Probably. But words can't be taken back. I was at Maisie's the other day. She's so wise. She said that words are the most potent poison of all.'

'She sounds smart. I can't wait to meet her.'

'You'll like her, really you will.'

I smiled and kissed her, enjoying her embrace for a while, but soon realised that calling in sick was impossible. I had to confront Amalyn sooner, not later. Before Archie had time to speak to her again. I couldn't let Amalyn use him any longer. I dressed slowly. A few messages from Archie and Harold pinged on my phone, which I tried to ignore. *I'll get there when I get there.*

Then an email from Peter came through, chasing the injectable article already. It seemed I had to put up with nagging from him as well as Greg now. I groaned and left for work.

Amalyn was working in the lab when I arrived. I went and stood by her, watching her work. She didn't flinch, not one bit.

'Amalyn, my office.'

She followed dutifully, as every good intern should. I closed the door behind her. The room was airless as I hadn't turned my air con on that morning yet. *Let her sweat.*

I sat at my desk, leaving her standing awkwardly in the middle of the space. I just stared at her, waiting for her to speak first. She looked uncomfortable, shifting on the spot and flapping her lab coat in the heat. Eventually, she broke the silence.

'What can I do for you, Professor?'

'You can tell me why you have been disclosing company secrets to Professor Harold at ProLabs.'

Her eyes bulged. 'I haven't! I swear, I haven't!'

'Professor Harold seems very concerned that we are making the infusion injectable. The task I gave you to research.'

'He probably just figured it out. It's a good idea, a sensible development,' she said, sounding way too calm and collected. A well-practised fraudster.

'Don't lie to me, Amalyn. I saw you there.'

'Yes, I was there,' she said, 'but I wasn't disclosing any company secrets. I would never do that.'

'You need to start explaining yourself a little more articulately than this.'

'I know Harold. Did Archie tell you about my tattoo? The Golden Fifty? Harold is one of us.'

'Harold is part of some cess-pit anti-government organisation?' I laughed. 'That's ridiculous.'

'It's not anti-government, it's just a remembrance thing. We don't cause any trouble. I've met Harold lots of times.'

'And that means you had to visit him in his office personally?'

'Yes. It was urgent. We always meet in person. Too many people can check emails and phones. Ask Archie. And it really was urgent. I was worried he was going to pull out of the deal with BioLabs. I didn't want that. This formula is important, and I wanted to help. I had to tell him.'

'What does the deal have to do with you?' She was meddling in business that was nothing to do with her. *How dare she!*

'Because I work here. I'm the only Golden Fifty member who works here. I had to tell him he was wrong. That you're not the Poison Maker.'

Silence cut the air. Had I heard that right? 'Say that again.'

'I told him you're not the Poison Maker.'

I leant back in my chair, stunned, clueless about what to say.

'Many people thought you were, including Harold,' Amalyn said.

'What kind of nonsense are you and your weird little club talking about, to accuse me of such a thing?'

'Think about it. Your products are everywhere. This infusion, it's going to be in most of the food on The Raft. And you wrote about it in the press, really over-inflating what it will do. You could, if you wanted, do a lot of damage. But I know it's not you. I've checked the formula. And Archie adores you and I trust his judgement completely. I had to go to Harold and reassure him it's not you, that you're really good at your job.' I just stared at her, dumbfounded. 'Professor, come on, you have to believe me.' Her eyes started to moisten.

I sat still, shellshocked, gobsmacked. That someone, anyone, could believe I was capable of harming people, that I wanted anything else but to make the population healthy... I knew my demeanour was harsh, but was it so harsh that people thought I was so evil? Amalyn was right. That article had promised the undeliverable and had soured my reputation.

'Well, if what you say is true, where did Harold hear about the injectable from?'

'He probably just considered it himself, like I said. It's a sensible line of research. And a horrible way to poison everyone, if that really was your intention. Call him if you like and he'll tell you. He hates BioLabs' dominance and has been suspicious of the company for ages, and then when you started writing for the press, well, that made him sure the company was trying to hide something. Then it was that article, how it exaggerated so much. That tipped him over the edge a bit. I had to set him straight.'

My words had made Harold think that about me. Except they weren't my words. My words had been ignored, snubbed by the press and twisted to suit the Centre and whatever schemes they were concocting. Every article I wrote had been distorted. My articles had renounced the Perimeter and served the Centre only. No wonder Harold thought I was such a villain. I was not creating the poison Harold had suspected. The press just warped it to make it sound that way. It was like Grace said: 'words are the most potent poison of all'.

I sat bolt upright. I could feel my brain hurting as it coiled and uncoiled, righting itself, trying to click everything into place. Voids interwoven with knowledge, blankness sprinkled with discoveries. I had so many questions, but only a massive vacuum where answers should be.

I got up to leave. I had to stop this. My reputation was not going to be contaminated by the partisan elite and their enforcement of control. The lies about the population, the ghost apartments, my infusion, the penguins and trajectory— I was going to make them fill in the blanks and tell the truth. The lies were too much to cope with. I was Perimeter, not merely a ventriloquist dummy for the Centre. *I am Perimeter.*

I wasn't going to get any answers sat in my office, but I knew where to find them. 'I have to go.'

'Okay,' Amalyn said, her wet eyes staring at me. 'You believe me, don't you, Professor?'

'Yes. We'll talk later. Keep up with your work. I have to go.' And I ushered her out of my office as I bolted for the exit.

I ran out of the lab and hailed a Speedy Autocar, their maximum allowable speed almost twice that of the regular ones and their price more than double. I didn't care. I phoned Greg's secretary and was told what I suspected. He was in a meeting. He always was on Friday mornings, and I knew who with. It was the weekly press meeting, where he and Peter and whoever else would sit around a table and discuss what would feature in the news over the coming weeks. Friday mornings were the time for Greg's booming voice to be heard.

I phoned Archie and asked him to get me a permit for the Centre.

'What's with you, Sav? You were in the office for two minutes and left.'

'Sorry, Archie, this is important. Can you get me a permit?'

'Erm... not legally, obviously. You know I'd have to forge one.'

'Please,' I said, 'it's an emergency, no time to explain. Can you do it?'

There was a moment's silence before he answered. 'Yes, sure. It'll take an hour. I'll email it to you.'

'Can you make it more like thirty minutes?'

'Jeez. Slavedriver! I'll do what I can. By the way, Marcus is wondering where you are.'

'Tell him... I don't know, say I'm researching something.'

'I'm doing all your dirty work today, aren't I?'

'I'll make it up to you.'

'Several cups of tea tomorrow, please.'

And there I was, at the precipice, about to fall into the pit from which there was no escape. I could not have turned back. Every fibre of my body was pushing me forward, into the dark, the unknown. I had an inkling but no actual idea; fragments of information, but none of them fit together. I wanted a complete picture. Needed it. I felt my mind's mechanisms cranking, still rusty with foolishness, not yet the well-oiled machine the complete picture would bring.

My mind was whizzing the entire way to the Centre. The birds, the flu, the population, the ghost apartments. All of it was making sense, sort of. But it wasn't. So much of it I could not understand. But I knew who to confront. I knew who had the answers. The one who knew the truth was the one who was twisting it.

The strip billboards continued their constant stream of news, bombarding my brain with the persistent nonsense that I strained to keep out. They flashed blindingly, filling my head with the Centre's words. Always their words.

RenterRafts Developments announces new Perimeter building projects to help the growing population! Progress is paramount! Get on the waiting list now!

I rubbed my temples, feeling my pulse thumping through my head. *Why?* Was all I could think.

Just why?

I was on my way to find out.

28

Chapter 27

My blood and swab test after entering the development was less than forty-eight hours before, so I could pass the sanitary checks. Archie's fraudulent permit arrived just as the gates were in sight. It looked perfect, just like the real thing. I sweated and shook as they scanned my documents, but was waved through. As I was a previous visitor to the Centre, they were less cautious than the first time.

The car was sterilised, and I soon arrived at the Press Office. I marched straight in, past the obnoxious receptionist who called after me, saying the editor was busy and not to be disturbed. I ignored her.

Greg's two assistants were waiting outside the office. The usual one and another new one, her 'bigger abilities' very much on show. I ignored them too and walked into the office without knocking. Everyone inside jumped at the intrusion and stared at me. Greg and Peter were there, as expected, but so was the Minister of Impartiality.

I saw the poster again, the tacky, out-of-date collectable

that now seemed so fitting. '*Whoever Controls the Media Controls the Mind.*' It struck me how, in the century or more since it had been made, human evolution had taken barely a step forward.

'Savannah, nice of you to join us,' Greg said, his cheery tone at odds with the scowl on his face.

I looked straight at Peter. It was the first time I'd seen him in the flesh. The photo outside his office was overly kind, showing nothing of the hives creeping up his neckline and the dandruff littering his shirt. He was every bit Perimeter, yet he did the Centre's bidding like this? I stared for a moment, revolted at the sight of him.

'Why are you lying about the population? I know the apartments are empty. It's time you started telling the people the truth.' I was stunned by my outspokenness.

Peter's lips sagged over a sparsely toothed mouth that twitched into a half-smile. 'What's good for your curiosity is not good for all,' he said. The coolness of his voice gave me chills.

I looked over to the Minister of Impartiality, who sat back in her chair, arms folded over her ample chest, lips pouting like she'd had some sour IcyCrema. She said nothing but stared at me, her eyes icy daggers.

'Grab a seat, Savannah. We have a lot to discuss.' Peter's voice was so calm. Like a psychopath.

I obliged and took a seat. My heart was thumping. I could feel sweat running down my back.

'Professor Selbourne.' The Minister of Impartiality stood up, for no reason I could see except to leer down at me from her intimidating height. Her jewellery was particularly excessive that day. I was surprised she could move at all under the weight of it. 'It is quite improper for you to barge in here like this and accuse us of deception. We have enough to put up with from the rest of the Perimeter population without hearing such outbursts from you, a servant to the cause.'

'The cause? What cause? I just want the truth.' *I'll be damned if I'm a servant to this crap.*

The Minister stepped closer and loomed over me. I felt smaller than ever. 'Lies are a matter of perspective, Professor. The truth is as murky as the sea.' She straightened her skirt, then lifted her chin higher. 'In any case, it's convenient you are here since some of this meeting will concern you.' She sat back down in her seat and faced the other two. 'Gentlemen, where were we?'

They looked at their e-pad screens, disregarding me as if I were nothing more than a VitaBiscuit crumb.

'Tomorrow's headlines, ma'am,' Peter said, before I had a second to divert the conversation back towards me.

'Ah yes.' The Minister flicked through some pages on her computer screen. 'The Prime Minister wants a boost in popularity. A show of leadership is just what the public need to see.'

'Perhaps report a few more bird shootings?'

'Excellent idea, Peter. This drift to the mainland could really work in our favour. Saying that we'll arrive at the Falklands in a month was a stroke of genius. The Prime Minister can be credited with taking measures to delay our course and give us more time to study the flu. That'll be a great spin.'

They all nodded and murmured agreements.

I sat listening, silent in disgust, gripping the edge of my seat, my rage threatening to boil over.

The Minister squeezed a bony grin out of her rigid face. 'I feel more about RenterRafts Developments would be most suitable for the main headlines, though. We need to keep Dexter and the other CEOs happy. How about reworking Savannah's little piece about the new apartment blocks?'

'I can certainly do a decent edit on that.' Peter nodded and made some notes.

A loud ring ricocheted through the room. 'Excuse me,' the Minister said, 'I need to take this.'

She put her phone to her ear but didn't leave the room. After clearing her throat and painting on a smile, she answered.

'Jacob, wonderful to hear from you. No, of course we're not going to anchor, such silly rumours. Your loyalty is much appreciated. I feel sure that your medicine bill will be included in the Prime Minister's agenda … No, really, anchoring is not going to happen… interference, I agree… foreign invaders, absolutely not. We're in agreement. I'll let the Prime Minister know personally. Bye for now.' She hung up.

'Jacob is enquiring about his flu treatment. He wanted to remind me he is next in the cycle of Centre businesses' head-line promotions, after Dexter and RenterRafts Developments. According to my calendar, it's Jacob's turn in a month. Is that what you all have?'

'It's in mine,' said Peter.

'My time was all too brief, if you ask me,' Greg said. 'BioLabs should be up there again soon. Don't you agree, Savannah?'

'Huh?' I said, surprised a question had come my way.

'You agree BioLabs needs more press attention?' Greg said, his cheeks reddening with frustration.

'Well…' I sat up, searching for the withered voice in my dry throat. 'Maybe if I could study water contamination issues—'

'Our priority is to rid the streets of Alternates,' the Minister said, waving her hand at me as if I were a wisp of smog. 'There are still too many around, spreading nonsense. Do we have the latest stats?'

Peter handed her a printout. I sat there, feeling smaller with every passing second.

'Hmm. Well, it's moving the right way. But fewer Alternates still isn't none. Useless consumers cannot be tolerated. The flu medication: let's really push the need for that. Close all black-market loops so they're not buying it from just anybody. We need to start with some understated press articles for now, before we build more next month. Keep Jacob happy and keep the momentum up.'

'Bird sightings, flu reports from the mainland—I'll make sure it hits the right note,' Peter said.

'Professor.' The Minister looked at me, her lips pursed. 'What are people in the Perimeter saying about the flu and the trajectory? Is there much concern?'

'I think people would appreciate the truth,' I said through gritted teeth. The last word came with a shower of spittle.

'We have lost half our interns already,' Greg butted in. 'That's a sign that fear is mounting.'

'Good, good,' the Minister said, her mouth stretched to a sneer. 'We need caution, not full-blown panic and riots. Maintain stability but enforce the message that the Prime Minister and Blue Liberation are taking care of it. Everyone is safe now.'

'The truth!' I shouted this time. My whole body trembled with anger. 'I said people want the truth.'

The Minister leaned towards me, her perfume making my eyes sting, her scornful face mere inches from mine. 'And what truth is it you desire?'

How was that even a question? There is only one truth: the one without the lies. I narrowed my eyes at her, willing myself not to look away. My heart raced. 'The truth about the empty apartments, that you don't want the Perimeter to have children, that the trajectory is wrong. All of it.'

The Minister lowered her head. 'We do not lie, Professor Selbourne. The audacity of your claims is displeasing. I hope you are not about to go shouting these senseless claims from the rooftops.'

'What would it matter if I did?' I replied, shocking myself with my candour. 'My words are always warped to suit your agenda.'

They were all staring at me now and, despite my initial boldness, I felt I was being beaten into submission.

'Peter's articles are magnificent,' the Minister said, 'our messages are subtle. We merely educate, never dictate.'

Peter smiled a bitter smile at me, proudly showing off his Perimeter teeth. 'Subconscious coercion,' he said, almost in a whisper.

'Excuse me?' I asked.

Peter said it again. 'Subconscious coercion. It's a nudge, a gentle prod, to encourage acceptable behaviours.'

'But you're Perimeter. How could you betray your own people like that?'

'I serve the needs of The Raft. As we all should,' he said, his expression unchanged.

'Now, we have a lot to get through, and no time for outbursts and distractions,' the Minister said, giving me the side-eye. 'The focus at the moment must be on RenterRafts. Dexter apologises, he couldn't make the meeting today. He's at an auction for rare collectables. He's been very forthcoming with his support for Blue Liberation over the years. The scarcity of housing must be highlighted to keep the demand and rents high. Dexter, as usual, does not want just anybody living in his properties. So again, we come back to the question of the Alternates.'

I sat listening. *Just anybody.*

'As I always say, prison camps would be best,' Greg said.

The Minister and Peter both sucked their teeth. 'Now, Greg. We've had this conversation before. Blue Liberation is a party of choice. The Alternates must choose the right path of their own volition.'

Greg folded his arms and stuck his bottom lip out like a sulking child.

'Fertility rates are marvellously low. They'll die out soon enough,' Peter said.

'Not quickly enough,' the Minister said with a sigh. 'It's the honour of the people to serve those who have the birthright to rule. To do their part in supporting such a wonderful city. The last great city on the planet. It baffles me how we still have any Alternates at all. Some even come from good families. Quite how such anomalies happen is a mystery.'

My hands were clenching the chair so hard I felt the sides cutting into the skin of my fingers. I had listened long enough. I sat as straight as I could and raised my eyes to look them all square in the face. 'You know the water is polluted!' Every word forced its way out of my throat. 'You're making us infertile.'

The three of them looked at each other with raised eyebrows. 'Pollution is an ambiguous term.' The Minister almost laughed at me. 'And we certainly never caused it. Earlier generations caused the problem.'

'But...' I took a breath. 'The Great Sterilisation Project rid us of all of that. With sterility comes liberty. That's what we chant, that's what you tell us, that's what we all support.'

The Minister stood up again. I felt the vibrations of her footsteps as she paraded around the room.

'Sterility has two meanings, Savannah. "Clean", but also "unviable". We cannot have just anybody reproducing.'

There was that term again. *Just anybody.*

I had guessed the truth, but hearing the vulgar reality out loud hit me like a brick. I deliberated for a moment, searching my mind for the questions she couldn't dodge with tangents and waffle. 'How many people are there really on The Raft? Nowhere near one hundred and fifty million, I'll bet.'

'Not quite that many, no.'

'How many?'

'It's hard to know for sure.'

'Nonsense,' I said. 'Stop lying to me. Tell me the truth.'

She took a step back, thought for a second, then replied, 'About ten million.'

That knocked the wind out of me. My mouth hung open. 'That's it? Ten million?'

'The current population is enough to serve the needs of the Centre.' Her chin rose as she spoke, displaying her nostrils and angular jawline to me.

'But you're lying to us. It's propaganda. It's... it's poison,' I said. 'You create hype to promote whatever you choose, ignoring the brutal realities. Like before, when the seabed disintegrated. The press featured other headlines. You fuelled the blasé mindset and barely gave a column inch to the glaring reality that the country was crumbling away.'

'Imagine if we had reported that,' Peter said, sneering. 'The public would have moaned and we wouldn't have been able to mine what we needed to develop the country. All those gases and ore would still lie useless beneath the ground. Progress is paramount.'

'That's right!' Greg shouted, and fist-bumped the air.

'Peter is an excellent wordsmith,' the Minister said. 'We simply think of the articles that best suit the collective needs of The Raft and he and his team persuade the population to do their bit to keep it functioning.'

My eyes widened, the level of their deceptions sinking in. 'You poison everyone's minds with your lies. This is where the poison is made. It's words that cause the most damage. The poison is in this office. It's you.' I glared at Peter. 'You are the Poison Maker!'

A thin smile formed across his face. 'A silly nickname the Alternates insist on using. You think a slight embellishment of the truth is poison? Go ahead, tell everyone the water is contaminated, and watch them all die of thirst. Alternatively, help Greg make more money with bottled water. Which is more toxic, do you think? Our story or yours?'

Greg nodded at this. The Minister of Impartiality sat down again, her chair creaking under her weight. 'So, Greg, you've had your turn. It's RenterRafts' time to promote their business for now. They've done a great service to The Raft in ridding the Perimeter of outside space. We can't allow Alternates places to hide.'

Greg grunted, and Peter nodded so enthusiastically his cheeks wobbled.

'And with such a huge reported population,' said the Minister, 'Alternates will have to start behaving in order to get housing.'

More murmurs of agreement. I looked at all three of them, their smugness, their arrogance. Their pockets were more precious to them than the Perimeter.

'Now, for your next assignment.' The Minister turned to face me, keeping her chin high, the light from the window catching a necklace and dazzling me. 'There is a new article we'd like you to write about the dangers of the bird flu that is raging in the Falklands.'

'But I know nothing about the flu,' I said. 'Is there even a flu? The Falklands would be an ideal anchor point, the climate there is still favourable.' However hard I tried to project my voice, it sounded weak.

'Maybe include something about the need to end group gatherings around the Perimeter. Keep those Alternates apart,' the Minister said, as if she hadn't heard me.

'That's sensible enough,' Peter said. 'Perhaps also highlight the need for everyone to ensure they have access to healthcare, just in case the flu finds its way onto The Raft.'

'Excellent,' the Minister said. 'Remember to put the adverts in about training courses and how to obtain loans to fund them. The banks emailed me this morning about their new interest rates.'

'Don't forget to maintain momentum on the new infusion,' Greg said with a snort, rubbing his hands together.

'Of course, Greg,' the Minister said, rolling her eyes and giving him a sarcastic grin. 'How could any of us ever forget about you?'

They all laughed cackling laughs, holding their bellies as their glee filled the room. Laughing while they used our future as a bargaining chip, asking me to do something I couldn't even comprehend. I came here for the truth and instead they were burying me under more lies. I ground my teeth, heat welling up from my core.

'Is there really a flu?' I said, startling their laughter into silence. I couldn't bear it, their superiority thumping me in the stomach with every word. The three heads turned to face me, sneers spreading across them. I exhaled heavily, exasperated. I thought back to my own prejudices, my own preconceptions. How much of that had been instilled by the Centre, by their agenda? I had been subconsciously coerced my whole life. I could see it. All the headlines, all the hate they spawned, all to suit the wealth of the wealthy.

'Can we be sure there isn't a flu?' Peter said, his face as hard and cold as concrete.

'People are the flu,' The Minister said, her lips tight and eyes narrow. 'The isolation we all enjoy means we can account for every single person and pathogen. If that were to be uncontrolled and unscrutinised, if we open our shores to other life forms, of course there will be flu.'

The Minister sat up straighter and took a deep breath. 'This is a wonderful moment in our nation's history that you, Savannah, have been tasked with delivering. To help us stay clean from foreign filth and at the same time secure our economic balance. A whole nation playing a vital role, a cog in the machine that is The Raft. Every single Perimeter person supporting the Centre, helping keep The Raft in balance. With your help and allegiance, we can—to use Peter's words — subconsciously coerce an entire population to be modern and useful. To work in careers that enable us to progress. And progress is paramount.'

'We haven't had any disease outbreaks for decades,' said Greg.

'The filth has gone. Everyone is safe now,' Peter said.

'Our methods are effective. Savannah, as a scientist, you must agree,' the Minister said.

I cringed at her statement. 'It's not the science I hold in disrepute, but the politics that pursue it.'

'Oh politics, politics, politics.' She waved her hand at me. 'A scapegoat for anything people disagree with. Tough decisions are made by those who bear the responsibility to make them. Look how great and strong we've been since we broke free from the grasp of the mainland.' She held her fist to her chest and raised her chin even higher. 'Look how we've blossomed as a country. A picture of health. No foreign invaders and we've done marvellously. With sterility comes liberty!'

'Hear, hear!' Greg cheered.

I shot him a look. This had nothing to do with him. He was, as always, an obtrusive showpiece.

The Minister lowered her chin to face me and smiled in a sickly-sweet way that made me want to gag. 'I want you to know that we appreciate you, Savannah. You and your reputation make for an excellent marketing tool.'

'I consider myself more a person than a marketing tool.'

'And you're an excellent cog in the machine,' she said, ignoring my quip. 'I'm sure you'll write us a wonderful article about the flu on the Falklands that will probably save thousands of people from exposure to deadly infections.' She raised her chin high once more and pursed her lips. 'You have a grandparent now, I see. A babysitter, which is very favourable. And of course, your choice to continue to be loyal to Blue Liberation should be rewarded, as should your discretion.' She widened her mouth into a grin, flashing a mouthful of shining teeth. 'I will have the fertility clinic email you with an appointment this week.'

'Really?' I said, a little too quickly, my fists unclenching.

'Absolutely. I see no reason why not,' said the Minister. 'Far better to have you on board than in the sea.' Her eyes narrowed for a moment, before her tone lightened again. 'There's a large apartment with an excellent postcode that will be ready for you to move into. Close to your grandmother, but even more central. And, obviously, you deserve more than pay grade D for all of your wages, BioLabs included. Don't you agree, Greg?'

'Huh?' He seemed to have dozed off. 'Yes, of course, whatever she needs to keep her mouth shut.'

'Why don't we call it a C pay grade, then? The Autocar to work will be a bit more expensive for you, with your new address, so the extra money will be important. It's a wonderful apartment, spacious, with clean air outside.' She leaned back in her chair and folded her arms across her chest. 'So you see, Professor, that's an excellent arrangement, don't you think? A successful career, a child on the way, an adequate apartment. What more could you want?'

29

Epilogue

I'd like to describe my inner turmoil, my internal battle as I pitted my principles and my conscience against my personal desires. But that would be a lie. The day I crashed into the meeting in the Press Office was a year ago and things transpired exactly as the Minister had said.

Because I agreed.

Of course I agreed. What else was I to do? Me against the Centre? As Archie said, they'd spit me out and I'd end up destitute. And Grace, poor Grace. It would ruin her. So I did what I'd always promised her I'd do. I provided. I made her happy.

Grace is happier now, my smile forsaken for hers. She hasn't visited the docks since, and our freezer was scrubbed clean. Our son, Ethan, is a joy. He was born a healthy weight and has Grace's golden curls. She carried him, just as we'd hoped.

His eyes are dark like Grace's. The colour of the sea. When I hold my son and look into his eyes, I'm filled with love. But under that is a constant disgust at myself that I cannot shed.

My lies feel endless. Some days I feel as though I'm drowning in deceit. However much I love my child, he is a reward for my silence. That's a burden I can never explain. My heart smoulders with deception.

After becoming pregnant, Grace forgot all about the Poison Maker. I reassured her that Archie had proven it to be nonsense, and, with her dreams coming true, she moved on. She loved being pregnant. Every mood swing, every part that expanded, every sickness, even—she revelled in it. Her worries seemed to melt away. She's a wonderful mother, doting and caring. Every whine, every nappy change, she enjoys it all. She still cries sometimes. Ethan has cured many of her ails, but some remain. Her loneliness still lingers.

Our apartment is pleasant, with three bedrooms and a large IC. Grace's clutter looks tidy now. Everything has its place. It's high up and from one window we can see the fence around the Centre. When the light catches it, it glows like embers. We haven't met our neighbours, of course. The silence outside is echoed in the hallways. Every time I sit alone in the apartment, I feel more suffocated than when we lived in the smog.

Maisie is still with us. She has Ethan several times a week. Our new apartment is just half an hour's drive from hers, so she visits our apartment or we go to hers. She is frailer, weaker, has developed a cough. She still natters, still tells stories. And her sweetie tin is always full.

Archie and Amalyn's relationship has flourished. I wouldn't have bet on that lasting a month, let alone a year. They're taking it slow, he says. I feel foolish for ever accusing her of being disloyal. She is a kind and thoughtful young woman. We have become good friends and I couldn't be happier for Archie.

Amalyn and Mabel are the only two that lasted the whole

internship. Mabel's work on the water pollutants and vitamin absorption was excellent, and our next formula should yield even greater results. Human trials are due to start imminently. She stands up straighter these days. Her bent posture disappeared when her results proved worthwhile. She still accepts Marcus's affections. I have no idea if anything more is going on between them.

Amalyn carried on her research into injectables, much to Harold's dismay. It's still a long way off, but her dedication and resilience have proved valuable. She has the backbone required to work in the lab. She tolerates Greg's grunts and wandering eyes better than most. Her sassiness rids her of any vulnerability.

The Falklands were in sight for a while. I went to the edge to see the land. Unlike the previous mainland sighting, only a few people were on the streets this time. My article about the flu had been effective, it seemed. We swung very close to both the Falklands and South America. It was cool. Blissfully cool. The tinnitus of the air con filling the streets was quieted for a while, and the stillness outside was so peaceful. Not a sound, not a single sound.

When South America was in view, I saw trees, real trees. Archie had some old army-issue binoculars so I could see them clearly. Great tall structures covered in green, like mould. The troops were all stood at the coast again, but no shells came this time. A few people waved at us, as if welcoming us. We sent explosives into the sea to divert our course and back out we drifted. The flu was too infectious, the press reported. I never saw a penguin, though apparently a few were shot. That's what the headlines said, anyway.

Talk of the Poison Maker died down. When the flu amounted

to nothing and we dodged the Falklands, the Golden Fifty panicked less. A few of them went out to see the mainland. Just a glimpse. With heavy hearts and longing eyes, they watched as The Raft veered close and then drifted away.

As the conditions of our fertility treatment stipulated, I have continued to write for the press. First drafts, anyway, before Peter twists my words and adds the hyperbole. I feel a heavy weight crush my chest every time an article is released. More and more, Grace has started to believe what my articles say, her belief in me and the system that granted her Ethan now strong and absolute. The mind most poisoned is the one I love more than any other.

Every day I feel sad to think that I am contributing to the poison. I am helping the Centre feed the public lies, a pawn in their game of power. Archie will never know, as they have stunted his clearance abilities of late and his old hacking techniques don't seem to work anymore. Too many rules were broken, too little trust in the system. The powers of the Centre evolved to exclude him.

No more birds have been seen, and not a single insect, much to everyone's relief. The sight of that cockroach still makes me wake in a cold sweat sometimes. I can still feel its crunch vibrate through me. Since that day in Peter's office, I have often wondered: did my father's insect collection really cause an outbreak? The headlines that accused him fill me with doubt now. The articles that reported his treason read like an act of punishment for someone so vociferously against the way the world was changing. One way or another, he had to be silenced. I shudder to think of those boxes of filth, or when I look through his old book, the pictures of the creepers and crawlers make me shiver. But he believed they were good, that they could help. He was brave in ways I am not. He fought for the world he loved.

Don't judge me for my conformity, for giving in. For putting parenthood before principles. So much of what the Minister said that day a year ago made sense. I would be livid if my hard work had been rewarded less than an Alternate's. But the divide between the Centre and us I could never change, whatever I did. Perhaps, in decades to come, not only my science work but my press articles will still be read. They will think I'm from the Centre. They will think the whole world was like the Centre, since the Perimeter voices remain so small. The Perimeter will wash away into the ocean, adding to the murk. Perhaps, in that future, the gap between us and them will shrink, something bordering on equality or recognition by achievement emerging instead of place of birth. Perhaps people will be safe enough to read literature again. There will be room for art and music. My parents always wished for that. I'm not sure if I do, as what use are these things? I'm still a scientist, after all. Perhaps bugs will make a comeback. I doubt it, though. The world was poisoned for them long before it was for us. I'm merely speculating on what the future holds. How alien is the world of my reader, compared to the one I write about? What does a better future look like? Is it better at all? Safer, of course. That's all anybody wants. To be safe. To be liberated.

We still float, meandering with the ever-changing sea, feeling the full force of Mother Nature's displeasure at our meddling. The drones circle frequently, looking for what they never really say. Vermin, filth, hackers, Alternates. All the above, most likely. Showing off their technology. It's progress, they say. And progress is paramount.

Everyone is safe now.

A note from Emma

Thank you so much for reading The Poison Maker. If you enjoyed it, please leave a review on Amazon or Goodreads. Reviews are so important for authors and help other readers discover books they will enjoy. If you would like to get in touch or keep up to date with my other books, please visit my website www.emmaellisauthor.com.

If you subscribe to my website you'll receive a link to a short story Goodbye, Flowers. It is a prequel, set just before the anchors were destroyed. A little peek into The Raft before it started to drift, and giving a little backstory to the poison maker himself, Peter Melrose.

The next two books in The Raft Series are available now. The Invisible Kick: Expose the Poison is set six years after Savannah made her deal with the Centre Elite. Grace is happy. Ethan, their son, is healthy. Work is going well.

Then The Raft starts to shake ...

If you are in the mood for some more weird dystopian, check out my other series, the Eyes Forward. This series is set in a world where, thanks to a new drug that restores youth, the global population has skyrocketed and the government goes to increasingly extreme measures to reduce human numbers.

This series is packed full of fun characters and some sinister twists!

As a full-time nomad, I am lucky to spend a lot of my time among nature. The Raft is my worst nightmare. Too much grey, so devoid of life. There are a lot of metaphors for me in these pages. Some people who have read The Poison Maker have told me what they feel The Raft represents for them, which is often different from my own thoughts. And that's okay. Our differences add colour to this world. If we were all the same, The Raft would be on the brink of coming true.

Acknowledgments

I have many people to thank for helping me create The Poison Maker. My wonderful betas and critique partners, namely Danica, Cherrie, Kate, Ginny, Lisa and Mark. Their time and honesty helped make this book into what it is today. My editor, Graham Clarke, proved invaluable. And of course, my partner John, for giving me the time and space I need to write, for his support, patience and encouragement.

And thank you, for reading it.

Printed in Great Britain
by Amazon